Praise for *The Children's Day*

"This is one of those novels that has an entirely original feel ..."
—*Mail and Guardian* (South Africa)

"[Heyns] tempers his acridity with compassion and his witticism with mellow maturity ... You will not easily come across a ... book that recreates history as palatably as *The Children's Day*."
—*Cape Times*

"What sets it apart from the start is the quality of the writing: the humour, the wryness and Heyns' skilful use of the power of understatement."
—*The Sunday Independent* (South Africa)

"Michiel Heyns has produced a deftly written novel which makes a distinctive contribution to the growing corpus of autobiographical fiction ... [T]his is a lightly written, witty and entertaining book. Heyns has a fine style which deploys understatement and innuendo above the more obvious techniques of making a point, while the story posits the 'wordless' joy of childhood, the narration employs a witty, worldly, amusing and highly articulate style of telling ... Heyns is able to manage the narration with a light hand ... The book's climax is excellently brought off, and gives pause for thought in a reflective and entertaining manner—and yet the political, moral and philosophical content of the book remains profound ... a style that manages to be both upbeat and light, as well as socially and politically revealing. This is no small achievement."
—*Sunday Times Lifestyle* (South Africa)

THE CHILDREN'S DAY

MICHIEL HEYNS

Tin House Books

First published in trade paperback in South Africa by Jonathan Ball
Publishers (Pty) Ltd, 2002, 2008

Published by Tin House Books, Portland, Oregon, and New York,
New York

Distributed to the trade by Publishers Group West, 1700 Fourth St.,
Berkeley, CA 94710, www.pgw.com

Library of Congress Cataloging-in-Publication Data
Heyns, Michiel.
  The children's day/by Michiel Heyns. — 1st U.S. ed.
    p. cm.
  ISBN 978-0-9802436-6-6
  1. Boys—Fiction. 2. Villages—Fiction. 3. Apartheid—Fiction.
  4. South Africa—Fiction. I. Title.
  PR9369.4.H49C47 2009
  823'.92—dc22First U.S. edition 2009

Typesetting and reproduction of text by Alinea Studio, Cape Town

Printed in Canada

www.tinhouse.com

The introduction by A. L. Kennedy originally appeared in Bookforum.

"The Cool Web" by Robert Graves, from Robert Graves: The
Complete Poems in One Volume ed. Beryl Graves and Dunstan Ward
(2000), is reprinted by permission of Carcanet Press Limited.

Introduction

Simon is growing up in Verkeerdespruit, a stifling Free State village of gossip, ice-cream floats, churchgoing, emotional tension and transgression, eccentricity and strange joys. Heyns offers him as a clear-eyed and intelligent observer, a beautifully realized and honestly flawed personality. The adults around Simon exist within the savage fantasy of 1960s apartheid, navigating narrow paths between a multiplicity of visible and unspoken rules: a legion of racial, sexual, religious, emotional, and social limitations. Deviation from the norm is punished with a chillingly banal violence. Simon moves from the bewilderment and overmastering passions of childhood toward a consciously muted, but equally fierce adulthood, all within the self-imposed hothouse isolation of his elders—the casual bullying, the couples who finish each other's sentences, a doggedly racist telephone operator—the runaways, rebels, and freaks—human beings grown strange by feeding on their own harshly intoxicating dreams—human beings struggling in their sleep, edging toward terrible awakenings.

The Children's Day is a deceptively delicate book carefully constructed, both subtly funny and melancholy. It teases apart the layers of memory and winds its young protagonist deeper and deeper into his short but intense past and the aching dilemmas of his present. But under the novel's surface, Heyns sustains a tangible, steely fury—a real sense of absolute violence, abuse, loss, and deep wrong. In Simon's half-spoken relationship with the outcast Fanie we are offered a final sense of dangerous tenderness, potential self-knowledge, and painful change. This is an important, lovely, and thoughtful book.

—A. L. Kennedy

For Christine

In memory of Johan

THE COOL WEB

Children are dumb to say how hot the day is,
How hot the scent is of the summer rose,
How dreadful the black wastes of evening sky,
How dreadful the tall soldiers drumming by.

But we have speech, to chill the angry day,
And speech, to dull the rose's cruel scent.
We spell away the overhanging night,
We spell away the soldiers and the fright.

There's a cool web of language winds us in,
Retreat from too much joy or too much fear:
We grow sea-green at last and coldly die
In brininess and volubility.

But if we let our tongues lose self-possession,
Throwing off language and its watery clasp
Before our death, instead of when death comes,
Facing the wide glare of the children's day,
Facing the rose, the dark sky and the drums,
We shall go mad no doubt and die that way.

Robert Graves

December 6, 1968

"Tennis? Against the Clutch Plates?" Tony Miles exclaimed. "Do Clutch Plates play tennis?"

"Obviously they must, otherwise they wouldn't have invited us," said Mr. Moore.

"I've never heard of a Clutch Plate playing tennis, have you? Have you ever heard of a Clutch Plate playing tennis?" Tony demanded from the rest of us, and we confessed that we had never heard of a Clutch Plate playing tennis. A Clutch Plate was a boy from a technical school, which, in the snob's hierarchy of Wesley College, ranked below even the Afrikaans schools, the undiscriminatingly coeducational growth medium of Ball-Bearings and Buses, the male and female offspring respectively of the subspecies Hairyback Rockspider. The only sport we normally played against the Clutch Plates was rugby, because by and large that was the only sport practiced at these institutions — or so we assumed, rugby being the highest, indeed only, common factor of white culture in South Africa.

"Perhaps they've only just started tennis and want to improve their game," suggested Mr. Moore, our tennis coach. The Clutch Plates in question were from the Goldfields Technical School in Odendaalsrust, which had invited — challenged, said Mr. Moore — us to a tennis tournament.

"So we have to give up a Saturday to teach the Clutch Plates which end of a racket to point at us?" asked Tony. But Mr. Moore was adamant that it would be rude to turn down an overture like this: as children of privilege and culture, it was our duty to share our amenities and abilities with the less privileged. Though by no means convinced of this duty, we recognized that Mr. Moore had moved the question onto non-negotiable moral grounds, and we resigned ourselves to our own putative high-mindedness. Because our match roster was already full, the game was scheduled for the last Saturday of the school year. This was also the day on which, as a special end-of-year treat, we could ask partners from our sister school, Victoria High, to the weekly film show in hall — but, as Mr. Moore pointed out, that was only in the evening, and need not interfere with our sporting commitments. We could be back in plenty of time for the film.

7

Expectations were not sharpened by the news that the Clutch Plates had asked if they could come to us instead: it seemed they had only two courts, which they now realized would prolong the match unduly. "For heaven's sake," complained Stephen Maddox, "they haven't even got tennis courts and they expect us to play against them." But again Mr. Moore insisted that the gesture was not to be spurned: "It's possible that the boys want an outing to the city — and you don't really want to go to Odendaalsrust, do you?" This was unanswerable, and it was arranged that the Clutch Plates would come to us, our hospitality extending to a light lunch — which, given the quality of the cooking of Mrs. Cameron, our food matron, we could hardly decry as an extravagantly generous gesture. But, although it was assumed that the guests would return to Odendaalsrust after the tennis, there was nevertheless a sense that they were gate-crashing our party, and they were resented accordingly, even by boys who normally had nothing but scorn for the tennis team and its affairs. The resistance was so vociferous and so unabashed that Mr. Robinson, the headmaster, felt called upon to denounce in chapel "the unlovely pride that would discriminate against a neighbor only because he has not had one's own privileges." This drove the protest underground but did not temper it. It was generally felt that we were being invaded by Clutch Plates and that Wesley would never be the same again.

Half-Afrikaans myself, I couldn't bring myself to share my schoolmates' disdain of everything emanating from Afrikanerdom, but by the same token I was hypersensitive to any suggestion that I might myself be a Ball-Bearing. Fortunately, English was my best subject, and I in fact regularly came first in class in English. This was a mildly satisfying achievement, but at Wesley academic achievement came a poor second to sporting prowess and to such spectacular feats as stealing the bread pudding for the master's dinner out of the kitchen, like Sydney Broadbean, or setting fire to one's own farts, like Peter Emery. I did not envy these accomplishments — they seemed too much limited to the fact of their own performance and not to admit to degrees of excellence — but I did mutely cherish ambitions to show publicly and incontrovertibly that I was not of the common herd.

Tennis promised to become the medium to such distinction: though not, of course, commanding the unquestioning slack-jawed adulation that rugby inspires among even quite intelligent people in South Africa, it was respected at Wesley as the raison d'être of Wimbledon, which to the Methodist imagination has all the appeal of snobbery and privilege that it conscientiously affects to disapprove of. In Bloemfontein, in the dry heart of the Republic of South Africa, tennis seemed almost heroically perverse. To my own surprise, and that of most of my peers, I turned out to have what Mr. Moore called "an excellent eye," probably thanks to my early exposure to tennis on the bumpy courts of Verkeerdespruit, my hometown, where the uncertain trajectory of the ball had trained me not to take for granted any of the usual laws of dynamics, but to wait till the very last second before committing myself to a stroke. This gave an element of near-spastic whiplash unpredictability to my game, which proved confusing to my opponents, and by the time I reached the Fourth Form I was one of the school's best tennis players. Indeed, I was the number three player after two Sixth Formers, Tony Miles and Peter Emery; and Tony Miles, the head prefect and Victor Ludorum, was so invariably superior at everything except schoolwork that he was automatically discounted from competition. Thus I was in effect the second-best player in the school after Peter Emery.

On the day before the match Tony Miles reported sick to Matron with a sprained groin, sustained, he claimed, when lifting his trunk from its shelf in the cellar to pack for the holiday. Mr. Moore looked at him skeptically. "Are you sure of this, Miles?" he asked. "You're not always so forward with your packing."

"Of course I'm sure, sir," he replied. "You sprain your groin, you know all about it." There were appreciative chuckles from the band of admirers that always accompanied Tony Miles. They knew that Matron declined to examine anything between the belt and the knee: she just said, "Oh well, if it's down there you must be very careful with it," and prescribed aspirin or a Band-Aid and sometimes both, as the nature of the alleged injury dictated.

"I take it you won't be attending the film on Saturday evening, then," said Mr. Moore.

9

"I don't know, sir, I may just have to force myself — you know, as head boy I'll have to welcome the girls and all that." He limped away ostentatiously, to the appreciative chuckles of the band of admirers. So, by default, I was promoted to Number Two; and when on the same evening Peter Emery was incapacitated by burns sustained in a spectacular display after a particularly dour version of Mrs. Cameron's cabbage soup, I found myself Number One player. I was well enough read to know that many an illustrious career had been built on the fortuitous absence of the supposed star, for reasons by tradition mundane, but a sprained groin and a singed backside seemed excessively prosaic. Still, I consoled myself that if I gave a brilliant performance nobody could in all fairness regard it as compromised by the circumstances making it possible. Heroism, Miss Smithers, our English teacher, had told us, is largely a matter of being in the right place at the right time; but I knew that one had also to be the right man for the role.

The day of the tennis match was the first day of real summer: blazingly hot, with a sultry wind threatening under its breath of thunder and fireworks to come. A small group of us sat outside waiting for the arrival of the Clutch Plates, less as a welcoming committee than as a kind of screening body. Not that we could have sent them back even if they had arrived dressed in animal skins and wielding slingshots, but there's always a premium on having seen anything first, and there was a general expectation that the Clutch Plate Visitation would be one to remember.

The first disappointment was the Clutch Plate vehicle. We had fantasized freely and unkindly about a school bus covered in fun fur, or perhaps an army truck painted orange. What drove up was a nondescript and perfectly respectable Combi; and what got out was a group of ordinary, indeed rather intimidated-looking schoolboys, hardly the rampaging vulgarians of the Methodist imagination. They wore school uniforms — admittedly a not-very-attractive maroon-and-yellow combination, but uniforms nevertheless, complete with tie and cap and shoes and socks. As far as we could see they were not missing any limbs or even teeth, and they were not noticeably unwashed. They were six ordinary-

10

looking boys, except that they were probably unusually subdued. They had clearly had a hot trip: their hair was plastered to their foreheads, and those who had taken their blazers off had large sweat marks under the arms of their white shirts.

Tim Watkins, who was standing next to me, made the most of this by saying, "Jeez, you can see they're not used to wearing clothes, hey?" and after a quick survey of the arrivals, "Gawd, that one looks as if it's had rickets." I looked where he was pointing and there, blinking slightly in the bright sun, in all his ungainly serenity, was Fanie van den Bergh.

"Oh, that one?" I asked, as casually as I could. "I think I know him from … from the place where I grew up. He was one of the poor children."

1

1962

Children naturally take an interest in any newcomer, whether as object of their charity or as victim of their persecution. Thus even Fanie van den Bergh created a little hush of attention when he was brought into the classroom by the principal, Mr. Viljoen, and assigned a desk by Miss Jordaan in the front of the class, across the aisle from mine. On a first frankly exploratory stare, he seemed candidate for neither charity nor persecution — that is, he seemed just ordinary. He was very thin, but then so were many of the children in the class; he was poorly dressed in slightly grubby clothes, but again that was hardly noteworthy in Verkeerdespruit. He was wearing a pair of scuffed shoes, which did set him apart from the predominantly barefooted class, but that was understood as a concession to his first day at school. Verkeerdespruit people, my mother used to say, had to prove that they possessed shoes. I never wore shoes, not even on the last day of term when everybody else did.

In the course of the morning Miss Jordaan asked her new pupil a few questions, partly to make him feel at home and partly, I suppose, because she also felt a certain curiosity: she hadn't been in Verkeerdespruit long enough to have ceased hoping for an exception. Fanie certainly was not it: her questions elicited only the usual dour silence of ignorance or shyness or both. She and the twenty-five members of the Standards One and Two class settled down again to their routine, and Fanie van den Bergh took his unremarkable place in the unexacting primary educational system of the Orange Free State.

At first break what curiosity remained was soon satisfied: Fanie was willing to join in games of *kennetjie*, which suggested

12

an acceptable combination of conformity and defiance of authority: *kennetjie*, a somewhat rudimentary game in which the bat was a long stick and the ball was a short stick, was officially outlawed since Marius Venter had received a cut on his forehead while trying to field one of Louis van Niekerk's more vigorous efforts. Fanie was uncommunicative about his origins, though he admitted to coming from Ficksburg, which was neither near enough to make him one of us nor far enough to be exotic. He was nine years old, which was the standard age in our class, except for Tjaart Bothma, whose father had taken him out of school for a year because he had found a reference to evolution in our Nature Studies book. It was generally believed that Tjaart's father, who was known as *Bobbejaan-Bakkies* Bothma, Baboon-face Bothma, felt as strongly as he did about the theory of evolution because it accounted so unflatteringly for his own appearance; but we did not generally refer to baboons in Tjaart's company, because his year's advantage in age gave him a disproportionate advantage in size.

The only slightly unusual thing about Fanie was that he had neither brothers nor sisters: one-child families were not common in Verkeerdespruit in 1962. Although I myself was in fact an only child, this did not seem to require explanation, since I was used to our family being slightly different from the rest of the village. But Fanie was in every other respect so ordinary that even this slight deviation from the four-child norm of the time and place seemed an anomaly. His father was the new barman at Loubser's Hotel, replacing Schalk Redelinghuis, who, rumor ran, had drunk up all the profits. From this we deduced that his father was a man of sober habits, and Louis van Niekerk stated with knowing emphasis, "Then *that's* why he's an only child."

"Why?" I asked reluctantly, unwilling to give Louis an opening to show off his powers of deduction.

"Because his father's a barman, of course," he said smugly. "That means he comes home too late."

I wanted to ask too late for what, but since that was clearly what Louis van Niekerk wanted me to do, I simply said, "Oh," and pretended to take a thorn out of my foot.

So Fanie van den Bergh, having been explained and categorized, ceased to occupy our minds. Nobody was nasty to him, and some were friendly: those with no particular friend who thought that perhaps Fanie might be it, and others like myself who had been taught that one should be kind to strangers. I can't remember that I was ever given a reason for this precept, but I accepted it as I accepted that one should not wipe one's nose on one's sleeve or talk of kaffirs — a sign of our difference from the rest of Verkeerdespruit.

My father was the magistrate, and we lived in the second-biggest house in Verkeerdespruit after the *pastorie* — the third-biggest in fact — but the biggest of all belonged to Dr. Mazwai in the location and thus did not count. Nor did the *pastorie* really, because that belonged to the church, which meant that we paid for it with the sixpences we put in the collection plate. So it was possible to believe that we owned the biggest house in Verkeerdespruit, and I believed it. Apart from this, my father was English-speaking, which was if not unique then relatively rare in Verkeerdespruit; my name, Simon, was supposed to be pronounced in the English way, though this was regarded as an affectation by my peers. My parents came from the Cape, which was bigger even than Bloemfontein and generally accepted to be considerably more advanced. As for Verkeerdespruit ... Verkeerdespruit had no claims to the regard of the rest of the world. It featured in our school history book only as the home of a minor "friendly" native tribe — which meant that they had not put up any resistance to the occupation of their land by the Voortrekkers — and as the place where two Voortrekker leaders, having no enemy against which to unite, had quarreled with each other, causing one group to trek on in a huff to meet obliteration at the hands of a less docile indigenous community in Natal and leaving the other to settle what became, not very spectacularly, the white village of Verkeerdespruit. Even the name Verkeerdespruit, the wrong creek, had something depressed about it, as if the founders had recognized their mistake but lacked the initiative to do anything about it. The heroic group that had set off to annihilation elsewhere was commemorated annually in a lugubrious ceremony around the square of cement imprinted with the tracks

14

of the ox wagon that had visited Verkeerdespruit during the centennial ox wagon trek of 1938. The square of cement also bore the distinct imprint of a high-heeled shoe, according to popular legend belonging to the mayor's wife, who had a drinking problem.

All in all, my ambitions were larger than my environment. I knew, in any case, that I was going to be sent to Free State College in Bloemfontein after Standard Five. My mother said that after a certain age you needed more from school than what she called The Basics; Verkeerdespruit, she said, was probably as Basic as you could get without severe mental deprivation. So in being nice to Fanie van den Bergh I was simply demonstrating a standard of behavior more exacting than that of the rest of Verkeerdespruit. I told my mother about the new boy, and she went to visit his mother, as she visited all newcomers to the village, partly as her social duty, partly in her capacity as secretary of the *Oranje Vrouevereniging*, or OVV, a women's charitable organization that looked after poor white people. She reported that the Van den Berghs were indeed very poor and that she would have to make regular visits, which she did not look forward to because Mrs. van den Bergh talked incessantly and, though older than my mother, called her "Auntie."

Prompted, after all, to my own form of charity by my mother's news, I offered Fanie van den Bergh one of my sandwiches at break, but he declined — not very graciously, I thought. It was a white-bread sandwich, which was regarded as a delicacy, white flour not being subsidized like the brown flour that the poor people used. When I saw Fanie accepting a *vetkoek* from Louis van Niekerk, I concluded that he was not used to white bread and did not know that it was better for him than *vetkoek*. My mother did not make *vetkoek*.

In spite of this rebuff, I occasionally helped Fanie van den Bergh with his sums. He seemed more appreciative of this than of the sandwich, though he was satisfied to be given the answers and showed little interest in my explanations of how I had arrived at them. I couldn't help him with reading: explaining why a particular combination of marks means *dog* rather than *cat* was beyond my powers. It seemed to me that Fanie should be able to arrive at so simple a distinction without explanations. "Can't you tell the difference between *cat* and *dog*?" I'd ask in exasperation, and "No," he would reply stolidly.

"Then what's that?" I asked, pointing at Mrs. Maree's mongrel fortuitously trotting past the school fence. Mrs. Maree lived next to the school and regularly complained about some aspect of our behavior. Her dog, though, was friendly, and sometimes condescended to visit my six-month-old puppy, Dumbo.

"That's Skollie," he said.

"Yes, but what sort of thing is Skollie? A dog or a cat?" I added quickly, to narrow down the available categories.

"A dog, of course," he said, looking at me as if I were the moron.

"Then if you can recognize a dog when you see one, why can't you recognize the word when you see it?" I asked triumphantly.

He thought for a moment. "Because the word doesn't have a tail and ears," he said at last.

"But a cat also has a tail and ears," I pounced, delighted at having him play into my pedagogical strategy so obligingly; but he only said, "Not like a dog's." I heard later that he'd told Tjaart Bothma that I didn't know the difference between a cat and a dog, and I decided that Fanie van den Bergh was stupid. He himself seemed strangely unaware of this and went his way impassively, apparently unperturbed by his lack of prowess. Nor did Miss Jordaan try to bring home to him his hopeless state, as she did to some others in the class. This seemed unfair, since most of the chastised were in fact less hopeless than Fanie.

Having done my duty by Fanie van den Bergh, I was prepared to consign him to the obscurity appropriate to his gifts, and I stopped trying to teach him anything. I was still kind to him, of course, but there didn't seem to be anything much to be kind about. My mother unwittingly confirmed me in this conviction in her accounts of her visits to Fanie's mother.

"I don't know," she announced one evening after supper, "why we bother."

"Why we bother with what?" asked my father.

"Oh, with people who can't be helped, like Mrs. van de Bergh."

16

This interested me. "Why can't she be helped?"

"I don't think she wants to be helped. I took her that recipe book that we produced, the one with nutritious meals …"

"You mean *Healthy Meals for Large Families*?" my father smiled.

"Yes, and now she complains that it doesn't contain a recipe for *vetkoek* — I mean, *vetkoek*, the stuff is pure starch and fat, it's exactly the kind of thing we're trying to get these people to stop eating."

"Why does she want to make *vetkoek*?" I asked, pursuing a line of thought of my own.

"It seems her son has been nagging her to make it. I told her to tell him it's bad for him, but I don't think she believes me."

I nodded; so Fanie had after all preferred Louis's *vetkoek* to my mother's white bread.

"And besides," my mother continued, "she tells me she can't use the book because they haven't got a large family. She just doesn't see the point."

"And what is the point?" asked my father.

"Well, that the recipes are meant for people who are too poor to afford meat and eggs and things."

"Then why didn't you call it *Healthy Meals for People Who Are Too Poor to Afford Meat and Eggs and Things*?" my father asked.

"Oh really, John, that's not the point!" my mother laughed, and, in spite of her laugh, which I didn't understand, I could see what she meant. The point was that the Van den Berghs couldn't see the point.

So, unlike my mother, who kept trying to raise the Van den Bergh standard of living, I stopped bothering. Fanie van den Bergh took his place among the featureless objects of Verkeerdespruit and would have remained there had he not turned out to be, after all, exceptional.

This fact, startling in itself, was brought home to us in a sensational manner. We were mumbling and stumbling our way through Loud Reading — always a trial to me, who read ahead and then got impatient with the other children's halting progress. As a result my attention was at leisure to survey the rest of the

17

class, most of them with their eyes fixed rigidly on the page in front of them, terrified lest they be called upon to read.

Fanie's attention seemed more fixed than most: if it had been possible to decipher a word by staring at it, he would have been a star reader. He gazed at his book with what I took to be a craving to understand; then suddenly, without any preliminary, he fell sideways off his desk and slumped on his back in the aisle. This was so unexpected that my categories of human behavior were taken completely by surprise. As I stared at him in a kind of horror of incomprehension, he went completely rigid, arching his back and clenching his fists. By now most of the rest of the class was watching, though Miss Jordaan, intent upon helping the fumbling reader of the moment, was unaware of anything untoward.

Somebody giggled at the back of the class. "Fanie! Get up!" I whispered, more to reassert my own sense of normality than because I thought it would have any effect. The effect was in fact extraordinary: Fanie started convulsing rhythmically, knocking his head against the floor. By the time Miss Jordaan reached him, foam was appearing at his mouth and half the class was hysterical.

"Shut up!" she snapped in passing at Jesserina Schoeman, who was more agitated than most, and shook her arm roughly. Jesserina gulped and shut up. Miss Jordaan knelt by the frantically undulating body of Fanie van den Bergh and seized his shoulders. "Fanie!" she shouted, and I could see that she was almost as terrified as we were. Then she found a category.

"He's having a fit," she announced.

The information calmed us immediately. We'd heard of fits. The horrible visitation had been named, explained, tamed in our minds. The only person unaffected by this exorcism was Fanie, who continued beating his head against the floor, his eyes and mouth clenched tight.

"He's going to swallow his tongue," declared Miss Jordaan, reawakening the dread of the bizarre in our minds. She seized his jaw. "Get me a ruler."

Mine was closest. Miss Jordaan grabbed it from my fumbling hand and started prizing open Fanie's rigid mouth with her left hand, holding the ruler in her right. She forced his teeth apart just far enough to get her fingers clamped tight between his jaws. She screamed and hit Fanie on the head with the ruler. Jesserina Schoeman also screamed, and Miss Jordaan hit her on the leg.

This served to calm both Miss Jordaan and Jesserina, but it had little effect on Fanie. Miss Jordaan set to work at forcing open his jaws with the ruler and managed to extricate her fingers. I noticed with fascination that they were bleeding. Miss Jordaan by now had the ruler lodged in Fanie's mouth, and she relaxed.

"Now at least he won't swallow his tongue," she said grimly, in a tone implying that by rights he should be left to swallow it and be damned. Reassured, we forgave Fanie for biting Miss Jordaan and watched him more dispassionately.

The fit lasted about five minutes. Then the convulsions stopped abruptly, and Fanie went limp, his eyes still shut. The ruler fell from his mouth with a clatter, and I retrieved it, examining with interest the tooth marks in the wood. "Let me see," whispered Annette Loubser, and the ruler made its way from hand to hand through the enthralled class, witness to the passion of Fanie's fit.

We carried Fanie to the principal's office, the clearinghouse of all crises, and Mr. Viljoen drove him home. Miss Jordaan, her fingers bandaged from the first-aid tin in the principal's office, slightly pale with pain and shock, explained the fit to us.

"Some people get fits like this because of a disease they have," she said. "They're not dangerous," (glancing briefly at her bandaged fingers) "but you must be careful not to give them a fright or anything, because that can bring on the fit."

"What will happen to Fanie?" I asked.

"He'll be all right soon," she said.

"Fanie van den Bergh had a fit today," I announced at lunch. To my disappointment my mother did not seem as interested as this piece of news merited.

"Yes, he's an epileptic," she said. "His mother told me."

"An epi …?"

"An epileptic. Somebody who gets fits."

"He bit Miss Jordaan," I added, determined to wring some sensation from the story after all. This was more successful.

"Why? Did she try to open his mouth?"

"She was trying to put a ruler in his mouth to stop him swallowing his tongue."

"Tsk," my mother disapproved, "*that* old superstition. She should have turned him on his side." My mother had been a nurse — "a qualified nurse," I always distinguished — before she married my father. "Tell her she's lucky he didn't bite off all her fingers." I wouldn't have thought of telling Miss Jordaan anything like that, but I was always secretly gratified by my mother's criticism of our teachers.

The next day Fanie van den Bergh was back at school, seeming none the worse for his fit. He was given more attention than he had had since his arrival, but he proved as taciturn on this subject as on all others. No, he couldn't remember anything, and no, he hadn't bitten Miss Jordaan on purpose, and no, he didn't think it happened when he got a fright. Armed with my mother's superior knowledge, in fact, I had more to tell them than Fanie.

"My mother says she shouldn't have tried to put a ruler in his mouth, she should have turned him on his side. He's an epileptic," I announced. I'd practiced the word before coming to school.

"What does your mother know?" challenged Louis van Niekerk. As a policeman's son, he felt obliged to support me in disputes involving legal matters but driven to oppose me when he thought I was exceeding my authority.

"She's a qualified nurse," I replied unanswerably, and offered Fanie van den Bergh an apricot jam sandwich. This time he accepted, though without saying thank you.

Fanie's fit soon passed into history. We resolved not to give Fanie a fright, but since few of us would normally have thought of doing so, this hardly changed our lives or Fanie's. There was a brief revival of interest when Miss Jordaan appeared without her bandage, and we all craned our necks to see the scars left by Fanie's teeth. These proved to be disappointingly faint, and I decided that she had been unnecessarily harsh in hitting Fanie with the ruler, especially when she had been bitten because of her own ignorance.

Fanie returned to his previous position of tolerated obscurity. He did, though, emerge momentarily from near invisibility one

20

day when he turned up clutching a brown paper bag, shiny and translucent with grease.

"What have you got in there, Fanie?" Louis asked, though there was no mistaking the appearance of a bag of *vetkoek*.

"*Vetkoek*," Fanie said, half shyly, half proudly. "Would you like one?" And he took out of the bag the largest and most misshapen *vetkoek* I had ever seen. Mrs. van den Bergh was clearly still experimenting. I stifled a giggle, but Louis, ever direct, said, "Jissus, it looks like a cow pat. Here, let me taste," and he took the strange object and bit into it experimentally. "Tastes better than it looks," he pronounced doughily.

"There," said Fanie and extended a second *vetkoek*, even more fantastically shaped than the first, toward me. "A *vetkoek*."

"No, thank you," I said. "My mother says *vetkoek* is bad for you."

He stood with the *vetkoek* still extended in his hand, looking at it as if seeing it for the first time. Then he threw the spurned object over the school fence into the dusty street. Skollie trotted up, sniffed at it, and bore it off into Mrs. Maree's backyard. The next day at assembly the principal announced that Mrs. Maree had complained that we had been feeding her dog "rubbish" and that he had been violently ill on her lounge carpet. When I told my mother, she said that Mrs. Maree's lounge carpet was enough to make anybody violently ill without *vetkoek*.

About six months after Fanie's fit there was a commotion during break. I had been standing on my own, whittling chunks off the corner-post of the school fence. The wood was reputed to make you — or your victim — sneeze if you ground it fine.

Suddenly everybody was running to a spot next to the boys' lavatories, even the girls who normally preserved a chaste distance from this male preserve. I assumed there was a fight taking place, though I hadn't heard the usual rallying cry of "Fight! Fight!" and ran to share the excitement. But instead of two belligerent boys giving each other "cash," the circle contained only a writhing Fanie van den Bergh, obviously in the throes of another fit. We Standard Ones and Twos felt superior to the rest of the school in having witnessed this before, and slightly disappointed that they

21

too were now being admitted to the mystery of fits. Still, we were being looked to for guidance, even from the big children.

"What must we do?" asked Frikkie Steyn, a big Standard Fiver who had been elected head boy of the primary school because he could run faster than anybody else and who was now facing the first crisis of his leadership.

"Put your fingers in his mouth," suggested Louis van Niekerk, his malice aimed more against me than against Frikkie. He knew that I would resent having my mother's medical knowledge impugned, and he was right.

"No, don't!" I shouted, pushing forward. "Just turn him on his side."

Faced with the choice of either putting his fingers into the clenched and foaming mouth of Fanie van den Bergh or turning him on his side, Frikkie sensibly opted for the latter course. The effect appeared miraculous: Fanie relaxed immediately and lapsed into what seemed a deep sleep. Even I was impressed at the efficacy of my mother's remedy; the rest of the school was dumbfounded.

"You see," I shrugged, "it works."

"What must we do now?" asked Frikkie, and I realized that I had no idea. I had not pursued my mother's knowledge far enough. Reluctant, though, to relinquish the authority I had so unexpectedly gained, I bluffed it out.

"We must carry him indoors. He can't lie here," I improvised.

"Right, let's take him to the office," said Frikkie, assuming command again, and seized a leg. "You" — to me — "take the other leg, and you" — to two other boys including the discredited Louis van Niekerk — "each take an arm."

So the unconscious Fanie van den Bergh was ceremonially, almost processionally, carried to Mr. Viljoen's office and dumped on the floor. There was a sofa there expressly for occasions like this, but we didn't even consider putting Fanie on it: never a very clean child, he was now covered in the red earth of the playground. Mr. Viljoen was having tea in the staff room; while Jesserina Schoeman was dispatched to fetch him, Frikkie chased out everybody except the bearers. The expelled crowded around the door, perhaps hoping that Fanie would bite Mr. Viljoen.

Mr. Viljoen appeared, carrying his cup of tea, with Miss Jordaan in his wake. He hesitated and looked at her; she considerately relieved him of his cup, spilling some tea on Fanie's shirt; Mr. Viljoen kneeled next to Fanie.

"Fanie!" he said. "Wake up!"

To everybody's surprise, Fanie woke up. He looked blankly at Mr. Viljoen, who, slightly taken aback at the efficacy of his own authority, felt obliged to continue his ministrations.

"What happened, Fanie? Did you get a fright?"

Slowly Fanie van den Bergh's gaze shifted from Mr. Viljoen's face to the rest of us.

"What happened, Fanie?" Mr. Viljoen repeated. "Did you get a fright?"

Fanie's eyes flickered briefly at Mr. Viljoen, returned to Frikkie, on to Louis, without a sign of recognition or anything else, until they met my attentive regard. His eyes locked with mine. For a few seconds he seemed to be thinking. Then his dull face set into an expression of pure hatred.

"It was him," he said triumphantly, pointing at me. "He gave me a fright."

December 6, 1968

I had remembered, of course, that Odendaalsrust Technical School was where Fanie van den Bergh went after he left Verkeerdespruit, but I had not imagined that he would be a member of their tennis team, given the level of his involvement when I had known him. The Clutch Plate tennis team must be an even more desperate affair than we had surmised if it counted Fanie van den Bergh as one of its assets. He had shown, it was true, a rudimentary interest in the game in Verkeerdespruit, but that had seemed centred on Mr. van der Walt, the tennis coach, and I could hardly imagine him actually becoming a real tennis player, in the sense of owning tennis shoes and a racket and white socks: to me, Fanie would always be barefoot and slightly grubby. But, incontrovertibly, there he was with the other Clutch Plates, looking, in the school uniform, quite unlike Fanie van den Bergh, and yet also unmistakably Fanie in his general air of being lost but not minding, a kind of indifference to his own helplessness that was profoundly irritating to people who felt that he should mind.

I was afraid that Fanie would create some embarrassing recognition scene that would implicate me in his state of Clutch Platery. I had just about established myself as not really a Ball-Bearing, and to be hailed now in unambiguous Afrikaans would set back my redefinition of myself irretrievably. But Fanie was no more given to scenes than he had ever been. Seeing me, he registered as little surprise or anything else as if he had met me walking down Voortrekker Street in Verkeerdespruit. He did shamble over, though, in his knock-kneed sort of way. He was still recognizably the gangling boy of Verkeerdespruit, but there was also a sort of grace in the gawkiness, like that of a young animal finding its form. And his weak features had filled out: the strangely prominent bones of the head somehow gave shape where before they had only emphasized vacuity. His colorless hair was now definitely blond and, possibly because it was cleaner than it used to be, even had a shine to it.

Fanie came up to me and said, "Hello," in a flatly factual tone, without offering to shake hands. I assumed that the Clutch Plates weren't taught these refinements.

"Fanie," I said, and put out my hand. He took it tentatively and shook it in an unpracticed sort of way.

"Your parents both well?" I asked. Mr. and Mrs. van den Bergh had moved to Ventersdorp "to help my sister on the plot," as Mrs. van den Bergh had explained to my mother. "Can you imagine that?" my mother had asked. "Mrs. van den Bergh helping her sister pluck the chickens and slaughter the pigs?"

Fanie looked at me in an unhelpful way: the social formulae of Wesley College were clearly beyond him. "Are your parents well — with your aunt?" I tried again.

"No," he said in his loud and un-self-conscious Afrikaans, "My pa sê die plek ruik na hoenderstront" — My father says the place smells of chicken shit.

I caught Tim Watkins's eye behind Fanie's back: he was making no secret of his gleeful interest. Fanie's fellow Clutch Plates, though presumably by now used to the gaps in Fanie's social skills, laughed exaggeratedly to distance themselves from this latest *instance. I decided not to pursue the fortunes of the Van den Bergh family.*

"Is this your first visit to Bloemfontein?" I asked, without curiosity or anticipation: making small talk with Fanie van den Bergh was about as rewarding as feeding peanuts to a camel. To my surprise, though, instead of the hopelessly uninflected, literal-minded "yes" or "no" that was Fanie's inveterate contribution to an articulate community, he brightened as if at the recollection of some cherished memory. "No," he said. "No, I came here once with Steve. On his motorbike."

2

Winter and Spring 1963

In court they called him Johannes Jacobus van der Westhuizen, but to us he was always Steve. That was how he introduced — or rather announced — himself to us, as we gathered around the big black motorbike parked in the dust of the main street outside Steyl's café.

"Call me Steve," he said, less as an invitation to familiarity than as a rebuke to Kosie Opperman's "*Middag, Oom*" — Good afternoon, Uncle — in the indiscriminately familial vocabulary of the Free State child. And although I had never called a grown man by his first name, I could see the inappropriateness of the avuncular form for somebody so unlike the uncles of our acquaintance. In our town, uncles did not wear blue jeans and tight T-shirts; in fact, in our town nobody wore blue jeans and tight T-shirts except the *tsotsis* who sometimes came from Bloemfontein and even Johannesburg to visit friends and relatives in the location and so could not be said to be part of our town at all. "Tsotsi clothes" — that was all the explanation that was needed or given to justify parental extinction of any subversive sartorial ambitions among the children of Verkeerdespruit. "But why can't I have a pink shirt?" "Tsotsi clothes" — and that would be the end of that.

Steve did not look like a *tsotsi*. Apart from the fact that *tsotsis* were black and he was white, *tsotsis* were, in the received wisdom of childhood lore, quite puny — "That's why they go around in gangs" — and Steve was very big, with forearms thicker than those of Maritz the Butcher. Maritz was reputed to have stunned a runaway bull with one blow of his tremendous fist long ago. Nobody knew exactly how: the majority opinion was that he had hit the bull between the eyes, but a strong minority favored a chop on the back of the neck. Louis van Niekerk, challenged to ask Maritz himself, did so once, with all of us watching from outside the shop. We saw Maritz look at Louis impassively, then roll up his sleeves; Louis turned tail and ran and so did we all, to come to a halt breathlessly outside Dominee Claassen's *pastorie*, which we regarded as a sanctuary from any evil not perpetrated by ourselves. "What did he say?" we demanded from the panting Louis van Niekerk. "I asked him how he had stunned the bull and he said … he said he … he would show me."

Steve, though as powerful as Maritz, instilled no such terror. On his first memorable appearance, roaring down the Saturday-afternoon-deserted, winter-dusty main street, he had seemed like a creature of another essence, too marvelous to correspond to any of our categories of fear; and thereafter, though not overtly friendly and, when cruising slowly past up Voortrekker Street, not deigning to notice us as we ceased our games or conversations or squabbles to look at the big man on the big motorbike, he seemed nevertheless to enjoy answering our many questions when he parked outside Steyl's for a Coke, of which he had about ten a day. "My mother says Coke is bad for your teeth," I volunteered once, not knowing enough about motorbikes to ask a convincing question. I now knew, like everybody else, that the gleaming machine was a Matchless G9, but to my untechnical mind this offered no opening to conversation. "Your *mother*!" Kosie Opperman jeered, and looked at Steve to corroborate his contempt for such unmanly talk; but Steve looked at me attentively and said, "That's only while you're still growing. When you're big your teeth settle." He tapped his front teeth with a long fingernail. "See? I've got thirty-two of them, and they're all strong enough to bite off your fingers." Without warning, he took my hand and put my fingers in his mouth and bit them, quite hard but not so that it hurt. "Feel that?" he asked. "Sharp, eh?" and showed most of his thirty-two teeth in a mock-savage grimace. Kosie and Louis laughed mirthlessly, slightly resentful of the attention I was getting, but not wanting to ignore Steve's comic intent, and I could feel myself blushing, not with embarrassment, but with an unfamiliar kind of pleasure. At a loss for words, I examined the light indentations left in my flesh by his teeth.

Fanie van den Bergh, who was watching in his usual taciturn way, did not laugh with the others, but merely stared at Steve with the unfathomable gaze of the simpleminded. Then Steve winked at him — not an absentminded flicker such as Mr. Osrin bestowed upon us from behind his counter as he weighed groceries for a customer, but a slow conspiratorial wink that seemed to recognize Fanie as an equal and accomplice, combined somehow against the rest of us.

"I bet you don't know what *matchless* means," I said to Fanie. He transferred his heavy gaze to me, frowned slightly, then looked at Steve, who was watching him with a little smile. "It means — it means without equal," Fanie said, flatly and factually, his eyes still on Steve, whose smile now broadened into a grin. "That's right," I conceded magnanimously. "Steve must have told you." But Steve said, "Fanie knows more than you think — not so, Fanie?" Fanie continued to look solemnly at Steve, then shook his head and went and stood next to the Matchless and stroked the saddle.

Steve's arrival made more of a difference to Verkeerdespruit than even he could have imagined — not that he was modest, because he wasn't. But the swagger with which he got off the bike and flicked back the curl from his forehead, totally conscious of the gaze of the contingent of children gathered on the sidewalk, was more prodigious even than his vanity could conceive. How could Steve have known what it was for a child in Verkeerdespruit to see every day, actually living in Verkeerdespruit, an order of apparition that until then had manifested itself only in some thrillingly fearful Big City of the imagination? The TJ registration number gleamed at us like a mantra, calling up a different state of existence in gold-encrusted, skyscrapered, sinful Johannesburg. When Kosie Opperman's mother issued a ban on his association with "that white tsotsi," it lent to the privilege of Steve's company the added allure of illegitimacy.

Having had the protected childhood that was the only kind possible in Verkeerdespruit, I was used to piecing together my understanding of the great world from literature in the broadest sense, that is, almost anything that I could find to read in an

28

unliterary community. Steve, I learned from old copies of *Die Huisgenoot* in Mr. Welthagen's barbershop, where I reluctantly went once a month to have my head scraped with his blunt clipper, was not unique. "He's a ducktail," I announced one day as we were standing around outside Steyl's café hoping Steve would arrive. "You can see it from the way he combs his hair."

"What's a ducktail?" Louis challenged in a truculent tone intended to neutralize the humiliation of having to admit ignorance.

"They're people who drive around on motorbikes and comb their hair like Steve's," I said, conscious of a certain circularity of definition. This was not lost on Louis. "Big deal," he said. "So what?"

"They live in Johannesburg," I added, "and they have Sheilas. The Sheilas are women who smoke."

Louis wasn't going to be trapped into another admission of ignorance. "Then where's Steve's Sheila?" he demanded, and to myself I had to concede that Louis had seized the initiative. To him I said, "In Johannesburg, I suppose. Sheilas live on the streets."

"So? There are streets here, aren't there?" and Louis gesticulated indignantly toward the dusty waste of Voortrekker Street.

I laughed scornfully. "And what do you think a Sheila would do on Voortrekker Street?"

"Just what she does on the Johannesburg streets, I suppose," Louis countered. "A street's a street, isn't it?"

Looking at Voortrekker Street in the meager light of an unexuberant spring, its one café and two shops, its gas pump and its hotel, its ragged eucalyptus trees, I shook my head. "No. A street's not a street," I said, though without quite understanding what it was that I was trying to say. "No Sheila could live on this street."

The next time we were all congregated around the Matchless, Louis had his revenge. "Where's your Sheila?" he asked Steve abruptly, in the middle of a general discussion of cylinder heads. When Steve looked at him quizzically, he faltered slightly. "He" — gesturing toward me — "he says he read that all ducktails have a Sheila."

There was a shocked silence. Nobody else had thought actually to confront Steve on the ducktail question; though ignorant of the exact implications of the label, we guessed that it was applied to people by other people rather than by themselves. Steve was looking at me in what I uncomfortably suspected was amusement. Before I could extricate myself from my embarrassment, Fanie made one of his rare contributions. "Steve doesn't have a Sheila," he announced flatly and heavily.

I turned on him. "How do *you* ..." and then desisted. It was hopeless trying to get anything out of Fanie.

"That's right," Steve said. "I don't have a Sheila."

"Then not all ducktails have Sheilas?" Louis persisted, looking at me triumphantly.

"What's a ducktail?" Steve asked mildly. Louis looked at me in some consternation, but I left him to wriggle on the consequences of his own audacity.

"They ride around on motorbikes and ... have Sheilas," he said somewhat lamely.

Kosie Opperman, who was defying his mother's ban because she had one of her migraines and was lying in a darkened room, intervened authoritatively: "Well, then, stupid, Steve can't be a ducktail, can he?"

We were all still warily considering the logic of this when Steve got onto his bike and kicked it into life with that nonchalant energy that always reminded me of the way Gene Autry leaped onto his horse. "Don't believe everything you read," he said to me as he puttered off. Then he stopped. "Are you coming, Fanie?" he asked, and to our communal amazement Fanie got onto the back of the Matchless and disappeared in a cloud of dust, clinging to the back of Steve's black leather jacket.

Later I realized that by this time Steve's carefully groomed image must have been as out of date as everything else that ended up in Verkeerdespruit. But to us he seemed as modern as the passenger planes that flew high over our town, and as dangerous as the hidden blade of the flick knife he once displayed to us. "It's against the law to carry one of these," he said, and Louis van Niekerk and I looked at each other in silent acknowledgement of a force superior to our fathers' judicial authority. Steve was the decline of urban youth brought to Verkeerdespruit, the worst imaginings of *Die Landstem* and *Die Huisgenoot* made flesh. No matter that we had only the most generalized notion of the enormities of evil that we ascribed to him, or that he had taken lodgings with the ferociously respectable Mrs. Maree: to us he was the sinister stranger who rides into town on a black horse — except that he was on our side, fighting against the adult world of duty and obedience that we didn't have the initiative to defy.

"What's Jo'burg like?" I asked Steve one day. We had taken to calling it "Jo'burg" because that was how Steve always referred to it, with an easy familiarity I couldn't quite match.

"It's big," he shrugged, "and the people are rich."

"And the Communists?" I asked. Johannesburg had recently been revealed to harbor a nest of Communists plotting to overthrow the government, and the city now loomed in my imagination as a center of conspiracy and subversion in addition to its more traditional turpitudes.

"What about the Communists?" Steve asked.

"Are they ... are there lots of them?" I asked inadequately, realizing that I knew little about them other than their name.

"Sure," he said. "There are lots of everything in Jo'burg."

Louis van Niekerk chipped in: "My father says the Communists want to take over the country and give it to the kaffirs." Steve shrugged again. "They don't bother me, long as they leave me alone."

In the lurid light of the press reports of the time, Steve's nonchalance seemed brave to the point of sedition. Though I was by no means so emancipated from my class and time as to feel anything but horror for *Umkhonto we Sizwe*, Steve's cavalier indifference to their dire plots paradoxically struck me as very fine. To the glamour of his general demeanor was now added the thrill of recklessness, even lawlessness.

One evening at supper my mother asked me, "Have you also been hanging around with that man with the motorbike?"

I was chewing a slice of bread, and under cover of emptying my mouth I considered a noncommittal reply. "I ... I have seen

31

him around," I said.

"Have you spoken to him?" she demanded.

"A few times," I admitted.

"And what kinds of things does he discuss with you?"

"Motorbikes," I said, probably slightly too patly to reassure my mother.

"I didn't know you knew about motorbikes," she said with a slight frown.

"His motorbike has five hundred CCs and eight grease nipples," I volunteered, hoping that my mother would not ask what that meant. But she only said, "I can't see why a grown man would want to stand around discussing nipples with a group of boys. Doesn't he have friends his own age?"

"I don't know," I said dumbly.

"I don't think there are any men his age in Verkeerdespruit," my father contributed.

"There are plenty of girls his age," said my mother.

"Who?" my father asked.

"Well, there's Miss Jordaan — she's about his age. Give or take five years."

"Steve says he asked her out and she said she didn't want to be seen on the back of a motorbike in case she got a reputation." I hoped my mother would tell me what a reputation was, but all she said was, "It's odd, the things you can get a reputation for in this town." For a while we ate in silence and then she said, "Well, then there's Betty the Exchange."

"I think he does know Betty the Exchange," I said carefully. One morning on my way to Sunday school I had seen Steve's motorbike in front of the house where Betty had a room with Steyl, the café owner, and his wife.

"The poor girl," my mother said somewhat inconsequentially, and then turned to my father. "I don't think it's a good thing that he hangs around our streets," she said. "Can't he be stopped?"

"I don't see how anyone can do that, my dear," he said mildly. "He isn't doing anything wrong."

"I think he's a bad influence," she said.

"What's a bad influence?" I asked.

Uncharacteristically, my mother got impatient with my questioning. "Never mind what it is," she said. "I'm telling you he's a bad influence, five hundred grease nipples or not. Why doesn't he get a job?"

"Eight. And he does have a job," I added. "He helps Mr. Deyssel at the garage." Deyssel's Garage and Service Station was the sole source of gas in Verkeerdespruit, and the only center of mechanical expertise. People with new cars took them to Bloemfontein to be serviced, but for emergency repairs and for old cars Mr. Deyssel was deemed adequate. His business, though not exactly thriving, had survived quite steadily on this grudging clientele for as long as I could remember.

"I hope he can teach Deyssel the difference between a carburetor and a gas cap," was all my father said, which I took as some sort of endorsement of Steve's usefulness in the community.

One Saturday morning I was walking down Voortrekker Street on my way to Steyl's café with my dog, Dumbo, snuffling along as usual, when the great roar of the Matchless announced to Verkeerdespruit that Steve had emerged for the day. It was the first sunny day after an unusually good bout of spring rains; the night before, a thunderstorm had descended on us with such violence that Dumbo had sought refuge in my bed from the noise and the light, and from the deluge that followed. The normally morose landscape was responding brilliantly to the freshness and the warmth, and was sharp with the smell of vegetation. In the crisp air Steve's machine sounded deafening as it approached; then, unexpectedly, it decelerated and throbbed to a pause next to me.

"Hi," Steve grinned at me. "Want to come for a spin?"

If Steve had asked me whether I wanted to fly to the moon I couldn't have been more at a loss. It's all very well to be offered a *spin* as if one had one every day, but I literally didn't know how to get onto the back of a motorbike, and once there what to do with myself. Besides, after my mother's mutterings about Steve, I suspected that a spin on the back of his motorbike would count as a bad influence, not to mention the *reputation* which, according to Miss Jordaan, one could incur as a consequence.

33

"What's the matter?" Steve said, "Don't you want to come?"

"No — I mean yes," I said. "Yes, I want to come." It was as simple as that. Even getting onto the huge motorbike proved to be easier than I had anticipated, and once I was seated behind Steve, he turned around and said, "Just put your arms around my waist if you're scared you're going to fall off."

So I held on tightly and the machine leaped forward, leaving behind, it felt, my heart and bowels — along with a reproachful Dumbo, who stared after us dolefully for a moment and then turned back home. I shrugged off my guilt and surrendered to the roar of the bike. Voortrekker Street streaked past, suffused with a glamour I had not thought it capable of, the shop fronts glistening in the clean air, the eucalyptus trees sparkling with raindrops and sunshine. I was subliminally aware of Mrs. Opperman coming out of Osrin's and looking after us as we sped past out onto the Bloemfontein road, the only strip of tarred road in the area. Once we were on the open road, Steve turned his head back to me and said, "Hold on tight," and accelerated, and once again part of me was left behind as we leaped forward, to catch up with the rest of me only as the machine settled to a steady roar. I was sheltered from the wind by Steve's big back and, resting my cheek against him, I could see the landscape, transformed by speed and noise, reeling past, itself released from earthbound immobility. The power of the machine shook my whole body, but, feeling the strength of Steve's body responding with the movement, I was secure in being at one with the source of power and speed: the swerving of the machine, so terrifying to watch from the side of the road, was the smooth tilting of a single axle around a still point, at the center of which I was fused with Steve.

We rushed through the morning. I wanted it to go on and on, never to return to Verkeerdespruit and its pedestrian existence, always to speed through an empty landscape contained in noise and movement with Steve. But the machine started to counter its own momentum as Steve cut the throttle, and we glided to a halt. We were next to the bridge over the Modder River. For once the river had water in it rather than the mud it was named for, or the dust to which the mud was invariably reduced.

Steve turned round to me. "Hop off," he said.

34

For a moment I thought he was going to abandon me there, but he smiled at me encouragingly, and I got off the bike slightly less clumsily than I had feared. He pulled the machine up onto its stand and got off.

"It's warm when you get off," he said, and lit a Texan.

It was also very quiet on the deserted road. My body was still tingling with the vibration of the machine, and I felt out of breath. I looked at the blue sky, and felt the sunshine on my skin, and said, "Yes, it is," and that seemed enough, that and the prospect of going back again on the magic machine.

He pulled at his cigarette. "Fancy a goof?" he asked.

"Goof ...?"

"Swim."

"You mean here?" I asked.

"Sure, where else? There's a *lekker* swimming hole just under the bridge," he said. "I've come out here before."

"I ... I can't swim," I confessed. Not many Verkeerdespruit children could, for the simple reason that there was no large body of water available for long enough to enable us to get over our native fear of the foreign element.

"'S'okay," he said. "I'll piggyback you."

While I was still wondering over this novel form of transportation, he flicked away his cigarette and extended his hand and said, "Come on," and helped me down the bank.

Under the bridge he took off his T-shirt and boots and jeans, and I noticed that he did not wear underpants. My mother said only common people went without underpants; when I said that none of the boys in my class wore underpants, she said, "Exactly."

Steve said, "Come on, get them off, there's nothing to be worried about. Nobody can see us down here under the bridge."

I took off my khaki shirt and shorts, and then my underpants. I didn't know what to do with my clothes, but he took them from me, folded them, and put them on top of his. He glanced at me. "You're thin," he said, but I couldn't think of anything to say.

"Come on," he said again, and turned his back to me. "Get onto my back."

He went and stood below me so that I could reach around his neck; then he gripped my legs in his arms and walked into the water. He was slightly unsteady because the bottom of the river was very rocky, and there was a weak current. Toward the middle of the river the bank sloped down, and he let go of my legs and started swimming what I recognized as the breaststroke from the Esther Williams movies that came to the town hall. I could feel the rhythmical contracting and relaxing of his back and shoulder muscles under me, and my belly rubbed against the skin of his back. It was like sitting behind him on the motorbike, except that instead of the throbbing engine there was only the water washing over us, resisting us and yet sustaining us, Steve and I moving as a single unit of force escaping from the pull of the earth.

"You can help us by kicking your legs," said Steve over his shoulder and I started churning up the water behind us, happy in the knowledge that I was contributing to our progress. The Modder River is not a very wide river, and we were soon on the other side.

"Okay?" he asked, and I nodded and said, "Okay." Then I asked what I'd been wondering: "Where did you learn to swim?"

"The place I work at has a swimming pool for the workers," he replied.

"In Jo'burg?" I asked, and he nodded, but he didn't seem to want to talk about it, so I dropped the topic.

"Ready to go back?" he asked.

"You mean to Verkeerdespruit?" I asked, disappointed.

"No, back to the other side of the river."

"Yes," I said, although I wished I could say something that would delay our return.

"This time I'll swim on my back and pull you along," Steve said. "Come and stand in front of me and just lie back." I did so, and he put his arms loosely around my body and kicked with his feet so that we moved backward slowly. It went less smoothly than the first time, and we got water in our mouths and noses. Coughing and spluttering and laughing, we got to the other side. He pulled me out of the water.

I looked down at my streaming body. "I'm wet," I said.

He laughed. "Of course you're wet. That's what happens when you get into the water. We'll dry out in the sun."

He found his crumpled packet of Texans, lit one carefully so as not to get it wet, and sat down on a sandy ledge. "Come and sit next to me," he said, and patted the ledge.

I sat next to him, half leaning against his side. He put his left arm on my shoulder. "Next time I'll teach you to swim," he said.

"Really?" I asked, thrilled as much by the idea of a next time as by the promise.

The sun was warm on our bodies, and apart from the sound of a bird making a fuss in a *soetdoring* tree next to us, it was absolutely quiet. Steve's smoke drifted in the still air in front of us, the sweetish smell of the tobacco mingling with the scent of the first yellow flowers on the tree. He blew a smoke ring and we watched it hover in front of us before it gradually dispersed.

"Blow another," I said, and he did. The insubstantial ring drifting in front of us seemed to me the most perfect thing I had ever seen, but I was too shy to say so.

We sat for a while and then he threw away his cigarette, rubbed his hand across his stomach, and said, "I'm just about dry, how about you?"

"I'm quite dry," I said.

"Course you are. There's much less of you to get dry," and he ran his hand down my side. Then he got up from the ledge and stretched himself in the sun. I had never seen a grown man without clothes before, and I looked at the hair on his body and wondered why men got hair there, and what it felt like. I put out my hand and touched the hair on his chest. It was rougher than ordinary hair.

Steve said, "You'll have some of that too, one day. Plenty of time." But I looked at Steve's body, the broad shoulders and thick arms, the strong legs, and shook my head. I knew that my body would never look like that.

"Yes, you will," he said, misinterpreting my head shake. "It happens to everybody. It's natural."

I thought of Mr. Viljoen and Mr. Deyssel and Dominee Claassen and somehow I couldn't imagine that they had hair on their bodies, or that if they did it looked like Steve's. "It looks nice on you," I said, then blushed.

"Of course it does," he said, and put his hand behind my neck and pressed my head against his shoulder. "Time to go," he said. "Your old folks will get worried."

As we pulled on our clothes there was the sound of a car approaching, not very fast. As it got to the bridge it slowed down and stopped. A car door opened and slammed, and my mother shouted, "Simon? Are you there?"

"Your old lady?" Steve asked.

"Yes," I said. "I don't know how she knew I was here."

"Simon!" my mother shouted, sounding half angry, half worried. I fastened the snake clasp on the buckle of my belt and clambered halfway up the bank to the road and said, "Yes, Mom, I'm here."

"What on earth are you doing there?" she asked.

"I'm here with Steve," I said, thinking that the presence of an adult would make it all right.

"Yes, I know *that*," she said, but it didn't sound as if this made things any better. "Where is … he?"

"Right here, madam," said Steve behind me, and he passed me and pulled me up the last bit of the bank. My mother was standing next to the car with a scarf around her head. I could see that her hair was in curlers, which meant that she must have left home in a hurry. My mother said it was common to appear in public in curlers. My mother wore a hat to go to town, except when she was just going to Osrin's quickly to buy groceries.

Mrs. Opperman was sitting in the car staring straight ahead, as if she might be turned to stone if she cast an eye on Steve or me. Dumbo was in the backseat, uncritically overjoyed to see me.

"Mr. …" my mother began, and hesitated.

"Call me Steve," he said, in the same languid way he had introduced himself to us upon his arrival in Verkeerdespruit.

"Steve," my mother said, though I could see she didn't really want to call him Steve, "you can't just go off with our sons on the back of that thing."

"Why not?" he asked, as if he really wanted to know. "I bring them back, don't I?"

"Yes, but it … it's dangerous," my mother said. "They could fall off."

"No chance," he said. "I tell them to hold on tight and they hold on tight."

"Anyway," my mother said, and I could see she was coming to her real point, "I don't think it's right for a grown man to drive around with little children."

"Why not?" he asked again. "I like little children."

At this Mrs. Opperman could no longer keep her countenance. She turned down her window all the way — it had been open just far enough for her to hear what was happening — put her head out, and hissed at Steve: "Pervert!" Dumbo jumped on top of her and leaped out of the window to get to me. Since Dumbo was a large dog, this demonstration detracted from her dignity.

Steve looked at Mrs. Opperman, looked at me, shrugged, and said, "You know what the old lady's on about?" but Mrs. Opperman, having uttered her incantation, had closed her window again.

"Get into the car," my mother said to me.

"But I want to go back with Steve," I protested, devastated at the prospect of losing the trip back on the motorbike and quite prepared to betray once again the affection of the forgiving Dumbo.

"Listen to me," my mother said in a tone that she used very seldom, and that did not allow for argument, "and get into that car immediately." She opened the back door so imperatively that Dumbo jumped in in a cowed sort of way and licked the back of Mrs. Opperman's neck. She screamed and slapped at him; she missed and he nipped her hand playfully. I also got in, trying to catch Steve's eye; somehow I wanted to tell him I was sorry for having brought this punitive expedition down upon him. But he was looking at my mother, who was saying: "It's very irresponsible of you to take children away. I was very worried when the dog came home on its own. If Mrs. Opperman hadn't seen you leave with Simon and come to tell me, I wouldn't have known where he was."

"That's right," Steve said, "and he'd have been back before you knew it."

"In any case," my mother said, "I'm warning you to stay away from my son. If you don't, I'll report you to the police."

"Suit yourself," said Steve. "But why don't you ask your son's opinion?"

"I don't ask my son's opinion on such matters and you know very well why," my mother snapped and got into the car.

As we drove off I looked back, and Steve gave me a thumbs-up sign. I waved at him. After a minute or two the Matchless roared past our car. There was infinite contempt in the ease with which it swerved to pass us and then cut in front of us and left us behind.

There was silence in the car for a while. I scratched Dumbo's ears and he nestled up against me happily.

"But what did he *do* with you under the bridge?" Mrs. Opperman demanded suddenly.

"He didn't do anything with me," I replied, sensing obscure horrors lurking in her question. "We swam in the river."

"You *swam*?" my mother exclaimed. "Where are your swimming trunks?" I had an old pair of swimming trunks for our annual trips to the sea.

"I didn't wear trunks," I said.

"Then what did you wear?" my mother demanded.

"Nothing," I said.

Mrs. Opperman turned round to me. She looked as if she'd seen a snake. "You mean you were *naked*?" she exclaimed.

I nodded. Then, with a dim intention of warding off the wrath and revulsion facing me, I said, "But Steve was also ... naked." The word was a violation.

Mrs. Opperman said, "I think I've got a migraine coming on," and my mother asked me, very gently: "Simon, did this, er ... Steve touch you at all?"

Again I heard a world of adult anxieties in the question, and an unfamiliar instinct warned me not to tell the truth. So I lied to my mother for the first time I could remember, and yet it was not really a lie either, for I knew that what my mother meant was not what Steve had done. "No," I said. "He didn't touch me."

After this Mrs. Opperman visited all of our parents, and most of them forbade their children to talk to Steve. Jesserina Schoeman giggled when she told us that her father had said she was not allowed to talk to "the ducktail." "I told him that I wished I could, but that Steve only talked to the boys, and he said worse and worse," she told us. "What did he mean?"

"I think he meant that Steve is a pervert," I replied, remembering the term Mrs. Opperman had spat at Steve.

"What's that?" demanded Louis van Niekerk.

"I don't know," I confessed. "It's what adults call Steve."

So when Louis was angry with me for not allowing him to copy my homework, he told Steve that I had said he was a pervert and reported to me that Steve had replied, "Well, bugger him then," and Steve stopped even waving at me when he drove past.

After a while the only boy who was still allowed to talk to Steve was Fanie van den Bergh. Kosie Opperman reported that his mother had been to see Mrs. van den Bergh, but that, unexpectedly for such a mild and tractable person, she'd refused. "As long as it makes the boy happy," she'd said, and when Mrs. Opperman had threatened to report her to the OVV, Mrs. van den Bergh had said to her, "Mind your own business," which Mrs. Opperman said nobody had ever said to her. When I told my mother this, she said that she could see Mrs. van den Bergh's point, even though of course Mrs. Opperman was quite right.

As, in a sense, the cause of all this activity, I was the object of some curiosity at school. From Mrs. Opperman's reaction I knew that what I had done was open to disapproval, but by and large the other children were too envious to be censorious. Mr. de Wet, our teacher that year, made a comment about children who risked their lives and futures by consorting with strangers, but his formulation did not accord with any recognizable reality and was ignored as the kind of thing adults had to say as a token of their authority.

Around this time Steve disappeared from our streets, to the consternation of the children and the relief of the adults. It was just starting to seem that the problem of Steve had been solved when he reappeared one day, a week later, as nonchalant as ever. But now the OVV, of which my mother was the secretary and Mrs. Opperman the president, took it upon itself to rid the community of "the threat to the children of Verkeerdespruit," as Steve was described in the circular Mrs. Opperman composed and

41

my mother sent out, announcing a special meeting in our sitting room. This fortunately took place on a Wednesday afternoon when I was at home. Having opened in advance the little window in the corner of our sitting room, which my mother said the builder had put in because he had a window left over from building the police station, I could listen to the proceedings by crouching in the flower bed outside, hidden from view by the large aloe my mother had planted to obscure the little window.

It was an uncomfortable position, and the aloe was not a congenial kind of shelter, but I was rewarded for my endurance by hearing an unedited version of a meeting that I knew I would have been given only a very partial account of.

The meeting was opened, like everything in Verkeerdespruit from cattle auctions to baby shows, with scripture and prayer, in this instance conducted by the dominee's wife, on the principle perhaps that, being married to the Lord's anointed, she would have privileged access to Him. She read from Ezekiel what she called a message of comfort to the Lord's flock in times of peril: "And they shall no more be a prey to the heathen, neither shall the beast of the land devour them; but they shall dwell safely, and none shall make them afraid." She thanked the Lord for sending us shepherds who were dealing so fearlessly with the onslaught of Communism and other foreign elements. Perhaps judging that in dealing with an omniscient power it was indelicate to call things by their names, she referred to "the wise measures recently introduced" in acknowledgment of God's part in the passing of the Ninety-Day Detention Act, and asked Him to avert also "this new onslaught from the heathen and the beast dwelling in our midst."

Clearly, though, the job was not going to be left to God's unaided efforts, and the rest of the meeting was devoted to a somewhat unstructured consideration of ways to rid the community of Steve. Discussion was lively, the majority of women apparently favoring the simple expedient of driving him from their midst. I had visions of Steve on his motorbike, pursued out of town by stick-wielding members of the OVV. My mother pointed out that there were no legal grounds for driving anybody from one's midst without that person's consent.

"What about the Bantu?" Mrs. van Onselen demanded. "They're being moved all the time, and some of them are quite respectable."

"Yes," my mother said, "but that's because they're black. There's no law to move a white person from anywhere."

"Yes," Mrs. van Niekerk confirmed, "Piet says the police can't do anything to him until he's done something wrong."

"So must we sit around and wait for him to commit … some atrocity before we can get rid of him?" asked Mrs. van Onselen. "I must say, I don't understand the law."

"Dominee says" — Dominee Claassen's wife always referred to her husband as "Dominee" — "that the church can't do anything to this man because he doesn't belong to the Dutch Reformed Church."

"But," suggested Mrs. Opperman, "we can make it impossible for him to stay here if we deny him a place to live and work."

"How will we do that?" asked my mother.

"Well, fortunately we have both Mrs. Maree and Mrs. Deyssel here," Mrs. Opperman pointed out.

There was a silence. Mrs. Maree, Steve's landlady, was not a person who took kindly to being prescribed to by anybody. Then, in her emphatic, precise way she said: "Steve pays me ten rand a month for his room, and anybody who wants me to get rid of him will have to pay me ten rand a month. And Skollie likes him."

"Must our dogs choose our children's companions?" asked Mrs. Price, the English hairdresser, who was not really a member of the OVV, but who was attending because her son Desmond had asked her if he could have a motorbike when he turned eighteen, which request she ascribed to Steve's influence.

"Not if it's a useless ball of cotton wool," sniffed Mrs. Maree, in pointed reference to Mrs. Price's Maltese poodle, Fifi, which, much bathed and perfumed, graced her hairdressing salon, *Chez Boutique*. Once, when Mrs. Maree had taken her dog with her for her wash and set, an enraged Fifi had pursued the thoroughly cowed Skollie down Voortrekker Street. I knew this because Mary, the wife of our gardener, Jim, worked for Mrs. Price.

"Order please, ladies," barked Mrs. Opperman. "Obviously we can't force Mrs. Maree to give up such a lucrative arrangement.

43

We must consider other ways of persuading this man to leave our town. Now Mrs. Deyssel ... your husband employs him."

"I'm sure Fred didn't know he was a ... heathen and a beast when he took him on," muttered Mrs. Deyssel, a meek and not very enterprising woman.

"Nobody's blaming Mr. Deyssel; the point is, now that this man has shown himself to be a millstone and a stumbling block, don't you think Mr. Deyssel would consider terminating his employment?"

"You mean Fred must sack Steve?" Mrs. Deyssel asked.

"Yes."

"I don't know," said Mrs. Deyssel. "Fred says the man knows about engines. He says that nobody else could get that van of Vermaas's going."

"What is more important, the safety of our children or the mobility of Mr. Vermaas's van?" demanded Mrs. Opperman.

"I'm sure I don't know," said Mrs. Deyssel in a depressed tone.

"Well, I know," said Mrs. Opperman, "and I think you should talk to your husband."

"I can talk to him," said Mrs. Deyssel, "but I don't know if it will do any good. Last year I talked to him about washing his hands when he came in from the garage because he was getting my new lounge suite full of oil, but he said a man is master in his own house and doesn't have to take orders from his wife. So now I've put loose covers on the lounge suite so that I can put them in the wash when they get dirty."

"That was a good solution to that problem," my mother interjected, "but loose covers are not going to do us any good with this Steve man."

"No, I was just saying about talking," said Mrs. Deyssel, but she had lost the floor. Mrs. Dominee interrupted her.

"Mr. Deyssel is an elder on the church council, isn't he?"

"Yes," said Mrs. Deyssel. "He says he was chosen because they hoped he would service the dominee's car for free." A grateful congregation had given the dominee a Mercedes-Benz the year before, in recognition of his initiative in organizing a day of prayer for rain, to such good effect that the Verkeerdespruit came down in flood and washed away half the

44

location. Two people and a cow were drowned. The owner of the cow tried to sue the church but couldn't find a lawyer to take his case.

"Dominee has his car serviced in Bloemfontein," said Mrs. Dominee. "But what I wanted to say is that although this Steve is not subject to church discipline, Mr. Deyssel is, and perhaps if Dominee spoke to him and impressed it upon him that it was his duty to the community to get rid of this man …"

"I don't much like it," said my mother. "It sounds like intimidation."

"Well," snapped Mrs. Opperman, "if you'd rather have your son gallivanting in the nude with this man on his motorbike …"

"My son went for a swim with this man; there's nothing wrong with that."

"Then why are we having this meeting?"

"I agree that it's a potentially undesirable situation …"

"I should think it's a potentially undesirable situation. I shudder to think what would have happened if I hadn't seen the man sneaking out of town with your son on the back of his motorbike."

"And I'm very grateful to you for informing me so promptly; I'm just saying that there's a difference between swimming and … gallivanting in the nude on a motorbike."

"Ladies," Mrs. Dominee intervened. "Is it agreed then that I should talk to Dominee and ask him to talk to Mr. Deyssel about employing this man?"

There were mutters and murmurs and reservations, but eventually, when teatime arrived, the ladies of the OVV agreed: Steve would have to go, and the way to achieve this was to deprive him of a means of livelihood. The heathen was about to be driven from the land.

The next day, on my way home from school, I saw Fanie walking ahead of me. I walked slightly faster and joined him without any preamble. Preliminaries were never necessary with Fanie, whose command of social graces had not yet extended to the most rudimentary forms of greeting.

"Did you hear that Steve's going away?" I asked.

I'd counted on a reaction, and I was not disappointed. He stopped dead and looked at me uncomprehendingly with his light-blue eyes.

"Who … who says so?" he stuttered.

"My mother," I said blithely. "The OVV thinks he's a bad influence."

Fanie didn't ask me what a bad influence was, though he couldn't have known. Nor did he question the power of the OVV, having, as an officially underprivileged epileptic, been subject to the whims of official, semi-official, and amateur busybody organizations all his life. The Poor Whites were a much looked-after segment of our society.

"When?" he asked.

"When what?" I replied.

"When's he leaving?"

"Oh. I don't know. I don't think they've decided."

Fanie looked at me like a dog in pain and didn't say anything more.

Two days after, Fanie came to me where I was sitting on the playground frying ants with a magnifying glass.

"Steve says they can't kick him out," he blurted out.

"Oh, really?" Since I suspected he was right, I took refuge in sarcasm.

"Yes. He says he's got as much right to be here as any — bloody old bitch."

"I'm going to tell Mr. Viljoen you've been swearing," I said.

"I'm not swearing. That's what Steve said."

"Well, he'll discover his mistake," I said in the tone that my mother employed when talking about the bad service she got from Osrin. "He'll be out of here before … before he can drain his sump." I had learned something after all from the technical discussions next to the motorbike.

"I'm going with him," Fanie announced in his flat, dull way.

"Then he is leaving?"

"Yes, he says it's not as if it's a pleasure living in a dump like this."

"And where to?" I taunted. "To Jo'burg?"

46

"No. To Winburg. His parents live there."

"Winburg?" I screeched. "Steve's parents live in Winburg?" It was like being told that Gene Autry's parents lived in Bloemfontein; in fact, the idea of Steve having parents was unthinkable.

"Yes," he said. "He says I can be his brother." And Fanie smiled, and I realized that I'd never seen him smile before.

"Why should he want you as his brother?" I asked, taken aback.

"I don't know," he said humbly and walked away.

"You can't be somebody's brother if you have different parents," I called after him, but I don't think he was listening.

Fanie's absence from school was at first not commented on. He stayed away periodically, partly because of his health, partly, I suspect, because Mr. de Wet, our current teacher, terrified Fanie even more than the rest of us. I think I was the only one who noticed that Fanie's absence coincided with Steve's second disappearance from our village. The latter event in any case absorbed too much of everybody's attention to leave any of it for Fanie's absence from school. Steve's first disappearance had been part of his fascinating unpredictability; a second seemed premeditated, final. Children who until recently had vied for Steve's attention now all had an anecdote relating to what had become established as his bad influence. Nasie Grundlingh said that Steve had offered him a cigarette, but since Nasie was suspected of being a secret smoker anyway, this did not seem like bad influence as much as generosity. Annette Loubser said that she had seen Steve talk to two Bantus next to the road.

Kosie Opperman informed us that his mother took credit for Steve's disappearance, on the grounds that the dominee would never have gone to talk to Mr. Deyssel if she hadn't called the special meeting of the OVV. Apparently Mr. Deyssel, though initially reluctant to lose the only competent mechanic he had ever had, had eventually come round to seeing his duty as a citizen of Verkeerdespruit and an elder of the Church, and had told Steve he could no longer employ him. Mrs. Maree was considering suing the church for loss of income.

So, what with the speculation and perturbation around Steve's departure, it was only after three days that Mr. de Wet sent a note to Mrs. van den Bergh to ask where Fanie was. I was used as messenger, I suspect because Mr. de Wet guessed, correctly, that my ten-year-old sensibilities and snobberies would find a visit to Mrs. van den Bergh's slovenly home particularly trying.

I knocked at the unprepossessing front door of the Van den Bergh home and waited. There was a forlorn peach tree at the front door that had optimistically formed a few blossoms at the beginning of spring and now seemed to be dying of drought. There was, surprisingly, given the general lack of amenities, a doormat made of Coca-Cola bottle tops nailed to a plank. I wondered whether Fanie had made it. At length the mournful face of Mrs. van den Bergh appeared around the door.

"Yes?" she asked with that total absence of curiosity that she had bequeathed to her only son.

"I've brought a note from Mr. de Wet at the school," I announced.

"Oh," she said, wiping her hands and taking the letter hesitantly. She opened it, frowned at it for about thirty seconds, then handed it back to me and said, "Can you read it for me?"

I guessed that Mrs. van den Bergh couldn't read.

"Yes," I said, and opening the little note, read, "Dear Mrs. van den Bergh: Your son Fanie has not been in school for three days. I hope he is not seriously ill, but if so please let me know by return of post. Yours faithfully, B. de Wet (Class teacher)."

"Oh," said Mrs. van den Bergh. "Fanie's not here."

"Where is he?" I asked.

"I don't know," she said. "He went away."

"But where to?"

"I don't know," she persisted. "He's done it before. He did it when we were living in Ficksburg, too. That time he went to visit my sister in Ventersdorp. She lives on a plot with her husband, Derek." And she looked at me as if that explained it all. "My husband will give him a hiding when he gets back," she reassured me.

The police came to ask us all questions. When Mr. de Wet asked if anybody knew anything that might help the police in their investigations — the constable standing next to him looked slightly alarmed — I put up my hand.

"Fanie said something last week …"

"Last week? Why didn't you tell anybody?" asked Mr. de Wet.

"I didn't believe him. He said he was going with Steve."

There was a rumble of speculation in the class, and Mr. de Wet and the constable looked at each other.

"I think … if this boy can come with me to make a statement?" he said to Mr. de Wet, who nodded. I left a profoundly hushed class behind me.

"And you're sure he said Winburg?" Captain van Niekerk asked me.

"Yes, *Oom*," I said.

"And this Steve — what's his full name?"

"I don't know, *Oom*. But Fanie said they were going to stay with Steve's parents."

"Should be easy," Captain van Niekerk said to the constable. "There can't be many motorbikes in Winburg. Go and find the fucker."

Fanie was brought back the next day. There was a general consciousness of an enormity, derived as much from the cryptic mutterings of grown-ups as from our own uninformed speculations. As son of the man in charge of the processes of retribution, Louis van Niekerk was much in demand. "My father says he should be hanged," he said.

"My mother says hanging is too good for him," said Kosie Opperman.

"Captain van Niekerk says Steve should be hanged," I told my father.

He looked at me pensively. "Fortunately Captain van Niekerk is not the magistrate," he said.

My father, though, *was* the magistrate, and had to pronounce sentence. I read the report in *The Friend*. The magistrate had said that there were extenuating circumstances and that the accused had apparently not "interfered" with the child. He sentenced Steve to three years in prison for abducting a minor. Asked why

49

he had left home, the accused replied that he had felt restless. Asked why he had taken the minor with him, he said that he liked children.

So Steve disappeared from our midst, and I might not have heard of him again had it not been for *Die Landstem*, a national weekly that specialized in "human interest" stories. My parents did not read it — my mother said it was common and my father said it exploited the misery of the few and the boredom of the many — but on Saturdays, when I read magazines in Steyl's café, I sometimes stealthily perused an alluring item in *Die Landstem*. And there, a week or two after the trial, was a photograph of Steve; also a photograph of a woman with a beehive hairdo, pointing at a deep freeze. "A Wife's Grief," the headline shouted. "'My husband left me for a motorbike.'" It appeared from the story that Steve had worked as a mechanic at a gold mine in Welkom. His wife, Mrs. Soekie van der Westhuizen, said she had forgiven him for abandoning her, but was hurt that he had pawned the wedding ring she had bought him and exchanged their new deep freeze for a motorbike belonging to Mr. Stoffel Lemmer, a next-door neighbor. Mr. Lemmer was also interviewed and said he wanted his Matchless back because his wife, Mrs. Sarie Lemmer, had effected the exchange without his permission when he went back to Johannesburg "for personal reasons" soon after they moved to Welkom. Now that he had returned to his wife, he should have his rightful property restored to him. In this he was supported by Mrs. van der Westhuizen, who wanted the deep freeze back, but Mrs. Lemmer refused to return it on the grounds that it had been a legitimate exchange, and besides, her husband had come back to her only because his Jo'burg girlfriend had kicked him out when he ran out of money.

I did not have the money or the courage to buy *Die Landstem*, but I cut the report from *The Friend* once my mother had thrown it on the heap of things to be burnt on Thursday mornings by Jim, and I showed it to Louis and Kosie at break in the playground, on the rockery, where it was accepted that serious discussions took place. Their fathers got *Die Volksblad*, which had not seen fit to cover the trial. Louis's father, though at times more than prepared to share his views on the proper conduct of justice with his own family, more often assumed an air of professional discretion that maddened his wife and frustrated Louis.

"What's *interfered with*?" asked Kosie.

I was reluctant to admit that I had no idea. "It means that he didn't steal anything from Fanie," I said.

"What's Fanie got to steal, anyway?" asked Louis.

"Nothing. That's why Steve didn't steal anything," I explained, hoping that they weren't going to ask me what extenuating circumstances were.

"What's extenuating circumstances?" asked Louis.

For a moment I thought I might bluff that one out too, but the expression on Kosie's face told me that he was not convinced on *interfered with* and was going to be tough on *extenuating circumstances*. So I said, "How should I know?"

"Why didn't you ask your father?"

I could in fact probably have asked him, but I didn't want my parents to know that I had read the report on Steve's trial.

"Let's ask Fanie," I suggested, more to divert attention from my lapses and because he happened to be walking past at that moment than because I thought there was much point to it.

"Hey! Fanie!" shouted Kosie, and Fanie looked up with the unsurprised air with which he met all overtures.

"Come here," said Louis, with the ring of authority that he at times assumed as appropriate to his father's position and rank.

Fanie obediently enough shambled over to where we were sitting on the school rockery, and looked at us with as much interest as if we were outcrops of the rockery.

"What ...?" started Kosie, and then seemed to run out of nerve, so I had to step in.

"The newspaper says Steve didn't interfere with you," I said bluntly. He looked at me expressionlessly. Then he said, "Yes."

"What does it mean?"

Kosie looked at me as if to say *I thought you knew*.

"I don't know," said Fanie.

"Of course he doesn't know," said Louis under his breath.

"But what ... what is it that he didn't do?"

"Nothing," said Fanie.

51

"He didn't do nothing?"

"Yes … no."

"What do you mean no?"

"He did nothing."

"Did he or didn't he do nothing?"

"No."

"Did he … okay, what did he do with you?"

"Nothing."

"Where did he take you?"

"To Winburg."

"And what did you do there?"

"Nothing."

"Then why did they put him in jail?"

Fanie looked at me. "Did they put him in jail?"

For the first time it occurred to me that nobody had seen fit to tell Fanie what had happened to Steve.

"Yes. Didn't you know?"

"No."

Then he looked at us. "Why?"

"Why what?"

"Why did they put him in jail?"

"Because of what he did to you."

"But he … can they put you in jail for that?"

Louis and I pounced simultaneously. "For what?" he demanded, and, "Then he did something to you?" I asked.

He shook his head. "No. He … he …"

"If you don't tell us, I'll tell my father," said Louis.

"He …" Fanie got that fixed expression that by now I recognized. But he didn't have a fit. He stared in front of himself; then, absentmindedly, he bit the side of his hand, and said: "He kissed me."

"*Kissed* you?" I exclaimed in incredulous disappointment. My mother and father kissed me at bedtime, and when they were going to Bloemfontein for the day, and my uncles and aunts kissed me when they came to visit; I had never considered it to be something that one might do voluntarily or because it gave anybody any pleasure. People did kiss in movies, but people in movies also did any number of things that people in

52

Verkeerdespruit or even Winburg wouldn't dream of doing, like bursting into song in midconversation or dying for their beliefs.

"Kissed you?" I repeated, and he nodded, clearly still lost in his own thoughts. "Where was he going?"

"Nowhere."

"Then why did he kiss you?" Something in me rebelled against the idea of Steve's kissing Fanie, rebelled against anybody's kissing Fanie, and Steve's kissing anybody. I looked at Kosie and Louis; they were looking at me hesitantly, clearly expecting me to clear up the mystery.

"Why did he kiss you?" I repeated.

Fanie thought for a moment; then, "Because he liked me," he said, and smiled for the second time since I had known him.

A few months later *The Friend* reported that Johannes Jacobus van der Westhuizen, "the convicted child molester," had been killed by his cellmate in Bloemfontein prison. I asked my father why.

"I don't really know," he said. "Strange things happen in prison. But they're often very hard on child molesters."

"What's a child molester?"

"Oh. Somebody who interferes with children."

"But you ... the newspaper said that Steve didn't interfere with Fanie."

"Well, no. Not technically. But you see, that's not the way his cellmate would have seen it. To him, what Steve did would be molesting."

I thought for a moment. "Fanie said ... Steve kissed him."

My father looked at me inquiringly, but didn't say anything, so I carried on. "Is that what molesting means?"

My father seemed vaguely surprised. "Yes," he said, "I suppose that would count as molesting."

"So Steve was killed because he kissed Fanie?" I pursued.

My father thought for a moment, then shrugged slightly and said, "Yes. I suppose that's what it amounts to."

When I told Fanie this, he said nothing, only looked at me in that dumb way of his.

December 6, 1968

I did not relish being reminded of Steve by Fanie, whom I still held obscurely responsible for Steve's fate. I did not think, in fact, that it was quite decent of Fanie to refer so openly to a relationship that had, after all, attracted the punitive attention of the law: even if technically Fanie had not been the criminal, he had been the cause of the crime. But Fanie stood there as blandly as if he were discussing the price of pawpaws. I was acutely aware of the satirical attention of Tim Watkins; and Mr. Moore, too, was clearly waiting for us to stop talking so that he could administer his anxious hospitality. I sought refuge once more in the arid wastes of small talk, and said, "Hot, isn't it?" and Fanie looked around as if he hadn't noticed.

The Clutch Plates were accompanied by a youngish teacher who, it turned out, had known Mr. Moore at university. "That's Mr. Sanders," said Fanie. "He taught me to play tennis." To judge by Fanie's reverent tone, he hero-worshipped Mr. Sanders, as he had always worshipped anybody who seemed prepared to give him a scrap of time or attention. I tried to shrug off my own irritation, but I couldn't help resenting the officiousness of this man who had brought Fanie so unexpectedly all the way from Odendaalsrust to embarrass me. And there was a whole lunch to get through before we could wipe the courts with the Clutch Plates and send them home.

Fortunately, at this point the teachers started to herd us together for the promised lunch. "Come, boys," said Mr. Moore, "let's not keep Mrs. Cameron waiting. She has kindly prepared a special light lunch for the tennis players."

Tim Watkins made a face. "That means it's the usual stuff, just less of it."

Mrs. Cameron, our not-so-much-venerated-as-feared food matron, was the widow of a Methodist minister who, rumor had it, had died of an overdose of cream puffs at a church conference in Blackpool, an overindulgence directly attributable, in the school mythology, to the deprivations the poor man had suffered at home. "Come, this way," I said to Fanie, who seemed to be on the point of getting back onto the bus.

"I ... I wanted to get my racket and clothes."

"They'll be quite safe there. This isn't Odendaalsrust." I couldn't imagine in any case who would want to steal Fanie's tennis clothes. "Come," I said, and Fanie obediently followed me to the dining hall, where he, quite smartly for such a clumsy person, took the seat next to mine.

The lunch was, as Tony Miles had predicted, an economy version of Mrs. Cameron's usual sludge: a shepherd's pie made of lumpy gray potatoes and greasy mince not so much bound as glued together with stale bread crumbs. In deference to the athletic nature of the event the meal was intended to inaugurate, the perennial pale brussels sprouts had yielded pride of place to a wilted green salad every bit as damp and listless as the superseded sprouts.

Fanie was the only boy who did not feel called upon to pass a witticism on the appearance and consistency of Mrs. Cameron's shepherd's pie. He simply ate his meal with the stolid singlemindedness of the hungry. His table manners, I was relieved to note, had improved, in that his chewing was no longer quite as visible a process as it used to be, although he did still hold his fork as if it were a shovel.

He carefully scraped up the last bit of gristle from his plate and, without putting down his fork, demanded, "Is there more?" This set off the hilarity of the Wesley boys, who found it impossible to believe that anybody could want more of Mrs. Cameron's shepherd's pie, and of the Clutch Plates, who wanted to make it quite clear that, unlike Fanie, they had found the lunch below standard. Mr. Moore intervened. He quelled the mirth of his own charges with a pointed look and explained to Fanie: "We thought that since you'll be playing a hard game of tennis we should not overdo the lunch."

Fanie nodded, clearly not convinced. Then suddenly his brow cleared and he turned to me. "Do you know who I saw last year?" he asked, with that slight sputter of saliva that excitement always produced in him.

"No," I replied ungraciously. "Elvis Presley?"

He shook his head with a foolish smile. "No," he said. "No, nobody like that." He looked at me expectantly, as if he seriously expected me to guess. As I resolutely refused to be drawn into a *pointless guess, he announced, "Betty," as triumphantly as if he were reporting a sighting of the Virgin of Lourdes.*

"Betty?"

"Betty … you know, Betty the Exchange. She came to visit her cousin in Ventersdorp."

"Oh — Bet-ty," I said, as if dredging up a long-forgotten name from my memory, though Betty was now as clear to my mind as everything else that Fanie was forcing back so unconsciously and yet so relentlessly into the light of this day.

Summer 1963

In Verkeerdespruit, if you picked up the receiver and briskly turned the handle a few times, you got, if you weren't Dik-Willem Vosloo, the prompt and invariable response: "Exchange here, number please *nommer asseblief*," in the businesslike staccato of Betty the Exchange.

Betty had lived in Verkeerdespruit all her life. The only child of mature parents, she had completed Standard Eight, which was as far as the local school went. My mother had suggested to Mrs. Brand that Betty should go to Bloemfontein to matriculate, but Mrs. Brand had said, "The child is shy because of her chin." Betty had no chin. So Betty had stayed, and from being Betty Brand had become Betty the Exchange.

In other villages, so we were told, the exchange became part of the community, chipped in on conversations, listened in shamelessly, gave helpful hints and passed on useful gossip, and generally acted as if she were talking to friends, which in many cases she was. But not Betty. Her professional integrity recognized no friends and, with one exception, no enemies, once she was behind the counter in the post office with her earphones and her plugs. Furthermore, she refused to vary her identification formula: always "Number please" first, then "*Nommer asseblief*," with no regard to the government's expressed policy of linguistic equality and unexpressed policy of favoring Afrikaans.

That was how Betty made her one enemy. Old Dik-Willem Vosloo, whose mother had died of the ground glass put in her food by the English in the concentration camps, and who had once collected twenty-three pounds and eleven shillings so that the National Museum in Bloemfontein could disprove the theory

57

of evolution, refused to accept Betty's language policy and insisted that she should at least vary the formula to give Afrikaans an equal number of first mentions. He went to elaborate lengths to prove to his own satisfaction that Betty did in fact always use English first, phoning her ten times a day to ask the time (a service which in those days was provided free by the exchange), until she suggested that he should buy a watch; then he took a poll among his neighbors. Those of them who noted these things confirmed his suspicion that Betty "treated Afrikaans like a stepchild," as he put it to her when he finally lodged his complaint. "*As jy vir die goewerment wil werk moet jy die goewerment se taal eerbiedig,*" he said — "If you work for the government you must respect the government's language." And she made the concession of actually replying in Afrikaans: "*Nou draai dan maar jou slingertjie tot jou goewerment antwoord*" — "Then you can turn your little handle till your government answers" — and disconnected him. He complained to the postmaster, Klasie Vermaak, but Klasie had no authority over Betty or anybody else, being completely under the authority of Moeder, his grimly widowed mother. So Betty refused point-blank to heed Dik-Willem's frantic cranking; indeed, when anybody tried to reach Dik-Willem's number, she would say blandly, "That number has been discontinued" and disconnect the caller. Dik-Willem wrote to the postmaster general, he told my father indignantly, but without receiving any reply, prompting him to confess that he wasn't sure that the National Party government knew as much about such things as the Smuts government, which had had the English to show them how. For Dik-Willem to admit that the Smuts government had been capable of anything at all other than selling out the country to the English and the kaffirs was to make a sizeable concession, but that was not enough for Betty: she insisted on a written apology — in both official languages. She showed me Dik-Willem's letter one Saturday afternoon in Steyl's café, where she was having her weekly cream soda float. Dik-Willem had got Mr. Murray, the Standard Six and Seven teacher, to help him with the letter. In Dik-Willem's careful, large letters it was headed "Apology," and then continued: "I, Dirk Willem Vosloo, being of sound body and mind, do hereby wish to apologize to Miss

Elizabeth Brand for any offense he may inadvertently have caused on the occasion of his last telephone conversation with said Miss Elizabeth Brand on the fifth inst. (D.V.) Signed: DW Vosloo."

"And what did you do?" I asked Betty.

"I reconnected him, of course," she said. "I called him and informed him that his service had been reinstated and that in view of the special circumstances surrounding his case we wouldn't charge him a reconnection fee."

"What did he say?"

Betty laughed. "He said *Huh*?"

"But ... *why* won't you say '*Nommer asseblief*' before 'Number please'?" I asked.

"It's a matter of principle," she said firmly.

"Oh." I thought for a moment, but it still seemed no clearer. "What's a principle?"

"A principle is something that you're prepared to make yourself unpleasant about," she explained.

"Oh." This merely brought me back to my first question. "But *why* ...?"

"Why have principles? Because if you haven't got a chin you've got to have principles."

Betty's father, Mr. Brand the bank manager, was the most neatly dressed person I had ever seen. When he entered the bank from one of his outings into the village, he would nod at the black man permanently sitting at the front door of the bank; the man would get out a spotless yellow duster, kneel in front of Mr. Brand, and dust his shoes. Then Mr. Brand would nod again and go into his office. He was very polite, and when the Brands visited my parents for bridge, he would jump to his feet every time my mother left the room or entered it, and pull out her chair for her, which my father complained put him off his bridge. This made my mother uncomfortable, and she tried to get up from the table as seldom as possible; even so, tea and cake had to be served at half past nine, which created endless opportunities for Mr. Brand to perform his elaborate courtesies and irritate my father.

"Can't you drop Brand's wife a hint to tell him to relax?" my father asked my mother.

"No. I couldn't possibly," she said firmly.

"Why ever not?" he asked.

She looked at me with her not-in-front-of-the-children look, then shrugged and said, "Mrs. Brand wouldn't tell her husband. She's scared of him."

"How on earth do you know?"

"She told me that time when she was ill and I took her some knitting to do for the OVV. She broke down; flu lowers people's resistance to emotion."

"But why is she scared of him?" persisted my father.

"He kicks her."

"Kicks her? But … when …?"

"Usually at supper. He doesn't like the food she cooks."

"Then why doesn't she cook him something else?"

"She's tried everything, but he doesn't like any of it. He says she cooks like a Nazi." Mrs. Brand had been born Vorster, and her father had been a member of the *Ossewa Brandwag*; Mr. Brand was the chairman of the local branch of the United Party. Thereafter, whenever Mr. Brand leaped to his feet when my mother entered the room, I sat petrified with terror that he might kick her if the cake wasn't to his taste.

Mr. Brand died suddenly one day of anger, or so Verkeerdespruit interpreted the massive stroke that claimed him in the entrance hall of his bank, when the spotless yellow duster, leaving a hideous wet smear on the brilliant sheen of his black toe-caps, turned out upon outraged inquiry to have been used by a new bank clerk to wipe up the puddle left by Mrs. van Onselen's incontinent bulldog. Mr. Brand's last words were *"That* filthy animal?"* prompting Mrs. van Onselen to close her account and put her money in the post office, even though the bank accountant suggested to her that a Higher Hand had adequately avenged her bulldog. Mrs. Brand died a fortnight after her husband — of a broken heart, the village said. So Betty was suddenly left alone, and everybody thought that she would be rich enough to move away from Verkeerdespruit or at least be proposed to by one of the young farmers in the district after the third consecutive failure of the peanut crop.

"Oh, I was almost as popular as Ariana Jordaan for a while," she told me. "Koos van Biljon even took me out in his *bakkie* one Wednesday evening after rugby practice, and, what's more, paid for my milkshake."

"Don't men usually pay for the milkshakes?" I asked.

"Not Koos van Biljon. Koos van Biljon pays for nothing if he can help it. I know of women who have had to split gas costs when he took them for a picnic in the *bakkie*. *And* they had to make the sandwiches. He came to visit my mother after my father's death, you know — when she was sick and people were saying I'd be left well off — and he brought a box of Black Magic. I thought it was odd, you know, usually people bring flowers or something, but not chocolates; anyway, he offered around the Black Magic, and when he left, he took the rest of the box home with him. From next to my mother's bed. That's why he didn't bring flowers, although I wouldn't have put it past him to take those away with him as well. So for him to pay for my milkshake showed that he was really making an effort."

When the will was read, though, it transpired that there was almost no money, and it became known that Mr. Brand's daily outings had been to Loubser's Hotel, where Schalk Redelinghuis ran a bookmaker's business on the side, and that he had lost all his money on the horses. The house belonged to the bank. So after Mrs. Brand's death, Betty moved into a room in the Steyls' back-yard and took the job as exchange, where she had been working for two years when she defeated Dik-Willem Vosloo. "It's not heaven," she said, "and the Steyls have some funny habits …" Mrs. Steyl was Greek, with very dark hair and eyes.

"Like what?" I interrupted.

"Like chasing each other round the house with him blowing that hunting horn he bought in Germany. But at least I don't have to sit at a table with my father three times a day watching him nibble his food like a disapproving rabbit."

Every Saturday afternoon, when Betty came off duty ("Through to Winburg when Verkeerdespruit is closed," it said in the phone book), she would come to Steyl's café, where she had a mixed grill and a cream soda float. Her board with the Steyls included food, and on Saturday afternoon Mrs. Steyl couldn't get away from the café to cook something at home. On that afternoon the farmers brought their laborers in by truck to come and spend their weekly wages on paraffin and candles, burning up their money as fast as they could earn it, as Louis van Niekerk's mother said, and Mrs. Steyl had to measure out the paraffin and count the candles that they bought at after-hours prices from the café, while her husband manned the till and watched the customers so that they wouldn't steal. I once asked him if anything had ever been stolen from his shop, and he said, "No bloody chance, they wouldn't dare while I'm watching them." Mr. Osrin complained that the farm laborers always arrived too late to buy their provisions from his shop, which closed at one o'clock, but all the farms worked till twelve o'clock on a Saturday, so the farmers couldn't get the laborers to the village before one.

Because I was fond of reading and there was little variety of reading matter in Verkeerdespruit, I had got into the habit of reading all Steyl's magazines every week. He objected at first, and when I told my father this, he said perhaps if I was careful not to leave any marks on the pages and spent some money, Steyl wouldn't mind, and he gave me money for a cream soda float. My mother was a bit worried about my spending so much time with Betty. "She's a nice enough girl," she said, "and I'm sorry for her with that awful father of hers even now that he's dead, and that chin, but I wonder if she isn't a bit too cynical for you."

"What's cynical?"

"Oh, you know, people who don't believe in life anymore."

It had never occurred to me that life was something one could either believe in or not believe in, and certainly I didn't think that Betty's not believing in it constituted a reason for not seeing her. Besides, Dumbo liked the trip to the café and enjoyed lying under the table at Betty's feet. Betty said she liked him because he didn't ask her how she was managing without her father, and because he didn't think she wanted to marry him just because she liked him. She seemed to like Fanie van den Bergh for much the same reason — of the two, Dumbo was the more expressive by a long shot — and slightly to my chagrin he would sometimes join us as we had our cream soda floats together, she paging through *Personality*, I reading *Die Huisgenoot* and *Die Brandwag* — even

Rooi Rose, when I thought there was no chance of any of my friends coming in and catching me at it. Fanie did not read, merely sat, sometimes scratching Dumbo's ears, and accepted with ungrateful taciturnity the cream soda that Betty invariably bought him. Betty and I talked as we read, and Betty told me her ambitions, the main one of which was to go to Cape Town and have "an operation" — gesturing in the direction of her chin — and then to find a job there. She had been putting away most of her monthly salary, and she thought in another year she would be able to afford the trip. Every week she would show me a photograph of or reference to Cape Town in one of the magazines. "There must be more to life than a pair of earphones on your head," she said.

When Steve appeared in our midst, there was a further topic of conversation between me and Betty. I could tell her everything he had said and done, and she seemed not to get bored or impatient, as my mother sometimes did. Fanie, to my surprise, never joined in, though I knew that he saw at least as much of Steve as I. Betty, too, never admitted to knowing him, and I never asked her about seeing his motorbike in front of the house where she stayed. But I noticed that the time when Steve was absent from the streets of Verkeerdespruit, she went to Bloemfontein to visit her cousin for her annual leave.

After Steve's trial and conviction Betty didn't appear in the café for a few weeks. Nor did Fanie, but that was probably in deference to the aura of scandal that hung about him, thickly enough, it would seem, for even Fanie to sense. To my relief, he seemed to be avoiding me, too, which I ascribed to his embarrassment and guilt at having, in a sense, caused Steve's downfall. Betty, however, had not been publicly associated with Steve, and I could not account for her absence.

But one Saturday Betty was back in her usual chair, sipping a cream soda, and I sat down with her. I did not refer to her absence, and neither did she. We read in silence for a while because there didn't seem to be anything to say. At length I found a photograph of the Huguenot Monument and asked Betty, "Is that in Cape Town?" although I knew it wasn't, to get her talking about her plans again. But she only glanced at the photo and said, "I don't think so." Then after a short silence she added, so softly that I almost couldn't hear, "It doesn't matter anyway."

"Why, Betty?" I asked.

"I'm not going to Cape Town anymore."

"But why not?"

"I've lost my savings."

"Have you ... lost them on the horses?" I asked, having recently learned of that method of impoverishing oneself.

"No — although I suppose you could say I backed the wrong horse."

I looked at her in incomprehension. She took a sip of her cream soda and said, "Listen, I'll tell you because I'm not going to tell anybody else." She thought for a while, then shrugged and said, "I might as well tell you. You won't tell Fanie?"

"Of course not." I was not in the habit of telling Fanie things.

"Good, because it might upset him. You remember Steve?"

I nodded. Of course I remembered Steve.

"Well, I got to know him quite well." She blushed. "I ... well, if you must know, I went away with him for a few days."

"Oh I know that," I said, rather disappointed at the nature of the secret.

"How do you know? Don't tell me Steve told you."

"No," I said. "I didn't really *know*, but I guessed when you went to Bloemfontein the same week that Steve disappeared."

"Mm." She looked at me with a slight frown. "You know more than you let on, don't you?"

I thought this was quite an interesting impression to create, though I didn't think my guessing about her and Steve was such an achievement. I wanted to know what they had done in Bloemfontein, but I didn't want to spoil her impression of my omniscience. Fortunately she continued of her own accord: "We went to Maselspoort."

"Oh, to swim?" Maselspoort was celebrated for having the largest swimming pool in the southern hemisphere. It was a pleasure resort on the banks of the Modder River, commemorating the measles epidemic that killed off a large number of Voortrekkers on their way through.

"Well, we did swim, yes, though it was still a bit cold for that. We … camped there."

"In one of those tents?"

"Yes, in one of those tents." She paused, clearly reminiscing. She smiled slightly. "They wouldn't let us in at first."

"Why not?" The idea of a white person being refused admission to any facility struck me as monstrous.

"Well, the campsite was run by this couple, husband and wife you know, except all the work was done by a tired-looking black woman and this couple didn't do anything except guard the camp against the likes of Steve and me. You could see that their idea of a good time was to tell people they couldn't come into their campsite. They'd even developed a sort of team routine, with the husband beginning a sentence and the wife finishing it. I don't think she could have started a sentence on her own, but then I suppose he couldn't have finished one on *his* own, either. The man said he could see we weren't bad people but, and then the woman took over, if they let us in all our friends and relatives would be there next weekend. We said we had no friends or relatives, and then both said together it was a Christian pleasure resort."

"What does that mean?"

"Search me. In this case it meant they didn't want us in there with them. The man said that Maselspoort was founded on a place sacred to the memory of, and the wife said sixty-seven little trekker children who died of the measles in 1837, and the man said he could not allow this place to be desecrated by and the woman said alien influences — Steve and I had been speaking English to each other, you understand."

"Yes." I'd also spoken English to Steve. He had that strange kind of bilingualism that meant he spoke both languages as if the other language were his mother tongue.

"So I thought perhaps we'd have to go to Fourteen Streams, and I don't know if you know Fourteen Streams, but its idea of public facilities is fourteen bucket latrines spaced out at intervals between rows of tents. But then Steve turned to me and said, in Afrikaans for good measure, well, Miss Strydom, I suppose we'll have to mention in our report that we couldn't gain access to the area. And the man said what do you mean report, and the woman said nothing and Steve said we're from the Department of the Interior and we're investigating potential Bantustans. Now you know that everyone around here's petrified of being turned into a Bantustan, and this man said what do you mean, and the woman said Bantustan? Steve said well the government thinks that perhaps the Bantu will need a recreational area and he's looking into possibilities in the Free State, and the man said well this place is highly unsuitable and the woman said as was proved by the Voortrekker children all dying of measles, and Steve said that's not necessarily a disqualification for a Bantustan, but of course we can't tell without seeing the place. I then chipped in and said but from what we can see it seems like just the sort of place the department has in mind, just the right distance from the nearest white area. So the man said I think you're taking a chance, and the woman said the department doesn't employ people like you, on a motorbike *nogal*, and Steve said we all know the department's not what it used to be, and they both of them said you can say that again, and you could see they didn't really believe Steve but didn't want to take the chance, so the man said well, and the woman said as long as they don't interfere with the vegetation like the last man with the motorbike."

"What does that mean?"

"Exactly what I asked, what does that mean? And the man said what it means is he roared up and down on the lawn and through the flower beds on his motorbike and the woman said and he left scars that you can still see if you look carefully down there in the hydrangeas. In the end Steve volunteered to leave his bike at the gate as guarantee of our good behavior, and they gave us a tent and we stayed for four days. When we left, the man asked us if we'd enjoyed our stay and when we said yes he looked relieved and said I knew that if you got to know it you'd realize it was too good for the Bantu and the woman said they don't like water anyway."

"And then …?"

"And then we came back to Verkeerdespruit," Betty said, looking depressed.

"Yes, but …?"

"You mean what happened between Steve and me? I don't really know. Well, I can guess. You see, he sometimes visited me … you know, where I stay."

"Yes, I know," I said. "I saw his motorbike there on my way to Sunday school."

"Yes, well so did other people — I don't mean on their way to Sunday school, but on their way to somewhere. And at this stage there was pretty strong feeling against Steve anyway — you know …"

"Yes I know," I said, "because he took me swimming."

"Yes. Now their problem was that they couldn't argue that Steve was a danger to the children of Verkeerdespruit while he was seeing me …"

"Why not?"

"Well … it's difficult to explain to you what they think, if you can call it thinking, but what it amounts to is that he couldn't have done with you what they thought he was doing with you if he did with me what they thought he was doing with me — you understand?"

"No."

"Oh well, not to worry. The point is that they came to me …"

"Who are they?"

"Well, only one of them, but she claimed to be speaking on behalf of the community, by which she means the OVV, that woman with the deep voice …"

"Mrs. Opperman," I volunteered.

"Yes," she said, "Mrs. Opperman. Except she didn't come to me as she would have gone to … to Osrin to complain about the mouse droppings in his sugar. She lifted her receiver and when I said number please she laid into me and said do you realize you're being used, and I said no I didn't, and she said well you are. I deliberately didn't ask her what she meant but she told me anyway. She said that Steve was trying to, as she put it, *pass for normal* but it was just a trick. All this while I'm on the switchboard and Myra Brink is trying to get through to her mother in Vaalwater and Dik-Willem Vosloo is hogging the party line so Dr. Mazwai can't get through to Tinie Kolver about his pig that's run amuck in the location, and Mrs. Opperman carries on and on, more or less telling me that Steve would never have looked at me twice just, you know, because he liked me."

"And what did you say?" I asked, although there were lots of other questions I'd have asked if I'd known how to.

"I said I wasn't allowed to have private conversations while I was on duty and she said the safety of the children of Verkeerdespruit was not a private matter, it was of public interest and then I said if she was so concerned about the public interest I had just the person for her and I connected her to Dr. Mazwai and it took them five minutes to sort out that they were talking about different things and when Mrs. Opperman churned her telephone again I connected her to Myra Brink. Next thing she wanted to speak to Ilena Steyl so I connected her and listened in, which you know I never do, and Mrs. Opperman asked Ilena did she know I had been receiving visits from undesirable elements and Ilena said undesirable to whom and Mrs. Opperman said undesirable to the town of Verkeerdespruit and Ilena said I come from the ancient city of Athens and I cannot get agitated about a man on a motorbike not being desired by Verkeerdespruit. Then Mrs. Opperman said yes you Greeks and Turks and Mohammedans don't care about moral principles, and Ilena said don't call me a Turk and just because your husband ran away from you is no reason to deny other people some pleasure and Mrs. Opperman called her a heathen slut and slammed down the receiver. I phoned her and asked whether she had concluded her call, and if so, please to turn the handle once. She almost cranked my ear off."

"What's a slut?"

"Not to worry, just Mrs. Opperman's way of insulting Mrs. Steyl."

"And then?"

"Well, I told Steve about Mrs. Opperman's visit and what she had said and he said it was time we left this dump. I said where to and he said what about Cape Town and I said that would be wonderful. He said he would go ahead and find a job and a place to stay, only he didn't have money, so I gave him my savings. So when Steve disappeared and everybody wondered where he was I thought I knew he was in Cape Town looking for a place to stay

68

and a job and when he had found one he would write to me and send me an address and a railway ticket."

"And then?"

"Well, you know. He was found in Winburg with Fanie van den Bergh."

"But why?"

"I have no idea. I thought you might know."

"No," I said. "Fanie said Steve liked him."

"Yes, and I thought Steve liked me."

"Fanie said Steve said he could be his brother."

"Oh well, that must be it, then," she shrugged. "Though it beats me why men are always looking for brothers. I've never looked for a sister. But what really gets me is what he spent my money on in Winburg. I don't think the place even has an OK Bazaars."

"He didn't return your money?" I asked.

"He wouldn't have gone to the trouble of taking it in the first place if he was going to return it, would he?"

"You mean he stole your savings?" I asked incredulously.

"No. I gave him the money."

"But so that the two of you could go to Cape Town together."

"Yes."

"Then he did steal it," I insisted. "Why didn't you tell the police?" I asked indignantly.

"You won't understand," she said, looking down into her cream soda and stirring it with her straw. Then after a moment she said: "I didn't want him to go to jail."

"But why not?" In my world people who stole had to go to jail. For the moment, in my indignation on Betty's behalf, I forgot that the person I wanted put in jail was Steve, and that Steve was in jail anyway.

"Because I loved him." The straw made a slurping sound as she sucked up the last little bit of her cream soda.

I looked at her in incomprehension. I had read stories in *Rooi Rose* in which people declared their love to each other, just as they killed each other or went to New York — but for a real human being, one who worked in the exchange and drank cream sodas, who lived in Verkeerdespruit — for somebody who was sitting at the same table as I, and who could reach across and touch me, to claim to *love* somebody ... or to love *Steve* ... seemed a desecration alike of my memory of Steve and of my friendship with Betty: a kind of indecency imposed upon me. I felt outrage and embarrassment overlaying a deep sense of exclusion, and I also started squashing the ice cream in the bottom of my glass, ruining the float in order to give Betty time to regain her senses. But instead of taking the opening I was giving her to change the topic, she said, slowly and deliberately, "And I still love him. I love Steve."

Without even finishing my cream soda, I got up. "I'm ... I'm ..." I hesitated, and then said, "I'm *glad* he stole your money!" and jumped up and ran out of the café. When I got home I realized that I'd left Dumbo behind and I went back for him, but Betty had left.

December 6, 1968
"So how was Betty?" I asked.

"She was all right," replied Fanie, taking a bite out of the green apple Mrs. Cameron had provided for dessert. I waited in vain for some elaboration of this bald proposition, but he proved no better at following up his own conversational gambits than those of other people.

"Jissis, this is a sour apple," he said, which was the first time I had heard Fanie van den Bergh comment on the quality of anything placed on his plate, as it were, by destiny or any other agency.

"It's a Granny Smith," I countered. "They're supposed to be sour."

"Oh," he said, with a docility more like the Fanie of old. One of his school fellows, though, overhearing my comment to Fanie, muttered, "Fok die granny ook," which means roughly "And fuck the granny too," which set off Clutch Plates and Wesleyans alike, though possibly for different reasons. Elated with his success, the Clutch Plate said, "Ons wil hulle susters hê, nie hulle grannies nie" — We want their sisters, not their grannies — which outraged the Wesleyans and convulsed the Clutch Plates.

70

Mr. Moore wisely pretended not to hear. "Well, I imagine it's time we girded our loins for battle," he said brightly. "Simon, since you and your long-lost friend are so engrossed in your conversation, why don't you take our visitors and show them where the change rooms are?"

"Yes, Mr. Moore," I muttered with bad grace. The last thing I wanted was to have my completely fortuitous acquaintance with Fanie van den Bergh elevated into a friendship. My mother used to say that the main disadvantage of living in Verkeerdespruit was that your friends were people who, given a choice, you would go out of your way to avoid. But I could see that I was probably the most appropriate person to lead the Clutch Plates to their dressing room: apart from being able to speak Afrikaans to them, I was marginally less likely to be openly rude to them than my more uninhibitedly snobbish fellow Wesleyans. The visitors were to use the dressing rooms in the rugby pavilion.

I led the way, flanked by the assiduous Fanie and followed raggedly by the increasingly confident and thus outspoken Clutch Plates. "Die kos is maar net so kak soos ons s'n," declared the largest of the Clutch Plates — "The food is just as shit as ours." There were assenting guffaws. Clearly, if Wesley had been disappointed in its expectations of the Clutch Plates, the disillusionment had been mutual.

Fanie alone seemed impervious to disappointment and delight alike, stolidly possessive as he was of my company. He seemed to take for granted that his place was by my side, which is to say that mine was by his. In Verkeerdespruit it had been easy to ignore him, mainly, I now realized, because he had made it possible for me to do so; here he presented himself as if he had claims on me, based on our common past and, to some extent, a common history. Nor was it only a matter of his unfamiliar new insistence, a quality almost physical in its intrusiveness, but also of the complex of associations that his presence activated in my own mind. It was not that he had featured at all largely in that childhood; but seeing him now, I realized what a constant if peripheral presence he had been. Looking back, I could make out the self-effacing, knock-kneed figure of Fanie van den Bergh dogging the edges of my early life, uninvited, undemanding, and yet undeniably present.

71

Now, he was still just Fanie van den Bergh, but he came burdened, or armed, with much of what had brought me where I was. It was to get away from the gormless maladroitness of backwater living, the skinny elbows and scabrous knees, the chilblains and runny noses and ringworm and horny heels and cheesy foreskins, the unenlightened gape and awkward stutter, that I had come to Bloemfontein — itself hardly a metropolis of culture and style, but at least some degrees evolved from the dust in which all of Verkeerdespruit seemed to have its being. Fairness reminded me that Fanie, too, had evolved beyond Verkeerdespruit, and as far as I could tell no longer had ringworm or horny heels, but my Wesley College standards reassured me that the Clutch Plates, lost in their dark domain of oil and grease, were hardly on a higher level of evolution than the dusty denizens of Verkeerdespruit.

In the bright sunlight outside, while Fanie was tying his shoelace for the sixth time — he seemed not yet to have fully mastered the intricacies of owning and managing a pair of shoes — I tried to examine him dispassionately, not as the unwelcome envoy from my past, but impersonally, as a boy of about my age. His rather pale skin was smooth, a fine down starting to show on the upper lip; his face was unblemished except for a light scar on his left temple — and that scar established again, between this boy of about my age and myself, the bond of the past, for I recognized it as the mark left by the edge of my desk, when Fanie fell against it in Mr. de Wet's class.

1963

At the end of Standard Two we moved to a new class, which, although ostensibly a rung up the ladder, entailed a demotion from lording it over the Standard Ones to being lorded over by the Standard Fours. But it was more than the loss of caste that made us dread the transition: it was the knowledge that we were moving into Mr. de Wet's class.

Mr. de Wet was odd, even by the standards of a school that had to accept such teachers as were desperate enough to apply to Verkeerdespruit, and odd beyond even the oddness that children ascribe to anybody not conforming in every respect to their idea of normal humanity. His short body, though powerful and broad-shouldered, seemed to be warped somewhere: not quite a hunchback, not quite a limp, more a list to one side. It was probably a minor hip defect, but at the time his oblique scuttle formed part of the mystery and menace of the man. His face was very square, his jaw set very tight, and his head would have been impressive in a monumental bust carved into rock; but it was too big to match his squat body and, being carried at a slight angle, seemed forever on the point of toppling off its precarious perch. His speech, like his body, was not quite deformed and yet not quite normal either: it was really no more than extreme sibilance, but again the elusive nature of the disability made it more sinister than a straightforward impediment would have been. But Mr. de Wet's most fabled and feared attribute was an ophthalmic peculiarity that inclined him to focus some twenty degrees to the right of wherever he seemed to be looking. It owed its notoriety partly to the fact that it was a deviation that could be demonstrated only in action, as it were: to look at Mr. de Wet looking, he seemed merely to have a slightly more intense stare than other people. Without actual experience of this obliquity, it was in fact difficult to see why previous generations of Standard Threes had evinced such horror at what seemed to be at most a slightly disconcerting peculiarity. "Just you wait," they said when questioned on the point, "just you wait."

Mr. de Wet was known as Ssscorpion, in reference to his sibilance and his mode of motion. Years later, in training camp, I saw a group of recruits pitting a scorpion and a spider against each other in an ammunition case, and I recognized then the accuracy of the unkind genius who had first discerned the similarity between Mr. de Wet's progress through his class and the nervous scamper of the scorpion, its sting poised like a vicious standard.

After the slightly gushy, sweet nature of Miss Jordaan, Ssscorpion came as a shock, and he knew it. "We've got a fresh crop today," he said on the first day, grinning conspiratorially at the Standard Fours, who, relieved to have graduated from the position of victims to that of collaborators in Mr. de Wet's humor, grinned back grimly, no doubt recalling their own terror the year before. We stood mutely; there seemed to be no way of averting a wrath as irrational and unpredictable as Mr. de Wet's.

"You've all been ssspoilt," he hissed at us. "You've been treated like sssugar mice. Well," he said, pausing for effect, "I have sssugar mice for breakfasssst."

The Standard Fours tittered obligingly, and we looked at Mr. de Wet, all trying as hard as possible not to look like a sugar mouse. "Sssome of you," he said ominously, "think you're very clever." He directed this observation at Fanie, who once again had the desk next to mine. "Well," he said, still to Fanie, "you're going to find out your missstake. You're going to find out that you're not half as clever as you've been allowed to think you are."

Fanie stared at Mr. de Wet, presumably as mystified as the rest of us, except that Fanie registered mystification no more vividly than any other emotion. There was something so grotesque in Fanie's being accused of intellectual presumption that I choked back a giggle.

Mr. de Wet came walking toward me, his eyes still fixed on Fanie. "Why are you sniggering?" he demanded, and I looked at Fanie in perplexity; he was not known to snigger.

"Don't look away when I'm ssspeaking to you," Mr. de Wet hissed, and slapped me on the side of the head. Then he sidled back to the front of the class. "I'll teach you sssome respect for authority," he said. "Classs sssit." As I slid into my seat, rubbing my cheek, I recollected Ssscorpion's famous obliquity of vision and ruefully reflected that half had not been told me: he had so *obviously* been looking at Fanie.

What made this such an insidious deviation was that in order to allow for the defects of Mr. de Wet's vision, one had to distrust one's own; no matter how often one had mistakenly interpreted the direction of his gaze, one always made the same mistake again, because it was so hard to believe that Mr. de Wet did not see what he seemed so obviously to be looking at. In any case, it would have taken more confidence in our own powers of geometry than any of us possessed to have calculated the degree of error and compensated for it. Not long ago, while having my eyes examined, I asked the ophthalmologist, "Is it possible to have a deviation that makes it look as if you're looking at something you're not looking at?"

"Yes," he said, deftly juggling his little lenses. "Macular degeneration. No sign of it here. Now — which is the sharper, one or two?"

It seems strange now that we so unquestioningly accepted not only Mr. de Wet's authority but also the apparent hatred of us that that authority gave him license to express. We never asked each other why he should seem to hate us: we simply accepted that he did, and hoped that somebody else would be selected that day. His favorite method of terrorism was to place himself straight in front of his victim, so that, whatever the direction of his gaze, the victim knew for once that he — or even she — had been selected. Then Mr. de Wet would pose whatever question he had thought up for the day, stand back, and wait for the mumbled "I don't know, sir," which was the invariable response. "I can't hear you," he would say in a quiet voice. "Don't mumble and don't look down and ANSWER ME!" The moment the panic-stricken victim started speaking, Mr. de Wet would close his fist lightly with the thumb resting upward on top of the other fingers and bring the hand thus armed swiftly and sharply under the chin of the stuttering child. When well-timed, this maneuver caught you with your tongue between your slack jaws, causing you to bite your own tongue with some violence.

"Bitten your tongue, have you?" he would say with feigned concern. "You shouldn't mumble like that," and away he would sidle, looking almost human in the glow of his pleasure. If, on the other hand, the blow was ill-timed and the victim managed to escape unbitten, Mr. de Wet would sourly retreat to his desk and inflict various refinements of torture on us for the rest of the day.

Nobody thought of complaining to some figure of authority, the principal, a parent, about this treatment: to us, Ssscorpion *was* authority, or its representative in our midst. A system of education based on the belief that all authority is derived from God does not encourage its victims to complain about the treatment meted out to them. We accepted Mr. de Wet as our doom for the next two years, and it is likely that this is what our parents would have advised us to do in any case if we had complained to them; my mother, though suspicious of authority and scornful of our teachers, did not believe in parents' intervening on their children's behalf, on the grounds that this simply caused the children to be victimized. Mr. de Wet himself assured us periodically, when he was moved to admiration of his own methods of education, that he was acting purely from a concern for our education and moral welfare: "Love without dissscipline is sssentimentality," he would say, "and dissscipline without love is tyranny; but love with dissscipline is the nourishment of the sssoul." Those sitting in the front row had learned to close their exercise books during these eulogies, so as not to get them blotted with the liquid sibilance of Mr. de Wet's enthusiasm. Children had been punished — by Mr. de Wet — for blots on their exercise books caused by his wet sputter.

For Mr. de Wet's delight in inflicting torment was coupled, and I now believe intimately connected, with a simpering and yet bullying sentimentality. Not that we recognized it as that: we merely cringed away from his effusions as we did from the slaps and jeers that so often followed them. Nothing served so well these two impulses of Mr. de Wet's soul as the business of essay writing, which enabled him to set us the most impossibly exalted topics and humiliate us most basely for failing to live up to the nobility of the theme. One particularly successful topic was announced simply as "Something I love."

"Use your imaginations, children," he said. "Free your ssstarved little sssouls from their tiny prisons inside those dirty little bodies and for once let them breathe and ssspeak."

Mr. de Wet was strong on soul, perhaps because his body was not in all respects satisfactory. On this occasion, as so often before, our souls failed to rise to the occasion. The class sat in dumb despair for the hour allowed for the release of their souls and produced, in most instances, a few pathetic lines of insincere gush on a subject on which the writer had obviously never before wasted a thought, not to mention a stirring of the soul. The delightful part of the exercise for Mr. de Wet was in then obliging us to read our fraudulent little raptures to a giggling and yet terrified class, while he himself hovered around the reader, right hand at the ready.

Jesserina was the first victim. "Something I love," she read, and then started giggling.

"What's the matter, Jesss-erina?" asked Mr. de Wet, scuttling up to her. "You were sssupposed to write on sssomething you love, not sssomething that amusesss you. Now carry on." He went and stood next to her and stared attentively at a spot twenty degrees to the right of her face.

Jesserina desperately gulped down her hysteria and started again in a quavering voice. "Something I love," she read as fast as possible, "is the sound of rain on the roof after a drought and the smell of the raindrops on the dusty ground and the sight of the sunset over the veld." She stopped abruptly and said, "That's all."

"Mmm," said Ssscorpion, in a tone that we had learned to recognize with relief as the hum of a frustrated urge to inflict punishment. "Your sssoul hasn't travelled very far from home, has it?" He scuttled on. "Now Tjaart," he said, fixing his gaze on Japie Dreyer, "you tell us what you love."

There was a nervous titter in the class. Our terror could not altogether dispel our sense of the incongruity of Tjaart Bothma's loving anything other than the rugby ball that he took everywhere with him as if hoping to hatch it. He got to his feet heavily and read haltingly in the deep voice that had earned him the prominence he normally enjoyed among our squeaky trebles: "Something I love. Something I love is my mother and father and sisters and brothers and all our cows." The titters turned into giggles. Tjaart's father, old Koot Bothma, was about the most unlovable human being in the district of Verkeerdespruit, with the possible exception of his wife, Ralie, who had once concussed her husband by throwing the telephone at him. Telephones in those regions were heavy and wooden and fixed to the wall. My mother said it wasn't nice to damage government property but she could see Ralie Bothma's point. As for their cows, Koot Bothma's dairy had two years earlier brought a particularly nasty epidemic of brucellosis upon Verkeerdespruit and its neighbors as far as Clocolan, not counting the tractor salesman from Pretoria who had drunk a glass of milk at breakfast in Loubser's Hotel to dilute the hangover he'd incurred the night before in an attempt to liven up a Tuesday evening in Verkeerdespruit. *Die Landstem* had reported the incident under the headline "Hangover cure almost kills man: victim vows to keep to brandy."

"Sssilence!" hissed Mr. de Wet. "Tjaart, just because you've grown up with cattle doesn't mean we want to listen to cow dung." We roared with the laughter of pent-up fear, knowing that this was allowed, indeed expected, whenever Mr. de Wet's jokes were at the expense of one of us. "Sssilence!" he hissed again, but with a pleased sort of sibilance, like a snake trying to purr.

It was my turn next. So intimidated was I by authority that I deferred even to as perverted a representative of it as Mr. de Wet; and I never quite lost an absurd hope of after all pleasing this man whose pleasure lay in the pain of others. So I had taken the topic seriously and had earnestly reflected on something I loved. This proved to be unexpectedly difficult, like writing an essay on the smell of snow or the taste of persimmons. I had heard of love, of course, but mainly as something that parents felt as a matter of course for their children and that children were duty bound to feel back. It did not seem to be the stuff essays were made of. In Sunday school I had learned that love was unselfish and put the happiness of others before its own, like Jesus getting crucified or little Racheltjie de Beer freezing to death trying to keep her younger brother warm in the anthill. It seemed an impractical sort of emotion, and I couldn't remember ever experiencing it, until I thought of Dumbo. After all, I almost never forgot to feed him, even when it was inconvenient for me, and when I went out in the afternoons, I usually took him along even if it did mean walking rather than cycling. This seemed incontrovertible evidence as defined by the best authorities. "Something I love," I read. "Something I love is my dog, Dumbo. He is called Dumbo because when he was small he looked so much like an elephant and ..."

"Jumbo," said Mr. de Wet.

I looked at him inquiringly. "Dumbo," I said.

"Jumbo," he repeated. "Elephants are called Jumbo."

"But ..." I began. One did not lightly contradict Mr. de Wet: it was so obviously what he wanted. But he had sniffed the heady smell of insubordination needing to be corrected.

"But what, Sssimon?" he asked in his most reasonable tone, the one that we knew to herald the lightning strike of the clenched hand.

"But my dog is called Dumbo," I said, except it came out as *Ut my og is alled Umbo*, as I tried to keep my tongue clear of my teeth.

"That I do not doubt," he said sweetly. "But then he is not called after an elephant. Perhaps he is called Dumbo because he is very dumb?" he suggested helpfully, the lightly clenched hand swaying by his side. The class tittered obligingly.

"Dumbo was the name of an elephant in a film," I explained, even while knowing that Mr. de Wet did not want an explanation. He wanted a disagreement.

"Are you sssaying I am wrong?" he asked.

"No," I said desperately, and then did not know how to continue. "No," I repeated lamely.

"If I'm not wrong I must be right, not ssso?"

"Yes, Mr. de Wet."

79

"Then your dog was not called after an elephant after all?"

"No, Mr. de Wet."

"Then why did you say it was?"

"I don't know, Mr. de Wet."

"SSSit down, SSSimon. If that's the best you can do for something you love, I advise you to give up love as sssoon as posssible."

I was relieved to escape without physical injury, but my dignity was rather bruised; and when I went home that afternoon I felt somehow disloyal to Dumbo when he bounded up to me, boisterously unaware of my treachery. I was sure that this was the effect that Mr. de Wet had calculated, with his preternatural sense of how to inflict pain; what I couldn't understand was why he would go to such elaborate lengths to do so. Most children accepted unquestioningly that Mr. de Wet's methods were simply his methods, and as such did not require any explanation. I, however, was puzzled, not so much at the unprovoked violence of his general demeanor as at the unmistakable targeting of myself. Used as I was to being the teacher's favorite, the best reader, the quickest at mental arithmetic, and probably also the cleanest child in class (I had been the only one to escape the ringworm epidemic the previous year), I was unpleasantly surprised to meet a teacher who not only seemed not to appreciate my superiority but actually treated me as if I were the class dunce deviously trying to pass himself off as the star pupil. There was no point in discussing the puzzle with my friends, because they were merely amused. "Serves you right for always sucking up," said Louis van Niekerk, and even Fanie smiled faintly at the justice of it. Nothing was more of a mystery to Fanie than anything else.

So I discussed the matter with one of the few adults who wouldn't regard it as her duty to reconcile me to the privileges of authority, Betty the Exchange. In one of our Saturday afternoon sessions in Steyl's café I asked her, "Do you know Mr. de Wet?"

"Ben de Wet at the school?" she asked. "Yes. He phones his mother in Hopetown every afternoon from the phone booth in the hostel."

This was new light on Mr. de Wet. "Oh," I said. "Well, I think he's … strange."

"You bet he's strange," Betty said flatly. "He calls her *Mammie-lief.*" This was one of the few times I heard Betty repeat any of the conversations she must have overheard regularly from her lonely listening post in the post office. The idea of Ssscorpion calling his mother *Mummy dear* was grotesque, but I was too preoccupied with my own mystification to spare a thought for Mr. de Wet's filial devotion.

"Yes, but I don't mean like that," I tried to explain. "He's different from other teachers. He says I'm stupid." Saying it, I realized why I was telling Betty this: she wouldn't regard it as her duty to assure me that perhaps I *was* stupid and shouldn't be arrogant. Instead she said quite factually, "Yes. He's jealous."

"Jealous?" I asked blankly. I could see no relation between Ssscorpion and me that merited jealousy.

"Yes. Because of Ariana Jordaan." Betty and Miss Jordaan were known to be "best friends," which, as just about the only two unmarried white women in town, they had little chance of avoiding.

"But …" I started.

"Yes," she repeated. "Didn't you know that he was in love with her?"

"I knew he took her out a few times." He had brought her to the Saturday night movie in the town hall once, causing so much whispering and craning of necks that the projectionist had stopped his machine and told us to behave ourselves.

"Yes. Well, he asked her to marry him and she said no. In fact she said that he gave her the creeps. That is, I'm sure she didn't put it like that, but that's what she meant and that's what he understood. He said that she'd *mortified his pride.*"

"But …" I interjected, but Betty was now in full spate.

"Yes. You mean what does this have to do with you? Well you must know that you were Ariana's favorite pupil."

"Yes," I said.

"And teachers tend to discuss their pupils with each other."

"Do they?" I asked, less interested in the conversational opportunities of teachers than in my unexpected prominence in the intrigue.

"You bet they do. It can be very boring being trapped with a bunch of teachers. Well, Ariana told Ben about you while he was still courting her, and he came to see you as in some way specially favored by her. So that when he was rejected by her, you see, he took it out on you."

"How do you know?" I asked, in awe of Betty's omniscience.

"I don't *know*," she said, "but I'm not a fool, and that's what I think. Ben de Wet sees you as Ariana's favorite. And he's still in love with her."

"But that's unfair," I protested.

"You bet it's unfair," said Betty laconically. "But how else can he get back at her?"

Betty's explanation helped me as much as explanations of the inevitable ever can: it gave me a vantage point from which to survey my own helplessness. Since I now knew that Ssscorpion's displeasure had nothing to do with my efforts or abilities, I did not feel seriously challenged by his slights. Besides, apart from the initial slap, he limited his assaults upon me to verbal sallies, ridicule, and sarcasm, which, though unpleasant, lost some of their sting with familiarity. And so it might have remained had I not been emboldened by the knowledge of my special status in Ssscorpion's emotional world to test my own power to vex.

At the end of the previous year I had sent a Christmas card to Miss Jordaan, all the way to Calvinia where her parents lived. To my great joy I received a card in return, a gaudy and obviously homemade but to me beautiful confection of holly and sparkling snow. The latter was pasted onto the card and shed glitter all over our lounge carpet when I hung the card on the string strung annually for the purpose. But more precious to me even than the tinsel glamour was the inscription inside: "To Simon, with love from (Miss) Ariana Jordaan." It was written on a slip of paper pasted inside the card, and Louis van Niekerk said that it was obviously a used card that Miss Jordaan had recycled, but my mother said she'd probably just made a mistake writing the inscription the first time and hadn't wanted to scratch it out.

Once a week we had to hand in our classwork books to Mr. de Wet for inspection. The idea of the classwork book was that we could work in rough before copying the correct version into a neatwork book, but Mr. de Wet insisted that our classwork books should also be neat, and he was hard on transgressions. So receiving back the classwork books was always an anxious business; after he had examined the books in his own time, he handed them out, commenting on individual messiness or general obstreperousness as best suited his mood. At best it was an opportunity for him to exercise his sense of humor; at worst it turned into a full-scale torture session.

It occurred to me that it might be an interesting experiment to leave Miss Jordaan's card in my book as if as a bookmark. What I hoped to achieve by this I have no idea; I think I simply wanted to see what Mr. de Wet would do. I realized that this was unlikely to be anything very pleasant, but I reassured myself that since I was not supposed to know about his attachment to Miss Jordaan, my act could not be interpreted as deliberate. I counted also on his reluctance to admit publicly to his rejection; by and large I probably thought that by mortifying his soul a bit more I might avenge some small portion of the suffering he'd wrought upon us.

When the handing-out ritual came round again, Ssscorpion returned my classwork book to me without comment, usually a sign that he could not find anything to criticize or ridicule. I soon noticed, though, that the card was missing, and from the way Ssscorpion hovered around my desk while handing out the other books, I surmised that he was waiting for me to comment on its absence — which of course I could not do without forfeiting the pretense that I had absentmindedly left the card in the book. So I reconciled myself to the loss of my card as the price of my experiment.

But I should have known that Ssscorpion's displeasure was not to be bought off so cheaply. He had finished handing out the books and was walking past my desk as if on his way back to the front of the class. Suddenly he paused, as if in midstride.

"What's that?" he asked, and pointed at my desk as if there were a particularly vile substance smeared over it. At first I could see nothing, and he said, "Are you going to answer me?" still pointing.

I shook my head dumbly. I knew by now that Mr. de Wet's questions were never rhetorical: he expected an answer, if only so that he could ridicule or punish its inadequacy. So I took refuge in the flimsy all-purpose shelter of the tormented scholar, and said, "I don't know."

"You don't know?" he asked. "Your desk is covered in the stuff and you *don't know* what it is?"

He extended a finger and pressed it on a particle of glitter that had sifted out of the book.

"Get up when I'm talking to you!" he said. Dumbly I obeyed, and he took up my book again.

"It ssseems to be coming out of your book," he said, and took my book by one page so that it flapped open downward like a dead chicken. Silver glitter sifted down.

"Look classs, a sssnowstorm," he hissed. "Sssimon's book has produced a sssnowstorm." There were dutiful chuckles, feebly hoping to propitiate or deflect the malice about to be released upon the class; but Ssscorpion was wise to the wiles of the terrified and rounded on the rest of the class. "If Sssimon can't tell us where the sssnow comes from, you'll have to help him," he said, and we knew an interrogation was in progress. "Sssit down, Sssimon." Keeping my book dangling down in his left hand he dragged himself around the class, picking victims at random, calling upon them to name the mystery substance. It was the old tongue-biting trick, presented as the consequence of my refusal to identify the offending substance. Since glitter was not a feature of the lives of Verkeerdespruit children, none of them knew what it was, although Bettie du Plooy did venture a guess that it could be cake decoration.

"Cake decoration?" Ssscorpion exclaimed. "Simon, have you been eating cake in your classwork book?"

"No, Mr. de Wet," I said.

"No, Bettie," he said. "Sssimon says no. Try again."

The terrified Bettie shook her head. "What was that?" he said politely, leaning forward. "I didn't hear what you said."

"I said …" Bettie began, and Ssscorpion's hand shot out like a snake striking. She squealed slightly as she bit her tongue.

"Sit down," he said, and moved on in his relentless progress through the class. He stopped in front of Fanie's desk, next to

84

where I was sitting mutely awaiting what I now realized was a reckoning.

"Fanie," he said, in his most pleasant tone, "can you help us?"

Fanie got to his feet. I could see that he was trembling.

"Come on, Fanie," he said, "I'm waiting for an answer."

Fanie started perspiring slightly. He licked his lips and prepared to say something; then his courage abandoned him and he stared down at his desk.

"Look at me when I'm talking to you," said Mr. de Wet, and Fanie lifted his clouded blue eyes at him. "Sssuch a sssimple question," Mr. de Wet continued. "What is this ssstuff that Sssimon has in his book?" and he opened the book at the spot where the card had nestled, leaving behind a particularly rich crop of glitter.

Fanie looked at the book and then looked at me in dumb anguish, and I slowly got to my feet. Ssscorpion shifted his gaze twenty degrees to the right of me.

"And why are you getting up?" he asked in his most reasonable tone.

"Because I can answer your question," I said.

"You've had your chance," he said. "It's Fanie's turn now. Sssit down," and the eyes swivelled back.

"The shiny stuff is glitter from a Christmas card," I persisted. "I used the card as a bookmark."

Ssscorpion had moved very quickly to stand in front in me. "And why did you not say so when I asked you?" he demanded.

"Because the card was from Miss Jordaan and was my own special card and you stole it," I rattled off desperately, but not fast enough to escape the lightly clenched hand. Except that this time it was not lightly clenched and seemed to be aimed at the side of my face. Or perhaps I ducked my head in an attempt to avoid the blow under the chin; it happened much too quickly for me to be aware of much except the astonishing pain in my jaw before I passed out. So I missed the excitement and had to be told about it by Louis van Niekerk when he came to visit me at home, where I was resting with a wired-up jaw. Apparently I collapsed forward on top of Mr. de Wet, Jesserina Schoeman got hysterical, and Fanie had another fit, cutting his temple against the side of my desk as he fell.

There was no explaining away my broken jaw, otherwise I do believe the school would have tried to do so. But this time they were up against my mother, who insisted that "something" had to be done. She agreed not to file a criminal charge of assault only on the condition that Mr. de Wet was reported to the provincial authorities in Bloemfontein. The school committee wrote a report and submitted it to the authorities. The authorities instructed the school committee to investigate the incident more fully and make a recommendation. "And I suppose the school committee will refer the matter back to Mr. de Wet and ask him to make a recommendation," my mother said.

"Not quite," said my father, who was on the school committee. "They'll try to avoid scandal, but I imagine they'll take a serious view of the offense."

"What will happen to Mr. de Wet?" I asked.

"I don't know. It's for the school committee to decide."

"But you're on the school committee."

"Well yes, but I can't decide for them. I'll tell you after the meeting."

A week later my father announced at the table: "The school committee has decided to recommend that Mr. de Wet be transferred to another school."

"To go and break somebody else's jaw?" my mother demanded.

"Well, they thought that perhaps there were special circumstances in this particular class …"

"You mean they think Simon deserved to have his jaw broken?"

"No, but the headmaster said that sometimes a particular teacher just has a difficult relationship with a particular class, and that a different environment might be better adapted to Mr. de Wet's teaching methods. It seems it's a matter of pedagogical dynamics."

"And the school committee bought that?"

"Well, Dominee Claassen said that the Bible teaches us to turn the other cheek …"

"Turn the other cheek!" my mother exploded. "Look at the

86

boy sitting there with his jaw wired up! Does the Bible say what you have to do if your jaw gets broken the first time round?"

"I did suggest that it was perhaps an unfortunate metaphor under the circumstances and that the man might not be fit to deal with children, but I couldn't very well push too hard, or people might think I wasn't objective, what with Simon being my son."

"I should have thought that it had been quite objectively enough established that your son's jaw was broken by this man. What do they want — an X-ray?"

"Well, nobody actually *said* anything, it was just an unspoken implication. In the end majority opinion was that he should be given another chance elsewhere."

"Majority opinion, my foot!" my mother said. "The majority of the school committee, perhaps, but did they think of consulting the children who have to put up with this man's *teaching methods*?"

This seemed like an opening for me to interrupt, so I asked, "Then Mr. de Wet won't appear in court?"

"No," my father said.

"Why not?"

"Well, he didn't commit a crime, you see."

"So he didn't … molest me?"

He looked half puzzled, half amused, and asked: "Why do you want to know?"

"Because — because they sent Steve to prison for molesting Fanie."

"I see. No, what Mr. de Wet did wasn't molesting."

"But …"

"Yes?"

"Why is it molesting for Steve to kiss Fanie but not for Mr. de Wet to break my jaw?"

My father looked at my mother, but she just shrugged. "You explain it, you're the magistrate."

"Well," said my father, "it's all a matter of definition, don't you see?"

"No."

"Oh. Do you know what I mean by a matter of definition?"

"No."

"Oh. Well, if I say something is a matter of definition, I mean that a word means something because it's been decided that that's what it means."

"Like the Sabotage Act," my mother said.

"Yes," my father said, "I suppose like the Sabotage Act. Have you heard of the Sabotage Act?"

"I've seen it in the papers." The Sabotage Act had been passed the year before.

"Well, then, sabotage used to mean planting a bomb and blowing up something; but the Sabotage Act now defines sabotage in such a way that it can mean, well, lots of other things."

"Anything that the government regards as a threat to itself," my mother interjected.

My father carried on. "So sabotage is now, as I was saying, a matter of definition."

"And who makes the definitions?"

"The people in charge, the people who make the laws. In the case of the Sabotage Act, the law defines certain acts as sabotage and punishes them accordingly; in Fanie's case, the law defines a grown-up man kissing a boy that he's not related to as molesting, and sends the man to prison."

"But why?"

"Well, as punishment for the crime, and to protect other people."

"You mean because he may kiss other people too?"

My father looked at my mother and sighed. "Not quite. Let's just say for an adult to ... be too fond of children is not ... natural."

"Is it natural for an adult to hit children?"

"Well, not *natural*, perhaps, but it may be necessary if the adult is in a position of authority."

"I'm sorry," my mother broke in. She didn't normally contradict my father in front of me. "But you're not going to convince me that it was necessary for that man to break Simon's jaw. He's a sadist and he should be removed from his position of authority."

"Well, yes," my father said. "I agree with you, if the man is a sadist he must be removed from office. But by the committee's definition he isn't a sadist."

"Then the committee should have its definitions shaken up. What's the point of being a magistrate if you can't see to it that justice is done?"

"Well, I don't have jurisdiction outside the court."

"And soon you won't have jurisdiction inside the court either, the way things are going."

"That's not really the point, is it?" asked my father.

"I don't know," my mother said. "Perhaps that's the real point."

At the end of that year Mr. de Wet was transferred to Bantu Education and disappeared from our lives. I saw him again years later. I was in my uniform in Pretoria; he was waiting for a bus on Church Square. He looked older, of course, but when the bus arrived he scuttled toward it with the same fierce energy that had so terrified us in that stifling classroom. Seeing that mad little scurry, I moved forward on an impulse of sudden hatred, and blocked his path. All the things I had felt as a child came back to me with a clarity I had not known at the time; I now knew the injustices he had wrought upon us, and could name to his face the distortions of his spirit. I could confront the man with his own misshapen soul and bring him to account for the terror he had inflicted upon trembling children. I was considerably taller than the hunched figure of Mr. de Wet, and I gave him time to take me in before I spoke. But as he lifted his head, he seemed oblivious to my presence, for all that I was standing right in front of him: he was reading an advertisement on the side of the bus. Short of grabbing him by the throat there seemed to be no way of claiming his attention. And then I remembered. Allowing for a deviation of twenty degrees, he must have been looking straight at me. Indeed, he was waiting for me to speak, with that air of polite attentiveness that had so terrified us, and instinctively I glanced down at his hand for the dreaded half-clenched fist. But the hand that used to shoot out so swiftly was dangling by his side motionlessly, except for the telltale tremor of Parkinson's disease. He put out his hand with the uncertain movement of a blind person, and I realized that indeed he could not see me, or see more of me than a vague outline — that macular degeneration had run its course.

Looking down at the half-blind, trembling, misshapen man, I could not pronounce my flaming curses, my indictment of my childhood and this man's part in it. What did come to me was almost as surprising to me as it must have been to him. "Ben de Wet," I said, leaning forward so that my face filled whatever vision he had left, "Ariana Jordaan will never send you a Christmas card now."

December 6, 1968

Fanie, having carefully, with the meticulousness of the unpracticed, tied his shoelace with a double knot, came clumping up to where I was waiting for him. His teammates, apparently quite used to these delays, were daring each other to steal the roses in the Garden of Remembrance, while very unconvincingly pretending to be admiring them. They knew and I knew that I would not be able to lift a finger to prevent their running riot in the rose garden if they so wished, and they were clearly weighing up the eventual consequences against the present satisfaction. To my considerable relief, the door to Mr. Robinson's house, which fronted onto the rose garden, opened, and Mr. Robinson himself appeared, his clerical dog collar looking reassuringly authoritative: surely even a Clutch Plate would not dare to defy such a potent symbol.

Mr. Robinson blinked vaguely in the bright sun; not a very perceptive person at the best of times, he was clearly at a loss to account for a group of schoolboys in unfamiliar uniform in front of his house. "Ah, good morning, boys," he said, in his ponderous manner. "Admiring the roses, are we?"

There were mutters and giggles from the Clutch Plates, but no articulate response. Mr. Robinson, used to addressing dumbstruck assemblies of boys, was not deterred by this lack of engagement. "I think you will find that we have some rare species here," he continued. "The rose you are admiring is the Rosa Damascena Bifera Officinalis." He paused, and, not one of the Clutch Plates taking up this conversational gambit, he must have sensed a certain lack of reciprocity in the conversation, for he cleared his throat and said, "But then, as the poet says, a rose by any other name would smell as sweet, not so?" He peered at the now

90

thoroughly cowed little group in front of him and, recognizing my uniform if not my face, said, "Who are your visitors, boy? Are you not going to introduce them to me?"

It occurred to me, madly, to say to him, a rose by any other name would smell as sweet, *but instead I muttered*, "Yes Mr. Robinson, sir. These are the boys from the ... from the Technical School."

"Ah yes, the little tennis team," he said. "And very welcome they are, too, to Wesley College." He now addressed himself to the Clutch Plates. "I am the Reverend Mr. Robinson, headmaster of Wesley College, and I am pleased to have this opportunity of welcoming you personally to our school. I trust that young ... this young man is looking after you well?"

He paused for a reply, but received none, so carried on. "I hope that this will be the first of many visits, and that you will have a splendid, er ... tennis match."

The Clutch Plates continued to gape in silence, and no doubt Mr. Robinson would now have terminated his monologue to his own satisfaction, had Fanie not seen fit, with quite un-Fanie-like initiative, to announce, in his best English, "I come from the same town as him," pointing at me. "He was together with me in the class."

It struck me that this was the second time that Fanie had denounced me in public: once, long ago, to accuse me of having caused his fit, and now this claim of a common origin. Of the two, this one seemed far worse; apart from anything else, I could not deny this charge, could not even openly resent it.

"Splendid, splendid," said Mr. Robinson, looking at me, I thought, as if he were reconsidering my right to be at Wesley College. "But I suspect you're in a hurry to start knocking those balls about, eh? Run along then, and may the best team win."

Mr. Robinson retreated into his house, and the Clutch Plates regained their voices and their critical faculties. The Main Plate indulged in what he imagined was a killing imitation of Mr. Robinson's manner and accent. I pretended not to notice. "Come on, Fanie," I urged, "the dressing rooms are just down there."

"We have to get our tennis clothes first," he announced. "You know, in the bus, where you said we should leave them."

The bus was on the other side of the school. "Then why …?" I started, and then shrugged it off. It was impossible to get Fanie to explain his behavior. "Come on, then," I said, and turned round to lead my little band to the bus. The other Clutch Plates, to my relief, did not question my authority, but straggled along behind Fanie and me, the apparently inseparable sharers of a common childhood.

I stood outside the Combi, waiting for the Clutch Plates to sort out their complicated belongings and trying to shake off the spell of forgotten things. Fanie appeared at my elbow, carrying an untidy bundle and a tennis racket. "Do you like Bloemfontein?" he asked. I looked at him in amazement. Fanie never asked questions; or if he did, they tended to be monosyllabic expressions of mystification rather than actual applications for information, as this one arguably was. Though not in itself a riveting question, it represented a revolution in intellectual inquiry for Fanie.

"Bloemfontein?" I replied rather lamely. Feeling I should come up with something profound in response to so unusual a probe, I did not want to seem naively impressionable, and yet I had to bear in mind that for Fanie, coming from Odendaalsrust, Bloemfontein still had the mystique of the metropolis. "Yes," I said weightily, "I suppose it's a fair enough place, if you bear in mind its relative isolation from the rest of the country, not to mention the rest of the world."

But Fanie had lost interest.

"Ja," he said, "Trevor het mos altyd gesê dis 'n kak plek," — Trevor always used to say it was a shit place.

5

1963

Klasie Vermaak, the postmaster, had lived with his mother for as long as I could remember, in a dark house behind a high hedge on the outskirts of Verkeerdespruit. The house was called Ebenezer. Mrs. Vermaak was called Gertruida, but nobody dared call her by her first name; she let it be known that to be called by anything other than the name bestowed upon her by marriage would be disrespectful to the memory of her husband. This husband, Gerhardus, had died so long ago that I had only a vague recollection of him — a tiny, bent man entering church five paces behind his wife, catching up with her just in time to stand back to allow her to enter the pew first, like a tug ushering an ocean liner into port. After his death she gave all her "sinful" dresses to the OVV's jumble sale and went into a mourning from which she never emerged — with one notable exception — till her own death ten years later. My mother said, though not to Mrs. Vermaak, that she was pleased to get the dresses for the jumble sale, and she hoped that Mrs. Vermaak's gesture gave her husband more joy in death than she had given him in life.

I knew Mrs. Vermaak as a grim-faced black presence sometimes to be seen sweeping the steps of her house — the cleanest house in Verkeerdespruit, my mother used to say: "You feel as if you should tie a duster to your ankle when you go in, so as not to leave a mark on the floor." She did not keep a servant, Mrs. Vermaak explained to my mother, because servants left more dirt than they removed. She believed that when God created the earth, the devil created dust to discredit Him, so that people would curse God for his creation. My father said this theory made as much sense as any other, and it also explained why South Africa was such a dusty country.

Mrs. Vermaak did not encourage visitors because they brought dirt and germs, but she tolerated visits from my mother in her capacity as secretary of the OVV because she felt, she said, she had to do "her little bit to help her neighbor." So far she had done nothing to help her neighbor other than the donation of her clothes, to which she referred as "my sacrifice." Her husband's death was "my loss" and her son was "my responsibility." My mother once took along Lida Mouton, the undersecretary of the OVV, and poor Lida was left completely bewildered trying to distinguish between Mrs. Vermaak's sacrifice, loss, and responsibility: she expressed sympathy with the sacrifice and gratitude for the loss, and looked so blank in the face of the responsibility that Mrs. Vermaak asked my mother in a very audible whisper, "Is she one of the railway Visagies?" The railway Visagies had twelve children with, my mother said, the intelligence of one fairly average child shared among the dozen.

My mother did not enjoy these visits, which were indeed quite pointless as far as promoting the aims of the OVV was concerned, but she felt, she said, that Mrs. Vermaak needed some human contact to take her mind off dust.

"She's got her son," my father said.

"Yes, poor man," my mother replied. "But he doesn't count as human contact."

"Why not?" I asked.

"Have you ever heard him *say* anything — I mean about anything other than stamps and postal orders?" I had to admit that I hadn't. Klasie was famous for once having taken out Selina Kotzé, the stationmaster's daughter, and not saying anything all evening — "Not a single bloody word," as she reported to Betty, "except *Ouch* when I slammed the car door on his finger." It was possible that Klasie's taciturnity was a consequence of a pronounced stammer he developed when nervous or excited, though the Verkeerdespruit theory was that the causation worked the other way around, and that Klasie stuttered because of lack of practice in talking.

About Klasie I knew more than most people because of my friendship with Betty. Not that there was much to know. Although in theory Betty worked under Klasie, in fact she told him what to do, and he did it cheerfully if a little absentmindedly. They had an excellent relationship, based on her good-humored acceptance that her lack of a chin would always cause her to be underestimated and his readiness to have his authority usurped by somebody as unthreatening as Betty. Klasie was the mildest person I had ever met. He had inherited or had had terrified into him his mother's cleanliness and tidiness, and the Verkeerdespruit post office regularly won the prize for the best-kept post office in the eastern Free State. He insisted that the water in the stamp-wetting machines should be emptied out at night and refilled every morning to prevent mosquitoes from hatching in them. The only time he ever showed any temper was when a new counter clerk, Sientjie Visagie, the twelfth of the twelve railway Visagies, licked a stamp to stick it on an envelope. "D-d-d-d-do you think Mrs. M-m-m-maree wants to carry your s-s-s-s-spit in her handbag?" he shouted at poor flustered Sientjie. Betty, who witnessed the scene, intervened to point out that Mrs. Maree wasn't going to carry the letter anywhere, since she was having it stamped for posting; upon which Klasie subsided immediately into his usual taciturn mildness, although Mrs. Maree, having been alerted to a sense of her own grievance, pointed out that she didn't want to send Sientjie's spit all the way to her sister in Eendekuil either.

Klasie spent his weekends pursuing his hobby, which was the battlefields of the Boer War. He got into his Morris Minor as soon as the post office closed on Saturday morning and drove off to a favorite battleground or, more rarely, one that he had not visited before. This much was common knowledge because one of his mother's few topics of conversation other than her loss and her sacrifice was "my son Herklaas's hobby." She did not seem to realize how dusty all these battlefields were, or perhaps she accepted that dust would be the natural element of the English, who stood to the rest of humanity on the ladder of creation as dust stands to honest soil. In any case, Klasie always washed his car the moment he got home from these expeditions, before he even went into the house to greet his mother. Mrs. Vermaak believed that Klasie was going to prove that the Boers had in fact won the Boer War, by showing conclusively that all accounts of the war had been falsified by English historians, it being a well-known fact that the English had invented reading and writing and could therefore clothe the truth in their image, as it were.

I was intrigued and slightly alarmed at the possibility of a revision of the history I had so painfully memorized at school, and asked my father what would happen if Klasie managed to prove his, or at any rate his mother's, theory.

"Will England give us back our country?" I asked.

"It's just done so anyway," he replied. This was a few years after South Africa's secession from British rule and the declaration of a new republic. "I don't think England wants us particularly."

"So what's the point of Klasie's hobby?" I demanded.

"What's the point of any hobby?" he asked. "What's the point of stamp collecting or flower arranging?"

I thought. "Well, if you collect stamps you've got the stamps, and if you arrange flowers you've got the arrangement; but Klasie … Klasie has nothing. He doesn't bring back anything from his trips."

But one day Klasie did bring back something from one of his trips. His name was Trevor.

"Where did Klasie meet Trevor?" I asked Betty.

"I don't know," she said. "I suppose on one of the battlefields; it's not a bad place for a Boer and an Englishman to meet." For Trevor was English. But this fact, momentous enough as it was in the light of Mrs. Vermaak's lifelong perpetuation of the Boer War, paled into insignificance on one's first view of Trevor. His hair was bright yellow, unlike any hair I'd ever seen. It was very long in front, so that he peered at the world through a golden fringe, except for a few moments after he'd flung back the fringe with a toss of his head, which he did to emphasize any of the many phrases that he felt needed emphasis, as in 'Well! I *suppose* you could put it like that,' when I asked him if he'd met Klasie on a battlefield.

But this was much later, when he had got into the habit of joining Betty and me, and occasionally Fanie, in Steyl's café on Saturdays while Klasie was wrapping up the week's business at the post office. Initially he was as much of a mystery to me as to

96

the rest of Verkeerdespruit, including even my mother, who didn't normally confess to failures of comprehension. "What I can't understand," she said, "is how he persuaded Mrs. Vermaak to take him into her house. With a *pink* shirt."

Trevor took to joining Betty and me because he met Betty through Klasie and found her, as I did, a congenial and receptive audience. What's more, she and I were two of the very few people in Verkeerdespruit to whom he could speak English. His Afrikaans was more than competent ("You don't grow up in fucking Bloem without getting to speak the fucking *taal*"), but he found it a relief, he said, to speak a language that didn't strain his jaw as much as Afrikaans ("It's how they get those square *jaws*, you know — from jutting them out to make those gggg-sounds."). Trevor didn't like the Afrikaners. He said they looked like pigs, smelled like camels, and thought like sheep. Furthermore, he said, they were fucking up the country with their notion that they were the chosen people. He had an apparently endless variety of names for them, Crunchies being his favorite but by no means his only. Until I met Trevor I had no very strong sense of English and Afrikaans as two distinct groups defined in opposition to each other: since my father was English and my mother Afrikaans, I was both, and I could not easily imagine a split between the two parts of me. Of course, I had heard anti-English comments from the less-enlightened Verkeerdespruiters, but had accepted my mother's explanation that that was just a feeling of inferiority expressing itself as hostility. With Trevor evincing a similar antipathy to Afrikaans, I was led to reconsider the nature of the split between English and Afrikaans. Was there perhaps a real difference, and if so, what did that make of me, who in a sense carried the difference in me? Could one be part Crunchie and part non-Crunchie?

In any case, the fact that I could speak English served me well in this instance, in that it led Trevor to include me in his confidence, as he sat recounting the story of his arrival in Verkeerdespruit, with many an emphatic flick of the blond fringe, and Fanie sitting by impassively, scratching Dumbo's ears. He couldn't in fact have understood more than Dumbo did, but by the same token seemed no more perturbed than Dumbo by his incomprehension. Apparently Klasie had found Trevor next to the road just outside Bloemfontein, trying to hitch a ride to Durban. ("Bloem was a bit, you know, *crunchy* for me; I thought Durbs would be more my style. All those *beaches*, you know, not like fucking Maselspoort with all those fat hairyback brats peeing in the water. And those Boer matrons in their *bathing costumes* like bags of mealie meal. And the mustache-and-paunch brigade drinking brandy and Coke.") Trevor was the first English person I'd heard swearing, which he did constantly in spite of Betty's objections to his doing so in my presence ("The boy knows the words — don't you? Of course you do — so why should it harm him to hear somebody *use* them?") He'd been beaten up by three men in a *bakkie* who had objected to his pink shirt. ("These three retards, you know, throwbacks to their grandmother's relationship with her Bull *mastiff*, built like double-seater shithouses all three, stopped and offered me a lift in the back on top of a load of very *ripe* compost and when I said, in quite a *friendly* fashion, you know, no thank you, not in my best clothes — I always wear my best clothes for hiking, you never know who you might meet — they took *violent* offense and kicked me and punched me and called me things you wouldn't *believe* and I'm not going to repeat in front of the boy because they're words I hope you *haven't* heard, in fact they called me some words *I* hadn't heard before and there aren't many of those, I can tell you, and they left me in the dust with a bleeding nose and torn clothes and my hair in a *mess*. So that when Klasie came along, bless his sweet soul, I was really *not* looking my best, you can imagine, but he took me in anyway, unlike the fat farmers zooming past in the Mercs the government gives them for not growing any more mealies. When he stopped and said, 'D-d-d-d-do you need help?' I couldn't even say something witty like 'N-n-n-no, I *always* hang around here with a bleeding nose and torn pants.' I just said yes thank you very much, God bless you, or something like that because I was speaking The Chosen Language and I don't know how to say God bless you in Afrikaans, which may say something about Afrikaans and the Afrikaners, all of them except Klasie even though he does wear a *hat* when he's driving, which is something I've always said proves that the Afrikaners haven't caught up with the twentieth century because what's stylish in an ox wagon is just not *practical* in a Morris Minor but where was I? I said yes thank you and when Klasie said where am I going I said Durbs actually but where are you going and when he said Verk-k-k-keerdespruit I said sounds like *fun*, take me there. And by the time we reached Verkeerdespruit he'd offered me board and lodging for free until I found a job. Which I've since discovered is more than Klasie has ever said to anybody, so I really feel quite *flattered*.")

"So here I am," he'd say, surveying Steyl's café through his fringe, with the Saturday afternoon crush of farm laborers, the Coca-Cola cooler, the plastic container of stale Chelsea buns on the counter. "It's not exactly *Durban*, I suppose, but there's more to life than beaches. And Mrs. Vermaak's food is good if you like it heavy with lots of fat and sugar. Not to mention other home comforts."

This gave me the opportunity to ask what all of Verkeerdespruit wanted to know. "But how …?"

"But how what, Smartypants?" He called me Smartypants because I was always reading.

"But how did you … I mean why did Mrs. Vermaak let you into her house?"

Betty intervened. "Mrs. Vermaak doesn't as a rule welcome people into her house. And you …"

"I what?"

"Well, for a start you're English …"

"And for a finish I dye my hair and wear pink shirts? Yes, Klasie did seem to think it would be a problem to get me past Moeder, as he calls her, especially with me in my dusty and bloody *state*. Moeder is very proud of her house, he said, and when I said good, I'm sure it's a very nice house he said yes but she doesn't like people to visit and I said well then she can't be very proud of it can she because when you've got something you're proud of you usually want other people to *appreciate* it don't you now, I mean that's what pride *means* isn't it, and he just said not for M-m-m-moeder as if to imply that Moeder settled her own definitions."

"Then …?"

"Then how did I make my way into Moeder's mansion? I'd love to claim it was all my own cleverness, but fact is, it was Klasie."

"Klasie?" Betty and I repeated in unison. We both liked Klasie, but not for his cleverness.

"Yes, Klasie. Well. I helped a bit I suppose. I said to him while we were driving along, it's all a bit like that story in the Bible isn't it, the one we learned about in Sunday school, not that I was ever a star pupil, and he said which one and I said you know the one about the chap who gets beaten up next to the road and gets ignored *flat* by the priests and all the other shits and then this other really nice type comes along and picks him up on his *camel*, and Klasie said that's it, the G-g-g-g-good *Samaritan*, I've just had an idea, and if I'd known Klasie better at the time I'd have realized what a rare event I was witnessing but as it was I just said what's your idea and he said we won't clean you up, we'll show you to Moeder like that and when she asks why I'm bringing home a dirty Englishman, I'll say because it's in the Bible, in the story of the Good Samaritan. Moeder is very religious, Klasie said, and if it's in the Bible it'll be all right with her and I said then just about *anything* goes with your old lady and he said no only the things that people don't get p-p-p-p-punished for, which of course cuts down considerably on the list of things to do on a rainy Sunday, but what the hell you don't have many of those here, do you? So that's what we did, we played the Good Samaritan for all it's worth, and at first Moeder wouldn't buy it and said yes but the Bible said nothing about English people and Afrikaners and Klasie said why don't you phone Dominee Claassen and she did and apparently the dominee said yes he was sure the lesson of the Good Samaritan could be interpreted to apply to English and Afrikaans though he wasn't sure about black and white, and Moeder got quite taken with the idea especially as I was so grateful and so appreciative of her beautiful house — isn't it the gloomiest place you've ever seen, by the way?"

"I've never seen it," said Betty. "You're very privileged."

"Thank you very *much*, but I'm not sure how much longer I can survive the privilege. All the furniture has *claws* and creeps around at night looking for somebody to strangle or crush or

100

generally knock about with those *balls* they're clutching. I dreamed the other night that the sideboard was trying to get into my bedroom to rape me."

"Rape?" I asked.

"Attack me, you know, and do nasty things to me. You never can tell with sideboards." He winked at Betty and she changed the subject.

"How about a job?" she asked. Trevor had been a hair stylist in Bloemfontein. I asked him what the difference was between a hairdresser and a hair stylist, and he said a hairdresser *did hair* for Matric farewells and a stylist created beauty. "It's not as if Verkeerdespruit is crawling with job opportunities."

"You can say that again," Trevor sighed. "You'd think a place with so many ugly people in it would need a good hair stylist, but that Mrs. What's-her-name with the beehive ..."

"Mrs. Price," I chipped in.

"Yes, Mrs. Price, anyway she claims that it's all she can do to keep herself and her assistant as she calls that rather sweet *ousie* who helps her ..."

"That's Mary," I interrupted again, "she's married to Jim. Our gardener."

"Yes, Mary, anyway she claims there's only enough work for her and Mary."

"But why," asked Betty, "do you want to find a job here?"

"Well, I can't live on Moeder's charity and Klasie's income for the rest of my life, can I?"

"But what happened to your idea of going to Durban?"

Trevor smiled. "Let's just say that Klasie changed my mind," he said.

We soon discovered that Trevor's pink shirt was not the only color change in Mrs. Vermaak's life. Trevor was to be seen in Osrin's store going through his stock of paint and loudly commenting on the inadequacies of the selection. "Devon Cream! Gentle Ginger! Fawn Foam! Pampas Grass! Café au Lait! Parchment! Twenty different shades of invisibility! How *adventurous* can you get? No wonder this town looks like shit if this is their idea of color!"

So Trevor got Osrin to order Puce and Lime and Carnival Pink and Aquamarine and went to work on Ebenezer. My mother said the result made up in courage what it lacked in taste; when I asked her what this meant she said, "It means it's common but at least it's colorful." As for Mrs. Vermaak, she stunned the congregation by appearing in church in turquoise chiffon with a matching hat; I was the only member not taken by surprise, having been treated the day before to Trevor's version of what he called the Beautification of Ebenezer. "I said to Moeder now that the house was so cheerful and bright, she looked more and more out of place in her gloomy getup like Queen Victoria moping in her *palace* for years after Whatsisname died, and of course Moeder didn't want to be like Queen Victoria in anything, holding her personally responsible for the Boer War, and besides I told her the Bible said make a joyful noise unto the Lord and how was she going to be joyful in the black dress and besides she was still a young woman and had no call to look like her own grandmother; to be honest, I flirted *ever* so slightly with Moeder and I don't think she minded a bit. So I took her to Marnette's and made her choose the most colorful dress in the place. It's a pity the color was turquoise but it was either that or pink with sequins which I thought was a bit *young* for Moeder."

Trevor even went to the lengths of accompanying Moeder and her son to church; and between her turquoise dress and Trevor's pink shirt, toned down slightly with one of Klasie's broad ties, poor Klasie looked very somber indeed in his dark suit, a bit like a father accompanying his daughter to the pulpit, which is not to say that Mrs. Vermaak looked like a bride. But she did indeed make a joyful noise unto the Lord in her turquoise dress, and her habitually morose style of hymn-singing, my mother said as if complaining to the Lord about his favoring of others, yielded to quite a vigorous and assertive delivery, as if the Lord were her personal shepherd and nobody else had any rights to Him. Klasie was clearly terribly embarrassed, and at times looked as if he wished his mother wouldn't sing so loudly, and yet I thought he looked quite pleased, too, as if he were rather proud of this assault upon Verkeerdespruit sensibilities.

Because of course Verkeerdespruit was riveted. It would not be accurate to say that it was dumbstruck, for it was very vociferous in its astonishment; but it seemed more at a loss than usual as to an explanation of the phenomenon. Kosie Opperman said his mother said that the devil had come to Verkeerdespruit to tempt Mrs. Vermaak and that she had sold her soul for a turquoise dress, but my father said that he couldn't imagine what the devil would want with Mrs. Vermaak, and a turquoise dress was a bad bargain for the devil. Louis van Niekerk said that his father had telephoned Bloemfontein to hear if there was any criminal charge against Trevor, but they had never heard of him; they *were* looking for somebody called Gert Mostert who had beaten up a bookmaker for not paying out what he thought he was owed after the Durban July, but Gert Mostert was bald and fifty-five. Mrs. Dominee Claassen said that the dominee said the Lord worked in mysterious ways and perhaps this was His way of getting Trevor to church. Mrs. Deyssel said that it was odd that He should want that pink shirt in His house, because she certainly didn't want it in hers.

Only Betty seemed neither surprised nor perplexed. "Klasie is happy for the first time in his life, and so, amazingly, is Mrs. Vermaak. I don't care if Trevor is the devil himself; it's a soul well lost. Mrs. Vermaak wouldn't have been much of a pearl in heaven anyway."

The only aspect of the situation that needed explanation, as far as she was concerned, was how Mrs. Vermaak coped with Klasie's happiness, having become so accustomed to seeing him as her "responsibility." "What does Mrs. Vermaak make of your and Klasie's friendship?" she asked Trevor.

"Oh, she thinks it's very *sweet*, which it is when you come to think of it — in fact, between us, I could do with less sweetness and more action, if you know what I mean. Moeder says it makes her think of David and Jonathan."

"But doesn't she resent your ... influence on Klasie?"

"What *influence*? My dear, the man has influenced *me*; I haven't touched him, more's the pity. Can't you see how tough I've become?" and he pointed at the khaki shirt he was wearing, which he had tied in a rather bunchy bow under his midriff. "You should see the boots Klasie has ordered me from the co-op — they make me look like John Wayne."

One day Trevor announced that he had found a job: "Mrs. Price thinks she'll have something for me at the end of the month; nothing *artistic*, mind you, just washing hair and taking out curlers, but I'm sure I'll make my way into the creative department soon enough, once the ladies of Verkeerdespruit discover that there's life beyond the permanent wave."

"But how come Mrs. Price has a job for you now? Has business improved that much?"

"No, alas, but it seems the *ousie* is going to be given notice."

"Mary?" I asked.

"Oh, you know her of course. Yes, it seems some of the customers have been complaining about having their hair washed by a black woman, and have even started doing their own hair, and Mrs. Price says she can't afford to lose the few customers she has."

"What's it mean to be given notice?"

"To … well, to be told to find another job."

"Are you going to be taking Mary's job?"

"I *wish* you wouldn't put it like that. If I didn't take the job it would be just a matter of time before somebody else did; and I'm sure there are *lots* of other jobs for Mary."

"There weren't lots of other jobs for you."

"It's not as if I could become a domestic servant or something, is it? I mean, can you imagine me on my *knees* polishing the floor?"

But there weren't lots of other jobs for Mary. Because she was not from our region originally, she needed a permit to work there, which was granted only to "indispensable" workers. Without a job Mary couldn't get a permit, and without a permit she couldn't get a job. She had worked for Mrs. Price for eight years, which was two years short of the period required to qualify for residence in Verkeerdespruit under Section 10 of the Black Urban Areas Act.

My father explained all this to me when I asked him why Mary was sitting on the back step crying. She herself could tell me only that she was going to "the homeland." When I asked her where this was, she said, "I don't know, I've never been there. I grew up in Cape Town." It transpired that Mary's homeland was a place called Elukhanyweni in Ciskei, where her mother had been born.

My mother and father had one of their few public disagreements on the subject at dinner one evening.

"It's easy enough for us to employ Mary," said my mother. "She can help me organize the provisions for the OVV."

"That's not the point," said my father. "The law says she has to be employed by the same employer for ten years."

"And who's to know?" asked my mother. "It's not as if Mary is going to make trouble." "Trouble" was a vaguely defined term much used in those days to refer to anything black people did other than work where white people wanted them to work.

"Who's to know?" my father asked. "*I'm* to know; I'm a magistrate of this country and I'm paid to administer its laws."

"Even if the laws are insane?"

"Even if the laws are against the law," he said. "There's something called the Black Prohibition Interdicts Act that forbids me as magistrate even to hear an objection to a removal."

"How can you be part of something like that?"

"Do you want me to resign my job?"

"I don't know," my mother said. "I don't know," and absent-mindedly gave me a second helping of pudding before I asked for it.

I decided that Trevor should be made to know what his job implied. The next Saturday afternoon I waited for him in Voortrekker Street because I didn't want him to think I was using Betty as an ally. He came sauntering up Voortrekker Street in a lime-green shirt that Klasie had bought him at Osrin's.

"Hi, Smartypants," he said. "You shouldn't hang around on the streets. Hi, Dogface." He called Dumbo Dogface.

"I was waiting for you," I said.

"Were you now? I'm flattered."

"I wanted to ask you ..." I began and hesitated.

"Go ahead and ask," he said. "Your Uncle Trevor is always at your service for advice or requests."

This seemed promising, so I continued, "I want to *request* you to … not to take Mary's job."

He looked at me and sighed. "Is that all?" he asked. "But I've *explained* to you — I'm not taking Mary's job. I'm taking a job that Mary would have lost anyway."

"But if you don't take the job, Mrs. Price will keep Mary because she can't find anybody else to do the job."

"And if I don't take the job what will I do for a job?"

"But if Mary loses her job she has to go home."

"And if I lose my job *I* have to go home."

"Yes, but her home is in Elukhanyweni." I had practiced the name because I thought it sounded so terrible that it might convince Trevor. But he just shrugged.

"It sounds like more fun than Bloemfontein."

"But Jim is here — you know, her … husband."

"And Klasie is here — you know, my … husband."

"Your …?"

"Never mind. My friend."

"But you can find another job, and Mary can't."

"Why not?"

"It's the law. If she loses her job she has to go to her homeland. Only it's not her home because there's nobody there that she knows."

"It's not my fault, is it, the *stupid* laws the Rockshitters make? I'm *sick* of them and their rules and regulations, their thou-shalt-not-blow-thy-nose-with-thy-left-hand mentality. When you get older you'll realize that people like me and I wouldn't wonder you, too, are just as oppressed by their laws as Mary."

This didn't seem to me to make Mary's position easier, but Trevor pinched my cheek and said, "Come, I'll buy you an ice-cream soda." So a month later my mother packed Mary a picnic basket with a roast chicken and hard-boiled eggs, and put her on the train to Bloemfontein, with instructions on how to get to Elukhanyweni. My father had contacted the magistrate there and asked him to find Mary a place to stay. "She'll be looked after," my mother assured me. "Black people always look after each other."

"What does Elukhanyweni mean?" I asked, hoping to get some indication of the nature of the place from its name.

"Place of Enlightenment," said my father.

I went along to the station with my mother to put Mary on the train. "You must look after your things, Mary," said my mother. "There are people on the train who will steal everything you have."

"Yes, madam," said Mary. "I know. The train is not like Verkeerdespruit. There are bad people on the train."

Trevor was every bit as successful in his new job as he had predicted. He duly washed hair for a week, as Mary had done for eight years, and then started suggesting slight modifications to a style here, a new cut there. In a surprisingly short time women started making appointments specifically to be styled by "Mr. Trevor" himself. He changed if not the face then at least the hair-style of Verkeerdespruit. The beehive had of course made its way there, albeit a few years late, and most women with any preten-sions to fashion piled their hair on top of their heads for Saturday evening's film show in the town hall. Since the hall did not have a sloping floor, this made for serious visibility problems, and from the back row you could see a constant ducking to and fro of beehived heads trying to see past beehived heads and causing beehived heads behind them to duck in turn, thus setting up a kind of Mexican wave through the hall. Trevor did not so much abolish the beehive as redecorate it: where before his advent women had been content with the standard elongated cone, he introduced them to apparently unlimited variations, all based on the principle of dividing the cone in half and curling and teasing and perming and tinting the top half. This did not improve visi-bility in the town hall, but it did produce a greater variety of silhouette. For church on Sunday the same cascading curls could be tightened up with lacquer to look more restrained and to accommodate the hats that had never been an altogether happy combination with a beehive. In time Trevor even persuaded some of the bolder souls to *experiment with color* as he called it. "Why accept nature's limited imagination when you have so much of your own?" he would say. The results perhaps said more about Trevor's imagination than that of his clients, but they accepted such compliments as they got, and fielded the snide comments of less adventurous neighbors as if indeed their new tints were of their own making. Mrs. Olivier, whose gingery-gray hair turned into a rich auburn after a visit to Trevor, said to Louis van Niekerk's mother, "I feel twenty years younger," to which Mrs. van Niekerk replied, "You're as old as your husband thinks you are," which my mother said was unkind, because Mr. Olivier was known to like younger women.

The most startling change was in Mrs. Vermaak, whose iron-gray bun-and-middle-parting suddenly blossomed into a bouquet of silvery curls that looked positively frivolous — and a frivolous Mrs. Vermaak was a contradictory concept, like a pink ox wagon or a cuddly rhinoceros. My mother was taken completely un-awares when she called upon Mrs. Vermaak on OVV business. She started giggling, which she had to disguise as a coughing fit, and Mrs. Vermaak told her not to bring germs into her house.

At this time Jim was found one Saturday afternoon in Voortrekker Street shouting things at passersby. He was obviously drunk, and three Standard Seven girls ran back to the school hostel and said he had sworn at them. When asked what he had said, they said they didn't know because it had been in black language, but they could tell it was swearing from the expression on Jim's face. The hostel warden phoned the police and the police sent a black constable and they locked Jim up. My father went to get him out, and the constable said Jim hadn't been swearing, he'd been shouting that he wanted his wife. My father asked them to let Jim go because he'd never been drunk before, and he brought him home and spoke nicely to him. Jim said he was sorry.

At this time, too, Klasie was made a deacon in church. There was a vacancy since Koos van Biljon had resigned because the church would not pay his gas expenses when he went on house visits to members of the congregation. There was some unpleasantness because he didn't want to return the black suit that came with the job, but in the end the church council sent a deputation to him of the biggest members, including Maritz the Butcher, and Koos van Biljon surrendered the black suit with bad grace to his successor. My father said that Dominee Claassen and the church council were probably worried about Trevor's influence and thought that by making Klasie a deacon they could exercise more authority over Ebenezer and its inhabitants. But Mrs. Vermaak told my mother that she thought Klasie had been elected because everybody could see the joy of the Lord in his face, and because he was a shining example of Christian charity to all. She saw it as a Sign that the black suit fitted Klasie "as if it had been made for him."

"Mmm," said Betty when I told her this, "I hope Mrs. Vermaak is right. I'm not so sure that it's the joy of the Lord on Klasie's face. But as long as it's joy, it doesn't matter where it comes from, I suppose."

Trevor found it all very entertaining. "The mealie-crunchers are a funny lot, aren't they? One day they beat you up and the next day they just about *adopt* you; and the funniest thing is the ones who beat you up perhaps understand you better than the ones who adopt you. Moeder, for instance, has really developed something of a soft spot for me," he said. "She has taken to bringing me coffee and rusks in bed in the morning, which has its inconvenient aspect of course …"

"What is an inconvenient aspect?" I asked.

"I keep forgetting you're listening, Smartypants. How would you describe an inconvenient aspect, Betty?"

"In this case I'd say it's when somebody brings you coffee and rusks when you don't want coffee and rusks," said Betty.

"Why don't you want coffee and rusks?" I persisted.

"Let's just say that when you grow up you'll find out that there are more important things in life than coffee and rusks, not that I'm exactly overwhelmed with *those* at the moment, but you never can tell and we live and hope and then the rusks may just become a problem, but we'll cross that bridge when we get to it. I *was* saying before I was so rudely interrupted that Moeder thinks I'm the greatest thing since whalebone corsets. Now if she *really* knew me, I doubt if she'd want me anywhere near her house."

"I don't know," said Betty. "After all, it's generally agreed that you're a good influence on Klasie."

"Ah, but you see, I'm doing my damndest to be a *bad* influence on him."

"Like Steve," I said, then wished I hadn't, because of Betty, but fortunately Trevor was talking so that she didn't hear me.

"And I can tell you," he continued, "being a bad influence on a country type like Klasie is *much* harder work than being a good influence. I should get a medal."

Trevor's fame as a hairdresser grew from week to week, so much so that women were even coming from Thaba Nchu and Tweespruit to have their hair done by him, much to the chagrin of the Verkeerdespruit women, who felt they'd discovered Trevor and shouldn't have to wait two days for an appointment with him. "It's not as if anybody in Thaba Nchu would have given him a roof over his head when he was homeless," said Mrs. Olivier. My mother shook her head and said, "It's wonderful what people will accept if they think it makes them look better."

Klasie seemed, as Betty said, very happy. "A bit absent-minded," she said, "but fortunately I'm there to see that the stamp-wetters get refilled, otherwise we might have had a plague of mosquitoes in Verkeerdespruit." The rest of Verkeerdespruit continued to speculate and to predict disaster: "You can't fly in the face of God's intention," Mrs. Opperman said to my mother, to which my mother replied: "Do you think it was God's intention for Mrs. Vermaak to spend the rest of her life in that black dress?"

With time, however, most people got tired of the unvarying repetition of the same speculations and predictions — not their own, perhaps, which retained for them the novelty and interest of all things one's own, but certainly those of their neighbors; and with this obstacle to the principle of reciprocity, commerce in the matter of Klasie, Trevor, and Mrs. Vermaak gradually dwindled to an occasional smirk when Trevor and Mrs. Vermaak made their colorful entrance into church, or a flutter of interest when Trevor devised yet another variation on the double-storey beehive.

One Saturday afternoon Betty and Trevor and I were once again sitting in Steyl's café, waiting for Klasie to come and collect Trevor for a trip to his favorite battlefield: "My dears, as far as I can make out one battlefield is pretty much like another and they all look like fuck-all ever happened there, in fact I suppose that's why the battles took place in the first place, what with there being nothing else to *do* there, I mean, you don't hear of the Battle of New York or of Rio de *Janeiro,* do you, just Magersfontein and Mabloodyjuba, but if it makes Klasie happy to show me a battle-field I'll happily see a *hundred* of them."

Klasie was late for the appointment, which was entirely unprecedented in anybody's experience of him: Klasie's punctuality was legendary in Verkeerdespruit. So when he eventually arrived, we were not surprised to note that he was agitated to the point of incoherence.

"I'm-m-m-m-m-m ..." he began, but Trevor got up and put his hand on Klasie's shoulder and made him sit down.

"There, there," he said. "Have a cream soda, it's *wonderful* for the nerves," and he made his jaunty way to the counter.

Klasie had been told that he could control his stammer by breathing deeply. I saw him inhaling and exhaling very deliberately until Trevor arrived with cream sodas all round. Then he said, still very deliberately and without a trace of a stammer, "*Hierdie fokken dorp,*" which means *this fucking town* but sounded like a Biblical curse coming from Klasie, who never swore.

We sat looking at him in awe until Betty said, "Tell us what happened, Klasie," and he took a deep breath and began.

"D-D-D-Dominee Claassen phoned just before one o'clock and asked if he c-c-could see me on a p-p-private matter. He s-said that he didn't want to dis-discuss it at home because it might up-up-upset M-m-m-m-m-m-m-mother." He was sweating slightly, but seemed to be calming down. He took another deep breath. Trevor started to say something, but Betty stopped him by shaking her head very slightly at him.

"S-s-so I said he must come to the post office when I closed, and he said but that's lunchtime c-c-can't I come earlier, and I said I'm s-s-sorry Dominee but the p-post office comes first and I

111

can't close early. S-s-so he came at one o'clock and he s-s-s-s-said that he had had c-c-c-complaints." Klasie paused again with the effort of getting the last word out.

"And I said c-complaints about what, haven't I been doing my d-duties as a d-deacon, and he said there was no p-problem there, but I had to remem-member that if I put on the b-black suit and appear before the c-c-congregation as a d-deacon I'm not just anyone, I'm setting an example, and there are m-m-members of the c-c-congregation who w-w-were deeply c-c-c-concerned about my f-f-f-f-f-friendship with Trevor." He glanced at Trevor and gave him a tight little smile. Then he carried on.

"He s-s-s-said he wanted to have my assurance that there was n-nothing s-s-s-s-sinful between us."

Trevor lifted his eyebrows at Betty but didn't say anything.

"S-s-so I said I c-can't give you an assurance because I don't know what you mean by s-sinful, and he said I mean love be-tween men and then ..." Klasie took a deep breath and completed his sentence in one rush "... and then I said to him then I'm a sinner because I love Trevor and I think he loves me and I can't see that it will make it more acceptable to the Lord if I lie about it and then he said I was living in mortal sin and I should get rid of Trevor and resign as a deacon and return the black suit as soon as possible and pray for forgiveness and I said I didn't need forgive-ness and I didn't need the black suit that smelled of Koos van Biljon's unwashed backside and I left him in the post office and came here." It was the longest sentence Klasie Vermaak had ever said, and he was exhausted with the effort, but his eyes were bright and he seemed almost glad.

"And now," he said to Trevor, "are we going to see M-m-m-majuba where the Boers *dondered* the English?"

There were aspects of Klasie's story that I found quite incompre-hensible, but I was used to feeling that the adult world conducted itself in ways mysterious not only to myself but also to itself. My mother once said to me, "When you grow up you'll discover that you don't know much more, you just get better at living with your ignorance." In this instance, Betty was slightly less helpful than usual: after Klasie and Trevor left, she just shook her head and said, "Bully for Klasie; I just hope he can handle what he's brought upon himself."

"What's that?" I asked.

"I'm not sure I know exactly. But we'll find out soon and it's bound to be unpleasant."

Betty was right. The following Saturday Trevor joined us, as usual, for cream soda floats; but he seemed preoccupied, and in the middle of a discussion of that night's film in the town hall — *On Moonlight Bay* with Doris Day — he announced, not without a certain dramatic flourish: "The dominee's done it."

"Done what?" Betty and I chorused, so loudly that Dumbo jumped up from under the table and started barking at Sarie Fourie, who was buying a white loaf. People said her father used the bread to filter the methylated spirits he drank on Saturday afternoons.

"Done just what I knew he would do. He's spoken to Moeder."

He paused for effect. Betty obligingly said, "And what did he tell Moeder?"

"He told her that her son was a Sodomite."

"A *what*?" I demanded.

"A Sodomite. An inhabitant of Sodom," Trevor explained. "You know, the city in the Bible that had something *horrible* happen to it because the Sodomites offended God, you know just how *touchy* God can be, so to answer your question a Sodomite is somebody who offends God and now Moeder is *furious* and says that God will destroy Ebenezer with fire and *sulfur* if she harbors Klasie and me in her house. The funny thing is that she seems to think it will be all right with God if Klasie moves out and *I* stay."

"And what does Klasie say?" Betty asked.

"Klasie says it's his house — it was left to him in his father's will — and he's not going to move out. But he doesn't want me to move out either, and to be honest I couldn't afford to — I mean Mrs. Price is still paying me what she *got* me for even though I'm bringing in new clients every day and doing most of her work for her because everybody wants me to style their hair. So things are

113

a teeny bit *strained* in Ebenezer at the moment. Who's for another cream soda?" He shrugged and smiled, but he looked less happy than usual. "Anyway," he said, "they can't say I didn't bring color into their lives. If it hadn't been for me this dump would never have known the two-tone beehive. And Klasie would never have known what he was looking for on the battlefields of the Boer War."

If it hadn't been for Dumbo I might never have known the rest of the story. Early one Sunday morning, before Sunday school and church, I discovered that he was gone. This happened periodically; my mother used to tell me not to worry, that dogs just liked to go and visit other dogs now and again, but I was always slightly restless until Dumbo came back, and I decided to go and look for him. I thought he might be visiting Skollie, whom I knew to be a friend of his. But there was no sign of him at Mrs. Maree's: Skollie was lying in his kennel, fast asleep, and when I said, "Where's Dumbo?" he jumped up barking and ran round his kennel three times and then collapsed in the kennel and was fast asleep again in five seconds. For the first time in my life I thought dogs were lacking in expressive abilities, and left in disgust.

I wandered to the outskirts of the town; Louis van Niekerk always said that Dumbo was "probably in the location" when he went visiting, but he said it in a tone to suggest that this was a lapse of taste or morals on Dumbo's part, and I had always resisted the suggestion. Now, however, I couldn't think of an alternative, and I wandered out on the Bloemfontein road in the direction of the location.

The morning was very quiet and I recognized the sound of Klasie Vermaak's Morris Minor before I saw it. I looked round, hoping to be given a lift as far as the location, but Klasie was driving much faster than usual and seemed not to see me. Trevor was sitting beside him, but he was also staring ahead of himself and didn't even wave.

Some hundred yards ahead of me, next to the sign with a crossed-out thirty-five, indicating to motorists that they had left Verkeerdespruit behind them, the Morris Minor came to an abrupt stop. I thought for a moment that Klasie had belatedly seen me walking and was waiting for me, but then Trevor got out and removed a suitcase from the boot. I noticed that he was wearing his pink shirt. He turned away from the car, but suddenly the driver's door opened and Klasie Vermaak got out, looking unusually purposeful. He walked up to Trevor and hit him, a not-very-professional blow under the chin; then he got back into the car, did a U-turn, and drove back to Verkeerdespruit.

Trevor was sitting on his suitcase next to the road when I got to him. He was rubbing his jaw and trying to rearrange his fringe, which was all over the place. He didn't seem to have shaved that morning either.

"Hi, Smartypants," he said, trying to smile. "Trust you to be around."

"Where are you going?" I asked, as a substitute for all the other questions I wanted to ask.

"I don't know," he said. "But somewhere out of this dump."

"Why ... why ... are you sitting here?" I asked.

"You mean why did Klasie throw me out of the car and hit me?" I nodded.

"We-ell," he said, still tugging at his fringe, "you might say it was a misunderstanding." He seemed to be thinking as he spoke, and his speech was altogether without the fringe-flicking emphasis of old. "And then again, perhaps it wasn't," he said. "You remember that Dominee Claassen came and put the fear of God into Moeder because of Klasie's friendship with me?"

I nodded; I had forgotten all about Dumbo in my fascination with Trevor's story.

"Well, she took it upon herself, as she said, to lead me back to the Lord, which meant mainly leading me away from Klasie. We had prayers in the evening in which the Lord was asked to protect the innocent against the plots of the wicked, which must have amused the Lord no end as it did me, but Klasie was not amused, what with having had to resign as deacon and now having his own mother declaring him to be all sorts of Old Testamenty bad news. He said I should explain to his mother that, you know, I didn't really *mind*, you know, being prey to the roaring lion and the stealthy tiger, but I said to him there wasn't much point in offending Moeder and being kicked out of the house and Klasie said it was his house, and I said yes but Moeder was in charge of it, and it was all very complicated, until this morning Moeder stormed into Klasie's bedroom and accused him, as she said, of polluting the house of his ancestors, and Klasie said if the house of his ancestors can be polluted by love then it's time his ancestors, as he put it, got their arses in gear, and then Moeder got hysterical and said but Trevor loves me, and then I said …"

"Were you there too?" I interrupted.

"Of course I was there. Oh. I mean, obviously Klasie and his mother made a noise you can imagine with Moeder having *hysterics* and I came to see what was the matter and what I said was yes of course I loved Moeder as a *mother*, I mean, what else could I *say*, and Klasie said and how do you love me and I said, you know, not knowing *what* to say with Moeder ready to have another bout of *hysterics*, and so I said I love you as a *brother* of course and then Klasie said p-p-put on your pink shirt and p-p-pack your bag and what could I *do* and I tried to explain, but Klasie just said, *Come on Boetie* and then he put me into the Morris Minor and the rest you saw."

Trevor's fringe had recovered something of its expressive emphasis in the telling of his story. He got up from his case and dusted his pants.

"And now?" I asked.

He shrugged. "Durban is just where it always was, I suppose. You might say I just took a long detour." He ruffled my hair. "Now run along, Smartypants. Nobody will give me a lift if they think I'm taking you along. Here's Dogface come to take you home."

Dumbo came trotting along from the direction of the location, looking shamefaced but pleased to see me. I decided to make him feel bad, and turned my back on him and walked home. He followed at a distance and wagged his tail every time I looked around. When I turned off Voortrekker Street Trevor was still standing next to the road, but when I went to Sunday school he had disappeared.

I told Betty this story, of course. She listened without comment and then said, "Who could have thought Klasie could hit anybody? But then, who could have thought Klasie would bring Trevor home?" She sipped pensively at her cream soda. "But perhaps now that he's discovered that he can *talk*, he'll get people to listen to him."

"And Mrs. Vermaak?"

"She'll just have to make her peace with Klasie and with Ebenezer's color scheme. Even the OVV will benefit, I should think. She's bound to sacrifice her sinful clothing all over again. So all in all Trevor was more of a good influence than a bad, I suppose."

"That's all right then," I said, finishing my cream soda. "Will Mary come back from Elukhanyweni now?"

December 6, 1968

I led the way at last to the dressing rooms, relieved that the end of my unwelcome custodianship was in sight. It could surely not be expected of me to accompany the Clutch Plates into the actual changing rooms. "The match is supposed to start at two o'clock," I said. "You'll find your way to the tennis courts?"

"Sure," said the largest Clutch Plate. "We're not stupid, just ugly." His fellows laughed raucously, Fanie abstaining as usual from the communal mirth. I beat an undignified retreat, leaving the Clutch Plates to their own mysterious devices (Tim Watkins had said, "Better make sure the lockers are bolted down") and resolving to have no mercy on the tennis court.

I went up to my own room to change for the tennis match. It was not a day for tennis or for any other form of physical exertion — the air was hazy with heat and almost opaque with humidity — and I was not in a frame of mind to face Fanie and his fellow Clutch Plates in any capacity, least of all as opponents in a farcical game of tennis. Why couldn't they practice against a wall or each other? Why did we have to dirty our tennis clothes to bring home to them their own place in the scheme of things? And why did we have to disrupt our preparations for the evening's social event for their sakes?

In fact I did not have very much in the line of preparations to make for the evening because I had not invited a partner. This

abstention I regarded as a principled stand against the super-
ficiality of the occasion. In spite of the feverish anticipation, there
were almost no opportunities to get to know any of the girls in our
so-called sister school, and most boys pretended to a much greater
degree of intimacy with their prospective partners than the restrict-
ed opportunities for contact afforded. Knowing a girl's name
constituted acquaintance, knowing that she knew one's name
constituted an understanding, and a shy smile and wave at church
were grounds for being ragged about the "case" one was presumed
to have. The girls, I gathered, were quite prepared to be phoned on
the basis of such rudimentary courtship rituals, and to be claimed
for whatever social function made a female presence necessary.
The boys from Wesley, though not as high on the social achieve-
ment scale as the boys from St. Andrews, still outranked Free State
High and Christian Brothers, and few boys were ever turned
down in their applications for partners. All that was required was
that one should wear long pants and not have too many pimples;
all that was required of a girl was that she should not be so fat as
to attract comment from one's fellows.

By the undemanding criteria of this social bartering I might
have found a girl willing to partner me to the evening's entertain-
ment; but, unlike most of my classmates, I had come, through my
primary-school exposure to the daily presence of girls, to discrimin-
ate between those that one would want to talk to for an evening
and those that one wouldn't under any circumstances want to
spend more than five minutes with. It seemed to me that the
Wesleyan principles of selection were hopelessly inadequate to
effect this primary division. This had been painfully demonstrated
to me the year before, when I ha.d dated one Rowena Glenn, who
turned out to be interested only in what my father did and where
we lived; when she found out that he was a magistrate in
Verkeerdespruit, she lapsed into an aggrieved silence that
somehow imposed itself even through the film of the evening —
That Darn Cat — at least until I fell asleep slightly less than
halfway into the film.

So for this particular evening I had not arranged a partner.
Originally we were going to see Romeo and Juliet: *Miss Smithers*
had told us excitedly that she had managed to arrange for a print

118

to be made available to us, even though it was a relatively recent film. But then Mr. Chalmers, the Scripture master, had read somewhere that the main actors were only fifteen and seventeen years old, and he ruled that it would "set a bad example to young people of an impressionable age." Miss Smithers was furious at what she described as "a slight to the Bard and a cultural impoverishment of our boys." The boys did not much mind the slight to the Bard nor even their own cultural impoverishment, until they found out that this entailed their being denied a much-discussed nude scene, after which they threatened to boycott the event altogether in the name of "cultural freedom" — a phrase supplied by my well-read roommate, Cavalla, from his following of the disturbances in France and elsewhere. For a while it seemed as if even Bloemfontein would be shaken by the Events of '68, but then it was announced that we would have The Sound of Music instead, and most boys felt it would be blasphemous and perhaps even unpatriotic to boycott that. The film was only about two years old and I was one of the few boys who had not yet seen it — partly through lack of opportunity, partly because my musical friend Hicks had told me, before he left Wesley the year before, that it was the kind of musical that gave music a bad name — but nobody seemed to mind seeing it again, on the hopeful theory that it was likely to reduce the girls to submissive and exploitable pulp. "Once they're crying and you've dried their tears with your handkerchief, you can do what you like with them," Peter Emery said. "Just make sure there's no snot on the hanky." Gottlieb Krause refused to go on the grounds that the film misrepresented the Germans. "I am told it shows Julie Andrews defeating the Wehrmacht by singing Do re mi," he said. Cavalla, on the other hand, said that the film trivialized history (he called it "Heidi meets the Holocaust") and also declined to attend. The combined stand of the non-English elements strengthened the case of those who maintained that a boycott would be subversive of Wesleyan values, and a full house was expected.

I took my clean tennis clothes out of my drawer. I wondered if I shouldn't have invited a partner after all, if only to be part of the general excitement. Cavalla had asked me why I hadn't invited anybody, and I'd said rather grandly, "I'm used to girls, I don't have to take them to The Sound of Music to sit next to them."

"Did you have a girlfriend in Verkeerdespruit, then?" he asked.

"Yes," I said. "Well, sort of."

"How can you sort of have a girlfriend?"

"I don't know. But I did. Her name was Juliana."

6

Spring and Summer 1964

Mr. de Wet's departure left us jubilant but teacherless. For a while we were put into the school hall along with the Standard Ones and Twos, but Miss Jordaan, whom we now regarded as somehow retarded because she had stayed behind with the Ones and Twos whereas we'd moved on, had lost her ability to hold our attention. Perhaps, even, the terror of Mr. de Wet had made her seem so tame in comparison that we had no respect for her authority. She scolded, and we punched and giggled and pulled and pushed, until one day Japie Dreyer, the biggest boy in class, frightened Sannie Terblanche — who suffered from weak nerves because her father had once locked her up for a week when her mother ran off with a fertilizer salesman — by putting a mole snake inside his shorts and allowing it to escape through his fly, and Sannie relieved herself on the floor, and Miss Jordaan had hysterics and then threatened to resign. I knew this because my father was on the school committee, and the school committee was now stuck with the job of finding a teacher for us. They found Mrs. Swanepoel.

Mrs. Swanepoel was the wife of the newly appointed Bantu commissioner. Whereas not even the most loyal citizen of Verkeerdespruit would have claimed metropolitan status for it, the town in fact had a large black population — confined, of course, to the sprawling location surrounding the white village. Verkeerdespruit was thus a more important posting for a Bantu commissioner than for, say, a bank manager or a school principal — or, I was starting to realize, a magistrate. Mr. Swanepoel took himself and his position seriously. He let it be known that he was on first-name terms with the minister and that he had left his children in

Rustenburg, his previous posting, for a "decent education." So when he was approached about the services of his wife (nobody thought of approaching her directly), he "hemmed and hawed," according to my father, "and then said that his wife had taught at Verwoerd Primary in Pretoria, where many of the Cabinet children went. I said that I didn't think this need be a disqualification, and he snorted and said he would think not, that in fact he thought that Verkeerdespruit was a step down for her."

"Fancy giving yourself airs because you've taught a bunch of little Broederbonders," my mother sniffed. "Verkeerdespruit may not be the center of the universe, but at least we're spared those fat men with mustaches."

But Mrs. Swanepoel didn't give herself airs. She seemed not to regard her illustrious teaching career as worth mentioning to us and won our confidence with a quiet kindness that we probably would have abused had Juliana not appeared. Juliana was one of the daughters sacrificed to the superior educational opportunities of Rustenburg; now that Mr. Swanepoel knew, as he said, that his child's education would be in good hands, she was brought from Rustenburg to be taught by her mother and to be adored by us.

Juliana came to us as if out of a luminous cloud, from faraway, exotic Rustenburg, where avocados and mangoes and bananas grew on trees and were to be had for the asking. Or so Juliana told me nonchalantly, once when I bragged that my father had brought us a pineapple from the Bloemfontein market. The school she had attended actually had a uniform and a school blazer, and when she appeared on her first morning in Verkeerdespruit, she was wearing a green jumper with a white panama hat and a blazer splendidly striped in yellow and black on a green background. But most miraculous of all was the fact that she wore a tie, also with yellow and black stripes. In Verkeerdespruit not even boys wore ties, and for a girl to wear a tie seemed so bizarre that had Juliana seemed at all self-conscious about it, she would probably have been the object of ridicule and practical jokes. As it was, she came into the class accompanied by her mother, smiled prettily at all of us, and sat down in the empty desk in the front row, which had been carried in by Paulus on instructions from Mr. Viljoen himself. Fanie van den Bergh, who sat on my right, was suddenly the much-envied neighbor of this magical creature, and I had to be content with a view of her prettily turned-up nose partly obscured by the vague outline of Fanie's profile.

"Class, this is my daughter Juliana," Mrs. Swanepoel explained redundantly. "I hope you'll all be nice to her and make her feel at home." Juliana was rummaging in her satchel and shook her curls as if to say that she was at home wherever she went and would consider attending to us when she had sorted out more pressing concerns. Her delicate pink-and-white complexion suddenly made everybody else in class seem coarse and chapped, roughened with the windburn and fever blisters caused by daily exposure to the harsh Free State weather.

Whispers were exchanged, and those in the back of the class got to their feet to get a better view of the newcomer. Japie Dreyer whispered something to Tjaart Bothma and they guffawed loudly; Jesserina Schoeman turned around to them and hissed "*Sies!*" which was our undifferentiated expression of disgust at anything that exceeded our notions of propriety or seemed threateningly incomprehensible.

"Quiet, class," said Mrs. Swanepoel in her mild way, and nothing better demonstrated the enhancement of her authority by her possession of such a daughter than the hush that descended immediately. We all got down to the challenge of impressing the new girl.

Her mother had told us, before she arrived, that Juliana was "very clever," and so she turned out to be. Even allowing for the fact that as her mother's daughter she had a better chance than us of knowing the answers to her mother's questions, she was impressively well-informed on everything from the Great Explorers to the Great Trek. And she was the only person of my age that I had ever met who had read more than I. Partly, I suppose, I resented the loss of my own supremacy in this regard, but mainly I was delighted to have somebody with whom to talk and exchange books. And I was not insensible to the fact that our shared taste for reading gave me a claim on Juliana's time that nobody else enjoyed. She was thoroughly contemptuous of the Verkeerdespruit public library. "It's so *childish*," she said as she surveyed the few shelves of Trompie and Saartjie, Enid Blyton and Hardy Boys, and I promptly betrayed all these companions of my happiest times. "You can't expect more from Verkeerdespruit," I said. "It's not a reading town." This last was a judgment I had heard my mother make in her capacity as library committee member. Juliana read Louisa May Alcott and Nancy Drew; she lent me her copies and condescended to being introduced to Robert Louis Stevenson and James Fenimore Cooper, which my father had given me. One of my happiest days was when she pronounced *The Last of the Mohicans* the best book she'd ever read.

All in all, Juliana's arrival seemed to me a vindication of my tastes and pursuits. Not playing rugby, I was set apart from most of the other boys by a subtle but absolute mechanism that invalidated whatever I achieved in any other field: if I could read better than anybody else, that was because I didn't play rugby; if I knew the text in Sunday school better than anybody else, that was because I hadn't been playing rugby the previous afternoon. If I had won the Nobel Peace Prize, Verkeerdespruit would have said it was because I didn't play rugby. The implication was that all my peers could have done likewise if they hadn't been so busy bruising and scabbing themselves and one another on the school rugby field. So if Juliana's company was a pleasure and an achievement that I owed largely to my reading, it figured to me as a reward for everything else, the esteem and admiration of the rest of the school that I sacrificed through preferring reading to rugby.

The Swanepoels lived a few miles out of Verkeerdespruit, not in the location, of course, but closer to the administrative office of the Department of Bantu Affairs, which couldn't be in Verkeerdespruit itself because it attracted Bantus. So Juliana and her mother were brought to school every morning in a Government Garage truck belonging to Bantu Affairs. Most of the Standard Four boys took to waiting for the cumbersome vehicle to rumble up in a cloud of dust; we would then rush upon it as if to turn it over or pillage it, but in fact eager only to pay homage to the occupants. We would stand back for Juliana to descend demurely from the cab of the truck and, as soon as she put foot on soil, we would press forward with hands extended for the magic burden; she would examine the savage horde with her sweet smile, then hand her neat satchel graciously to the favorite of the day with a "Thank you very much." The consolation prize was carrying Mrs. Swanepoel's briefcase, an unglamourous affair in thick leather that smelled of Pond's Cold Cream. The whole group would then scramble along to the school building, where by this time the bell was usually ringing for assembly.

Juliana was fairly impartial in the granting of her favor: she seemed to rotate the honor, but now and again, presumably not to be so predictable as to take the edge off the contest, she would confer her satchel two days running on the same supplicant. And some boys she seemed never to see: Fanie van den Bergh, for instance, though he sat next to her in class. To me it seemed only appropriate that the charmed world of Juliana Swanepoel should contain no Fanie van den Berghs.

The only boys in class who did not deign to scramble for Juliana's favor were Japie Dreyer and Tjaart Bothma, who ostentatiously kicked a rugby ball at each other while we were lining up for the charge. "What do you think she's going to give you for carrying her case?" Tjaart mocked. "A sweetie?"

"A toffee, I bet," Japie said, and the two of them collapsed into incomprehensible laughter. But where normally I'd have felt excluded from their merriment and intimidated by their facility with the rugby ball, I could now see both as simply a pathetic compensation for their own banishment from the enchanted circle around Juliana. Feeling sorry for Tjaart Bothma was a new and pleasant experience for me.

Because Juliana's father was the Bantu commissioner and mine was the magistrate, they saw a certain amount of each other professionally, and took to playing golf together. My mother, though never warming to Mr. Swanepoel, liked Mrs. Swanepoel. "She's a good type of person," she pronounced firmly. "I don't know why she married that pompous fool, but perhaps when he was young he had nice eyes or teeth or something." So the two families visited, usually for those afternoon teas that formed the sole break in the immense tedium of a Sunday in Verkeerdespruit. Juliana and I happily chatted about books over the tea and chocolate cake that we were allowed to carry out onto the lawn.

One day she asked: "Why is your father still stuck in Verkeerdespruit?"

"Same reason your father is stuck here, I suppose," I said, stung by the implication that Verkeerdespruit was a place one got away from if one could, though I had often enough cherished that suspicion.

"My father isn't stuck here," she said. "He came here on promotion, and he'll be promoted to a better place."

My misery at the prospect of her going to that awful *better place* with her father was deadened slightly by my resentment at the implication that there could be better places where I was not.

"That's because your father's in the Broederbond," I said, scared at my own daring. I had gleaned from my parents' tone that one did not mention the Broederbond in public. But Juliana seemed unperturbed.

"What's the Broederbond?" she asked. I realized that I didn't know.

"It's something you belong to so that you can get promoted to better jobs. That's why my father's stuck here — because he doesn't belong to the Broederbond."

"Then why on earth doesn't he belong?"

I realized I didn't know this either.

My spending so much time with Juliana exposed me, of course, to much teasing at school, but I complacently ascribed this to jealousy — jealousy of my favored position on the part of the boys and jealousy of Juliana's beauty on the part of the girls. At home our parents seemed hardly to notice how much time we spent together — I realize now that they must have adopted a deliberate policy of noninterference in a relationship that did nobody any harm and gave us much pleasure. The exception was Mr. Swanepoel, who joked heavy-handedly about my preference for his daughter's company. "Shouldn't you be out there playing rugby?" he would ask, or, "What? Aren't you tired of each other's company yet?"

One day, when her father made one of his ponderous comments at the lunch table, Juliana said to me, "Never mind, Simon, as long as we love each other we needn't mind their teasing." This embarrassed me horribly and pleased me tremendously.

One day she announced, "You must change places with Fanie van den Bergh."

Nothing would have delighted me more, since that would mean sitting next to Juliana, but I didn't think Fanie would be amenable to such a swap. "But why?" I asked, rather smugly expecting to be told that she wanted to sit next to me.

"Because Fanie gives me the creeps. He stares at me."

"What do you mean he stares at you?"

"He *stares* at me. Like that," and she fixed her features in an expression of ferocious, imbecile concentration. "He scares me, I tell you."

"But I can't just tell him to move."

"Yes, you can. I can't, of course, because it would seem … unkind, as if I were trying to get rid of him."

"But you are trying to get rid of him."

"Yes, but I can't tell him that. He's got his feelings, you know. If *you* ask him, he'll simply think you want to sit next to me."

"But why should he do it just because I ask him?"

"He'll do anything you ask him."

"He'll *what*?" The idea of my commanding Fanie's obedience was almost as alarming as it was bizarre.

"You'll see. Have you ever asked him to do anything for you?"

I reflected. On the whole I couldn't think of anything I would want Fanie to do for me. "No."

"Well, then. Try it and you'll see."

So the next day I approached Fanie at break.

"Fanie," I said, "won't you exchange desks with me?"

He looked at me uninquisitively. "If you want to," he said in his unemphatic way. I was amazed at how easy it had been.

"Thanks," I said. "I hope you don't mind."

"No, I don't mind," he said. "We can move now."

127

"Right," I said, and led the way to the classroom. We weren't supposed to be in the classrooms at break, but it was not the kind of thing Mrs. Swanepoel would make a fuss about, and Mr. Viljoen wouldn't come out of the staff room until he'd had his third cup of tea.

Fanie went to his desk. "You take the front," he said, "and I'll take the back."

"Do we have to move the desks?" I asked. "Can't we just move our stuff across?"

He looked at me in perplexity. "But you said you wanted to change desks," he said.

"No, no, no," I said in exasperation. "Or rather yes, I did say that, but I meant can we change places, can I sit here and you sit there?"

He stared at me. "You want to sit here?" he asked, pointing at his seat.

"Yes, that's what I said."

"I thought …"

"Yes, I know you thought I meant can we swap desks, but I meant can I sit there?"

"Next to Juliana?"

"Yes."

"Why?"

"Well, just because I'd like to sit next to Juliana."

"I also want to sit next to her," he said simply.

I could see that he had a point. But I *badly* wanted to sit next to Juliana, and felt strengthened by her own preference. "Well, yes, but you see, she doesn't want to sit next to you."

"You lie," he said without expression.

"Don't call me a liar," I said. "You can ask her. She says … she says you give her the creeps."

He looked down at his bare feet and then up at me again.

"Why?" I wished that Fanie would stop questioning the reason for things and just accept them, as befitted his intellectual level.

"I don't know why," I said. "You just do."

"Oh," he said. "Let's move, then." And he started collecting the scraps of paper and dry bread in his desk.

When we were nearly done he stopped, looked at me, and asked, "Do I give you the creeps too?"

"What has that got to do with it?" I asked. "It's Juliana who wants you to move."

"But you also want me to move," he said, factually rather than accusingly.

"Only because Juliana wants it," I said impatiently, wishing he could have spared us both the embarrassment of dwelling on the subject.

But he persisted. "You'd rather sit next to her than to me."

"Well, yes," I said. I almost added "Of course," since it seemed such a reasonable preference, but I reflected that perhaps it wouldn't seem as self-evident to him as to me. My forethought was wasted, though; Fanie started removing his odds and ends from my old desk, to which he had just laboriously transferred them.

"And where are you going with those?" I asked.

He didn't reply for a while, just carried the things to an empty desk in the back of the class, next to Tjaart Bothma's. "You can't sit there," I said. "You know Miss Jordaan said you should sit in the front of the class."

"That was long ago," he said, "when I was still stupid."

I resisted the obvious reply and shrugged. "Suit yourself," I said.

I was too pleased at sitting next to Juliana to spare very many thoughts for those feelings Juliana had assured me Fanie had, though I did say to her, "Shame, you know, I think he's quite hurt."

"It's not as if he knows that I don't want to sit next to him, is it?"

"I'm afraid he does. You see, he wouldn't move, and I had to tell him that you didn't want him next to you."

"Shame, I suppose that's why he's moved to the back of the class." She shrugged impatiently. "I don't know why you had to go and tell him. Now he's going to think less of me."

"But if he gives you the creeps, does it matter what he thinks of you?"

"Of course it does. You don't understand."

I didn't understand, then.

Since she had no occasion to doubt herself and her control of her own world, Juliana was extraordinarily good-natured. She never seemed out of temper or even petulant, which at the time I ascribed to her angelic nature, but which I can now see must have been simply complacency at not being thwarted, the satisfaction of always having her own way. This more skeptical hypothesis is supported by my recollection of the one occasion on which Juliana revealed what in a less besotted state I would have recognized as bad temper. It was one morning during the usual satchel rush; she and her mother had arrived a bit earlier than usual, and as she descended from her three-ton chariot (Bantu Affairs had big vehicles because in those early days of Bantustans they were designed to transport large numbers of people) Tjaart Bothma happened to be in the vicinity, though not part of the adoring throng. Juliana glanced cursorily at the little group jostling for the trophy and then said, in her sweet manner: "Tjaart, you've never carried my case."

He blushed — Tjaart blushing was in itself a prodigious event — took a step forward, then bethought himself, possibly because Japie Dreyer was approaching, followed by Fanie van den Bergh carrying the rugby ball; he mumbled, "I don't carry girls' cases," and went to meet his fellow heretic.

The rest of us took this as a sign to resume our scramble for possession, but Juliana tossed her curls and said, "Can't you leave me alone? I can carry my own case, thank you." We followed sheepishly, not even remembering to take Mrs. Swanepoel's briefcase.

It was not long after this that Juliana asked me, during one of our Sunday afternoon conversations on the lawn, "What do you think of Tjaart Bothma?"

"He's — not very clever," I said.

"Yes, I know. But that's not all that matters, is it?"

"I suppose not," I said, though in fact I had hoped it was.

"Why doesn't he like me?" she asked me, as if this were a phenomenon requiring explanation.

I was hurt that she should be so concerned about Tjaart Bothma's opinion of her, and said churlishly, "Perhaps he doesn't think you're pretty."

Unfazed by my malice, she said serenely, "No, it can't be that. Perhaps it's just a phase he's going through. How long has he had that rugby ball?"

"Ever since I can remember."

"Perhaps he'll outgrow it."

I laughed. Tjaart without his rugby ball was unthinkable, a logical contradiction, like a bicycle without wheels or like Juliana herself without her curls. "He'll never outgrow his rugby ball. He's got nowhere to grow to."

She looked at me without rancor. "You may be right," she said, "but I wonder."

Toward the end of the year disaster struck my little world. Mr. Swanepoel, having distinguished himself in administering the Affairs of the Bantus of Verkeerdespruit, was to be transferred — "on promotion," he insisted — to Pietersburg, where apparently there were even more Bantus than in Verkeerdespruit. Juliana seemed quite pleased at the prospect.

I was devastated. "But do you *want* to go to Pietersburg?" I demanded. "Can't you stay behind in the hostel?" I had counted on at least another year of Juliana's presence.

"And share a dormitory with Bettie du Plooy and Sarie Verster?" she asked unanswerably. Bettie and Sarie were notorious for their lack of personal hygiene, even in an environment not overly concerned with the mere washable surface of the body.

"You can stay with us," I offered wildly. "I'll ask my mother."

"I think Pietersburg could be fun," she said. "It's quite a big place, and it has a good school. Children come all the way from Rhodesia." I could see she was already excited at the prospect, and I was wretched. "Besides," she continued, "my father says Verkeerdespruit is going to be part of a Bantustan. I don't want to live in a Bantustan."

I was too miserable about her departure to give much thought to the consequences of the processes whereby Verkeerdespruit was to be declared the Traditional Homeland of thousands of people who had never seen it, whereas we who had grown up in it would be foreigners in our own village. To me, Juliana's voluntary departure was far more real than the forced removal of any number of people.

Some alleviation of, or at any rate distraction from, my woe came through Mrs. Swanepoel's announcement that the end of the year would be celebrated with a party — "an *evening* party," she specified, "if your parents won't mind." She added that she might even be able to organize a gramophone with records.

Some parents did in fact mutter about the silliness of allowing a bunch of twelve-year-olds to go out in the evening, but once introduced to the idea, none of the twelve-year-olds could have been kept from the party by mere parental authority. Jesserina Schoeman's aunt, who had been living with the Schoemans since the death of her husband, the previous dominee, let it be known that her late husband would not have approved of his niece's going to a party where anything could happen, even dancing; to which Jesserina's mother, who no doubt had had enough of the attributed opinions of her late brother-in-law, said, "Well, now that he's dead I hope he can see things in perspective." Jesserina's aunt retreated into hurt silence, but at family prayers that evening prayed long and tearfully that God should take pity on innocent souls abandoned to the world by those who should protect them from its dangers and temptations. Jesserina got the giggles — "I wondered if Japie Dreyer was a danger or a temptation," she told us — and had to be sent out of the room.

The party came to be the sole topic of conversation among us all. Perhaps rather carried away with the success of her inspiration, Mrs. Swanepoel had another idea. "I think it would be nice," she announced to the class, "if the boys all invited a partner to the party. There are fewer girls than boys in the class, but the boys who can't find a partner from this class can ask somebody from another class."

I turned immediately to Juliana and made little signs indicating "Will you go with me?" and she nodded graciously enough, though without any evidence of the rapture I felt on the occasion.

Mrs. Swanepoel's bright idea turned Verkeerdespruit Primary School into a battleground. The boys went ahead and asked the girls of their choice, regardless of their class affiliation, as transpired shortly before the party from the bitter tears of a small group of partnerless Standard Four girls. Lifelong friendships turned into savage enmity between the uninvited and the invited. As for those hapless but happy girls from other classes invited by the faithless swains of Standard Four, one Standard Three girl was slapped in assembly by a Standard Four girl (she promptly slapped back), and another, a boarder, had her bed apple-pied three nights in succession, it was assumed by the aforesaid Bettie and Sarie, who of course had not been invited. Parents protested to Mr. Viljoen, and he ruled that the spurned girls should be free to ask boys from other classes to accompany them. They did so with surprising alacrity and ambition, cornering such sought-after and previously undreamt-of trophies as Frikkie Steyn, the rugby captain from the Secondary School, and Henk Pienaar, a Standard Fiver originally from Kimberley, who was rumored to have a diamond-smuggling father. This caused mutters among the girls who had foolishly grasped at the invitations from their more callow contemporaries. Annette Loubser even asked Louis van Niekerk if he would "mind very much" if she didn't go with him; he said very firmly yes he would and what was more he would never fix her punctures again. Verkeerdespruit being a thorny sort of place, punctures were more frequent than parties, and Annette prudently decided not to jeopardize her cycling future for one evening of careless rapture with a Standard Five boy.

The only children apparently indifferent to the general excitement were, predictably, Tjaart Bothma and Japie Dreyer, who let it be known that it was a "sissy party" and that they weren't going to waste their time standing around with "a lot of girls." Fanie van den Bergh, who had become Tjaart and Japie's shadow since his move to the back of the class, had also not invited anybody to the party, but whether this was out of solidarity with his new friends or just his usual lack of initiative was not clear. When I asked him why he wasn't going, he just said, "Why do you want to know?" and since in fact I didn't particularly want to know, I didn't push the question.

Secure in the knowledge that I was going with the only person on earth I wanted to go with, I was indulgently mature about the perturbations around me. "You'd think it was the coronation of the Queen of England," I commented to Juliana, an event that my mother still quoted whenever she needed to imply the quintessence of much ado about nothing.

"Yes, it's not as if there's never been a party before, is it?" she replied, which was also not what I had hoped to hear. As far as I was concerned there *had* never been a party before.

I still have a photograph taken at the end of Standard Four by a traveling photographer. We are lined up against the wall of the school, those at the back balancing on rickety benches carried out of the school hall, those in front sitting with a kind of naive surrender on the rocky soil, all squinting into the bright light of a December morning. Hardly anybody is smiling: perhaps we were too intimidated by the occasion to pretend to pleasure or goodwill, or perhaps the photographer hadn't felt up to the effort of getting a smile out of the unfrivolous regards of his communal subject. In our near-unanimous scowl at the camera and our gray faces, in our motley clothes and rough bare feet, I now read a terrible deprivation not so much of material things as of spiritual sustenance: the flat Free State summer light blanching out all nuance and shade seems the proper medium for the hopelessness of our common presence in that particular spot of nothingness, that featureless instant randomly salvaged from the maw of eternity.

And yet what I most remember about that morning is my acute, almost painful, consciousness of the wonder of being in the same place and time as Juliana Swanepoel, the drab surroundings transfigured by her presence. And there she still is in the front row, prim in a jumper and white shirt. She now seems merely a fat little girl with a quizzically lifted eyebrow and rather affected curls, but at the time she was the brilliant, dimpled, rosy-cheeked, ringleted object of my devotion. Her mother sits behind her, stern in glasses and dumpy in skirt and twinset; again the camera has quite effaced the magic that as Juliana's mother she radiated. The photograph was taken on the morning of the party. For all the drabness of our clothes and the moroseness of our expressions, on that one day of all others our lives seemed

134

exciting, full of the promise of glamour and pleasure that we knew only from the old musicals we gawked at in the town hall on Saturday evenings. As for me, when I look at my own pinched anxiety on the grayish enlargement, I'm surprised that I can't discern what I know I felt — the exultation of the assurance that even if Juliana were going to Pietersburg, for one night I was going to be at a real adult party with her. I did not think of it leading anywhere, any more than one thought of the Bloemfontein road as leading anywhere but Bloemfontein — just to be there was enough.

After school, as we were waiting for the Bantu Affairs GG truck to collect Juliana and Mrs. Swanepoel, I said to her, "Can I cycle out and come in to the party with you tonight?" It seemed to me only appropriate that we should arrive together. "I'll sit in the back." This would also give me an excuse to go home with them after the party.

"Perhaps you'd better not," she said, and for the only time I knew her Juliana seemed slightly embarrassed. "In fact, I can't go to the party with you tonight."

I looked at her in utter incomprehension. After my weeks of anticipation, the idea of her not going with me was so inconceivable that I didn't even think to ask her *why*, any more than I would have asked *why* if I had been swallowed by an earthquake.

"The fact is," she went on, assuming a nonchalance that even in my disoriented state I could see was not quite real, "that this morning, just before we had the photograph taken" — and here she flushed with unfeigned pleasure — "Tjaart Bothma asked me to go with him."

"But …" I helplessly replied. There didn't seem to be anything I could say to such a flagrant breach of all known rules of conduct. Her behavior exceeded even the categories of outrage. Then something came to me. "But you said we loved each other."

"Yes," she said. "But that's different. This is a *party*."

I was going to ask her what the difference was, but the Bantu Affairs truck was rumbling up to take her away from me forever. "I'm sorry," she said, "I really am." And I do believe she was: she didn't want me to think less of her.

I have tried to read triumph, pleasure, exultation into Tjaart Bothma's stolid countenance, frowning at the camera from just behind me, minutes after claiming Juliana from me. But I can't see anything there, other than the common effort not to appear silly or weak to the camera, to face eternity with a square jaw and an unflinching gaze. But Fanie van den Bergh, standing next to Tjaart, for once seems amused, even happy; and I reflect how odd it is that the only photograph I have of Fanie should have captured that most rare event, Fanie smiling.

December 6, 1968

It seemed unconscionable that this day, which I had at most mildly dreaded as a day of bad tennis and uncomfortable sociability, should have turned, for me, into a forced march down some ghastly memory lane in the company of Fanie van den Bergh, as if Verkeerdespruit were some kind of lost Arcadia and we the only two survivors. The Clutch Plates, too, were proving more troublesome than they had, as barely tolerated guests, the right to be: instead of being suitably awed by the venerable age of the institution, they had made no attempt to hide their scorn for it. One of the many points of superiority of tennis to rugby, as far as I was concerned, was that in tennis, the weaker the opponent, the shorter the game. We could finish them off and send them home.

I stood next to the tennis courts waiting, with my teammates, for the appearance of the Clutch Plates. "What's keeping them?" asked Stephen Maddox. "Do you think we should send someone to show them how to tie their tennis shoes?"

"Who said they had tennis shoes?" countered Tim Watkins. "Perhaps they're putting on their soccer cleats."

I was not amused. Whereas I had, heaven knows, no particular tenderness for the Clutch Plates, I did feel in a sense implicated in their gaucherie, since one of them had claimed me as one of theirs. This made me resent my teammates' snobbery, and resent the Clutch Plates even more for bringing it upon themselves and upon me.

"*Simon, won't you just run up and see what's keeping them?*" Mr. Moore asked, as casually as if he weren't condemning me to yet another humiliating trudge across the school grounds with a train of recalcitrant Clutch Plates in tow. I knew better than to object: Mr. Moore, though very gentle in the exercise of his authority, did not tolerate insubordination.

"Yes, Mr. Moore," I said, only just suppressing a petulant sigh.

I arrived at the dressing rooms to find that the Clutch Plates were fully dressed, decently and unsensationally enough in tennis clothes, complete with tennis shoes. Even Fanie had the full complement of clothing, though his white shorts did have about them the depressed air of the unstylish charity of the OVV: they were all-purpose gym shorts with an elasticized waist and no fly, and they were very large and shapeless, as if they had been made from a pillow slip. Still, they were white and they were clean.

The Clutch Plates were standing around outside the dressing rooms as if expecting the tennis match to come to them.

"We're waiting for you," I said, probably a trifle tetchily, because the Main Plate, the one who had been responsible for most of the witticisms, said, in what I suspected to be an imitation of my tone, "And we're waiting for you."

I suppressed any number of crushing replies and contented myself with saying, "Well, here I am. Let's go to the courts."

As I had anticipated, Fanie once again attached himself to me for the walk to the tennis courts, apparently quite contented just to be there, for he did not initiate any conversation. I, however, found the silence uncomfortable. "So you've kept up your tennis," I ventured.

"Yes," Fanie replied. Assuming this to be the extent of his response to my conversational gambit, I was casting around for another, when he unexpectedly continued: "We have all-weather courts at school. Not like at Verkeerdespruit."

"Yes," I said with as much dismissive energy as I could muster, "that dusty old court." I thought of the dusty court, of Mr. van der Walt, and of Fanie sitting on the ground fondling Dumbo's ears, and I swallowed hard, my scorn overtaken by a sharp realization that Mr. van der Walt and Dumbo were gone, and that this strange boy was what had become of little Fanie van den Bergh, and that I was old enough to have lost something.

"Yes," I said, "yes." I reflected that I probably sounded just as idiotic as Fanie himself, but he just said, "Yes," as if he understood what I had meant.

7

1965

After Mrs. Swanepoel's departure at the end of Standard Four, we were sent a new teacher by whatever haphazard coincidence of motives constituted our collective destiny. In this instance, destiny, normally so cack-handed in its dealings with Verkeerdespruit, proved to be unusually benign: as if in recompense for our sufferings under Mr. de Wet, Mr. van der Walt was almost schematically the opposite. He was a tall, gangling young man with gentle eyes and a large mustache. He had come to Verkeerdespruit because he had failed his final year at university. This information I owed to my father's position on the school committee. Whereas he was careful not to discuss school matters in front of me, he assumed too readily that I was out of earshot when I was out of sight. Not that I eavesdropped: I would have regarded that as dishonorable, like cheating on a test — apart from being unnecessary, given the location of the stoop next to my father's study, where he and my mother had most of the conversations they deemed confidential. Just by sitting and reading on the stoop I was party to most of these conversations.

"He's a nice enough young man," my father said. "Probably a bit of a bumbler, but seems dedicated to the idea of teaching."

"I don't know," my mother sighed.

"What don't you know?" my father asked, as her declarations of ignorance were intended to make him do.

"I don't know why we always have to put up with teachers that nobody else wants."

"I know why," said my father. "It's because if anybody else wanted them they wouldn't come to Verkeerdespruit."

This apparently damaging comment did not at the time strike me as reflecting too adversely on the abilities of Mr. van der Walt. We were quite humble about our own status as a refuge for failed teachers, and unresentfully aware of the fact that most of our teachers had some entirely unpedagogic if usually quite harmless reason for teaching us. We were also resigned to the abrupt departure of those teachers with any ambition or ability to posts better fitted to their talents. Our present principal, Mr. Viljoen, was clearly one of these birds of passage. Although younger than most of the teachers, he was better qualified, and had come to us from a big school in Bloemfontein. "He'll stay until he finds a job as headmaster in a bigger school," my father predicted, in another one of my parents' "private" conversations. "Obviously a Broederbond application — you can tell from those black toe caps of his, not to mention the way Dominee Claassen and Jan de Vries pushed for his appointment. But I suppose he's no worse than the other applicants. And ambition's not always a bad thing, I suppose."

"He's not chosen his wife well, if he's ambitious," said my mother. "She seems rather colorless."

"That's all that's required from a Broederbond wife. They have to blend with the background and let their husbands get on with their careers."

"And make pudding," my mother added. "They must be able to make pudding." This was probably a reference to the previous headmaster's wife, who had been known as the pudding queen of the Free State: she had regularly won all the prizes at the Bloemfontein Agricultural Show, until her husband died of a heart attack and she went to live with her mother in Klerksdorp.

But if Verkeerdespruit did not keep its more career-minded inhabitants for very long, the others at least occasionally made up for their lack of success by the interesting speculation generated by their questionable past. The most intriguing refugee from the rigors of the more successful world was Miss Rheeder, the needlework teacher, the dominee's sister-in-law. She was a pretty and vivacious young woman who yet inexplicably failed to attract the usual complement of farmers-in-*bakkies* as suitors. On Saturday nights when we all went to see a film in the town hall, every unmarried woman teacher was almost invariably accompanied by a stout young farmer uncomfortably got up in blazer and tie for the occasion; but Miss Rheeder was always with her sister and brother-in-law, with whom she lived.

My interest in Miss Rheeder's case was prompted by the fact that my mother, normally so forthcoming about our teachers, had nothing to say about her other than a noncommittal "She seems quite attractive — very cheerful, I must say." She made Miss Rheeder's cheerfulness sound like an indiscretion or worse, which was unusual for my mother, whose own high spirits seemed at times assumed deliberately to irritate the lugubriousness that passed for respectability in Verkeerdespruit. So I deduced that Miss Rheeder had reason to be less spirited than she in fact was, and connected this reason with her odd failure to excite the usual rush of young farmers.

Though I was probably quicker than my contemporaries at fitting together apparently unrelated observations, I was hampered in my deductions by an almost complete ignorance of sexual matters. I had arrived, for instance, at the conclusion that kissing was both a much sought-after pleasure for oneself and a much-ridiculed weakness in others, and that adults were too old for it and children too young. I had guessed that there was, some-where, a key to the various mysteries of adult life, and had even conceived the suspicion that it was in some way related to the business of having babies; but I could not understand what connection there could conceivably be between the prosaic burden of childbearing (it was a much-repeated commonplace that the Bantu would be so much better off if only they didn't have so many children) and the half-guilty, half-gleeful excitement that I sensed whenever conversation transgressed into that area of reference. My friends were almost certainly better informed than I, but I balked at betraying my own ignorance and asking Louis or Kosie for enlightenment, and I suppose they didn't regard me as a worthy sharer of the sniggers I sometimes saw them exchanging at break or in class when the teacher was otherwise occupied. I suspect I wasn't an easy person to tell a dirty joke to.

But if I was underinformed, I was sensitive to the vibration of charged references. I remember paging through a *Ladies' Home*

Journal of my mother's and coming across a cartoon that I did not understand, and which yet impressed itself upon my memory as significant in its very unintelligibility. It showed two little boys with a huge dictionary on the floor between them, the one saying to the other, "Here it is — S-E-X." I concluded that the word was somehow the clue to that mystery the boys, like me, must have been looking for. I looked it up in our dictionary, of course, only to be told that it was "the quality of being male or female," which I knew anyway. Still, I saved up the word and watched for things to fall into place around it.

Clarity of sorts came one Saturday morning at the annual church bazaar. I was standing at the cake table while the dominee was opening the occasion with the obligatory scripture and prayer. The bazaar was an opportunity to buy the best produce of the district at relatively low prices, and the rule was that nothing could be sold before the dominee said, "Amen," so the end of the prayer was awaited with less Christian resignation than usual. Competition was especially fierce around the meat and cake tables, and my mother had left me at the cake table while she went off to stake a claim to a leg of lamb. My instructions were to buy back my mother's chocolate cake: as she was playing tennis that afternoon, she wouldn't have time to bake another for Sunday afternoon tea, and she didn't believe in serving other people's cake at her tea table. "And don't let anybody snatch it from in front of you," she warned. "They've gone and underpriced my cake." The prices were written on little slips of paper stuck onto the cakes with pins. Once Mrs. Theron had swallowed a pin and tried to sue the church, but she couldn't prove damages. "They really shouldn't put inexperienced people on the cake table," said my mother, looking disapprovingly at an unsuspecting Mrs. Viljoen, who had been put in charge of the cake table because her husband was the school principal. The cake table was the most important table after the pudding table, which was presided over by the dominee's wife.

While the dominee was praying I peeped at regular intervals to make sure that the cake was still where it should be. At least half the people around the table were evidently doing the same, opening their eyes at short intervals to check on the cake of their

142

choice. On the other side of me stood those people with no particular interest in having first choice of anything, who by and large managed better to preserve the decorum of the prayer. Next to me stood Mrs. Price, the hairdresser, with her sister, who visited her occasionally from Ficksburg. They were English-speaking and didn't respect our institutions, Kosie Opperman said; his mother washed her own hair so as not to enrich people who had already caused us enough sorrow and loss. Mrs. Price and her sister were whispering to each other under the prayer.

"That one," said Mrs. Price, pointing at Miss Rheeder, who was standing behind the pudding table with her head bowed; she was going to help her sister the dominee's wife dish up and serve the garish collection of gelatin-and-condensed-milk confections donated to God by the wives of the congregation.

"Oh yes, I recognize the face now," whispered her sister. "From the photos in the *Sunday Times*."

"Doesn't look as if pudding could melt in her mouth, does she?" asked Mrs. Price. "Much less kill her own baby."

"AMEN!" proclaimed the dominee, clearly aware of the ceremonial and practical import of his word, and instantly thirty cakes were snatched up from the table. But I had forgotten my mission in the fascination of Mrs. Price's conversation. She was saying, "In a position like hers I wouldn't wear those red shoes," and while I was wondering what Miss Rheeder's red shoes had to do with killing her baby, Mrs. Vermaas expertly swept up my mother's cake from the table in front of me.

"I … I …" I stuttered at Mrs. Vermaas, who was trying to attract the attention of Mrs. Viljoen, who was trying to take money from thirty people at the same time.

"Mmm?" Mrs. Vermaas replied, not very encouragingly.

"That's … that's my mother's cake," I explained.

"You mean she baked it?" she asked, impatiently brandishing a fistful of money at Mrs. Viljoen, who had just dropped the cash box. Behind me I could hear Mrs. Price's sister saying, "Well, I think she's got cheek, selling pudding at a *church* bazaar."

"Yes," I said to Mrs. Vermaas, "but she said I had to buy it for her."

"If she baked one she can bake another," pronounced Mrs. Vermaas. "Or otherwise she can buy somebody else's cake, like the rest of us." She slapped her money on the table and walked off.

I was torn between awe at the enormity of Mrs. Price's revelation and panic at my own hardly less grave failure to secure my mother's cake. I looked round, hoping to attract my mother's attention, but she was intent on paying for her leg of lamb; in the meantime cakes were disappearing fast from the table in front of me. In desperation I grabbed the nearest of the few remaining cakes and held out my handful of money to Mrs. Viljoen, who wasn't even attempting to give change. "It's all for a good cause," she said in a flustered way and stuffed whatever one gave her into the cash box.

I retreated from the fray with my trophy, a somewhat uneven white cake embellished with large red glacé cherries cut in half. My mother hated glacé cherries. She said they were common.

"What kind of thing is that?" she exclaimed as I approached her with my purchase. She inspected it with a mixture of scientific interest and disgust, as if it were a nasty little animal of an unknown species. Then she identified it. "You've gone and bought one of Myra Brink's flops, for heaven's sake. It'll taste even worse than it looks. Couldn't you …?" then she looked at me more closely. "Why are you so pale?"

"I don't know," I said, and suddenly wanted to cry.

"Never mind," she said, eyeing the cake. "I know what a crush it is. Go and put that thing in the car and buy yourself a bowl of pudding with the change from the cake." I didn't tell her that the change had gone to the good cause, and as I walked off I heard her mutter, "*Glacé cherries.*"

I pondered the mystery of Miss Rheeder for a week, and then realized that it was quite simple really: I could ask Betty the Exchange. She was different from other adults in that she never asked me why I wanted to know whatever I wanted to know, and different from my friends in never making fun of my ignorance.

"Betty," I said, as we settled down to our Saturday afternoon in Steyl's café and T Room. "Do you know Miss Rheeder?"

"Dora? Yes, slightly. She's a friend of Ariana Jordaan's."

"Is it true that ... she killed her own baby?" I tried to sound nonchalant while trotting out this atrocity.

"Yes," Betty said, opening her copy of *Personality*. "In Durban. She drowned it. She was given a suspended sentence."

"But why — I mean, why did she kill the baby?"

"She was ... not quite herself, the judge said. You see, she wasn't married."

"But then ...?"

"Then ...?"

"Then how could she have a baby?" I pretended to be leafing through a magazine to hide my embarrassment.

"Oh dear," Betty said. "I think you must ask your mother to explain these things to you. But you see, if you ... love somebody enough, you can have a baby without marrying."

"Oh." I sensed the proximity of The Mystery, but I didn't know how to ask what I wanted to know, so I asked again, "But why did she kill the baby?"

"The person she ... loved had left her."

"Oh," I said. "I see."

Then, "Is that what ... sex is?" I asked.

Betty smiled. "Yes," she said. "Pretty much."

"Then ... then what's the difference between love and sex?"

Betty lowered her copy of *Personality*, looked at me, and said, "Hell, Simon, if I knew that, do you think I'd be spending my Saturday afternoons in Steyl's café?"

But Miss Rheeder was of far less import to me than Mr. van der Walt, who had such a relatively simple reason for coming to Verkeerdespruit: his failure was of the unsensational sort appropriate to the general mildness of a man whose most assertive feature was a mustache intended, my mother believed, to hide a weak mouth — "All men with mustaches have weak mouths," she assured me.

"What's wrong with a weak mouth?" I asked, reluctant to believe that anything Mr. van der Walt had could be reprehensible.

"Well," she said, "you don't want to be weak, do you?"

"I don't know," I replied, in one of my more perverse moods. "What's the point of being strong?"

"If you're weak you get pushed around by the strong."

"So I must be strong to push the weak around?"

"No, to push back."

I decided that Mr. van der Walt was probably an exception to my mother's law of mustaches. After the terrors of Mr. de Wet, in any case, we were quite prepared to believe that Mr. van der Walt was an angel sent by Providence, and were less interested than we might otherwise have been in his reasons for being there. It was enough that he was there and that he seemed to like us.

We returned his liking with fervor and enthusiasm. We vied with each other to carry his case, to clean the board, to do anything that he seemed to want done — except that there didn't seem to be all that much that he wanted done. He was impartially friendly with all of us, which was on the one hand a bit unsatisfactory for me, who was used to being singled out for praise — but then, on the other hand, preferable to the kind of prominence I had endured under Mr. de Wet. So I happily enough accepted my share of Mr. van der Walt's democratic warmth. His mustache gave him a slightly mournful aspect, which rendered his dry jokes all the more delightful when they came. He stayed in the school hostel, so the boarders, usually the object of scornful pity for being dirty and hungry, became the envy of the rest of us. They reported that he sat with them at mealtimes instead of with the other teachers and that he had on occasion shared his pudding out between his neighbors. Hostel children had been known to mutilate one another for pudding.

If the rest of us idolized Mr. van der Walt, Fanie doted on him. He sat transfixed in class and stared at him solemnly, often for several seconds after the rest of the class had recognized one of his mournful comments as a joke and were outdoing each other in appreciative laughter. I had been taught, partly by my mother's precept, partly by my father's example, that there were more subdued ways of showing appreciation of someone else's wit, and I felt rewarded for my restrained smile on these occasions by noting Mr. van der Walt's quick glance in my direction. For the rest, I felt that there was a special bond between us because he was the tennis coach and I was the only boy in Standard Five who played tennis — "That sissy game," as Tjaart Bothma called it. In Verkeerdespruit, of course, rugby was the official boys' game — and indeed, played as it was on the stony, dusty patch of winter-parched veld that constituted the rugby field, it required that fine indifference to bruises and scabs that is the small boy's first claim to manliness. So it was a victory for me in my embattled sissy-hood that Mr. van der Walt turned out to be an excellent tennis player and showed little interest in rugby — where, in any case, his services were not needed, Mr. Viljoen himself being the chief rugby coach.

Tuesday afternoons, boys' tennis afternoon, were thus my favorite afternoon of the week. I was always early, and would collect the key to the tennis room (in fact a particularly dusty and dark little hole next to the boys' toilets) from a hook behind Mr. Viljoen's office door. Then I would drag out the net and wait for Mr. van der Walt to turn up to help me put it up. The few of us who played tennis took turns to play doubles on the uneven dirt surface of the school's tennis court, watched over patiently by Mr. van der Walt, ruling impartially and firmly on dubious line calls from his seat on the roller. There were many of these, owing to the faintness and crookedness of the chalk lines that Paulus, the school caretaker, renewed only twice a year with a watering can on wheels. Apart from Mr. van der Walt, the only spectator we attracted was Fanie van den Bergh, who sat mutely on the ground next to the roller, stroking the ears of my dog, Dumbo, who sometimes followed me to tennis and spent the afternoon sleeping in the dust. When one of us knocked the ball over the fence, which we not infrequently did, Fanie ran to retrieve it, and with a clumsy underhand stroke threw it back into the court. Sometimes the ball hit the fence and Fanie had to try again. Mr. van der Walt had suggested to Fanie that he should start playing tennis, but he just shook his head and drew circles in the dust with his big toe.

On special afternoons, after the rest of the players had left, Mr. van der Walt would play a game of singles with me, still watched by Fanie, who helped me take down the net after the game and store it in the dark little room. The key was normally entrusted to me to be taken back the following morning to Mr. Viljoen's office, which Paulus locked at four o'clock.

I had never discussed my knowledge of Miss Rheeder's past with any of my friends: it still seemed so incomprehensible a matter to me that I wouldn't have known how to broach the subject. I was in fact quite prepared to forget about Miss Rheeder: as needlework teacher she hardly impinged on my existence. But then it transpired that she was also a tennis player, and she started coaching the girls on Wednesdays. This would not in itself have been a threat to my Tuesday afternoons had she not started attending boys' practice as well, for no other purpose that I could see than to distract Mr. van der Walt's attention from our disputes. She sat next to him on the roller, and though he tried to pretend he was attending to our game, it was clear from their animated chatter that we were not of much more account than the August winds blowing around the dust we raised on the tennis court. Mr. van der Walt's inattention caused many of our games to deteriorate into mere squabbles, with him belatedly trying to establish peace and fair play when the dispute became too heated to ignore. Without Mr. van der Walt's authority the game suddenly seemed rather pointless, and on some afternoons there were only three players ill-temperedly banging balls at one another. Even Fanie stopped attending our practices, not, I imagined, in disgust at the deteriorating standard of the tennis as much as in protest at the chattering presence of Miss Rheeder on the roller. Perhaps missing Fanie's attention, Dumbo also stopped following me to tennis.

But much more disruptive to me than these effects of Miss Rheeder's arrival was her decision that she needed extra practice, prompting her to claim my place as Mr. van der Walt's singles opponent after our doubles battle. The first time this happened, Mr. van der Walt looked at me, I thought apologetically, and said, "Don't worry about the key, I'll take it back tomorrow morning."

"And the net?" I asked timidly.

"Do you think I don't know how to take it off?" he asked sternly; I was on the point of explaining elaborately when I noticed the twitch of his mustache signaling a joke, so I just smiled as best I could and left. I noted with some satisfaction that Miss Rheeder served underhand.

After this had happened three times, I was not surprised when Mr. van der Walt appeared one Saturday evening at the movies with Miss Rheeder, to the general hilarity and speculation of the town children. I had at least the consolation of being able to say, "Oh, didn't you know? Yes, they've been playing tennis together for *weeks*."

"*Tennis*?" exclaimed Louis van Niekerk. "You call it *tennis*? Indoor doubles, I suppose?" and he and Tjaart subsided into the kind of laughter I had learned to recognize as appropriate to The Topic.

"No, outdoors singles, actually," I replied, which reduced the two of them to hysterics. The movie — Hitchcock's *Strangers on a Train*, which was only about fifteen years old at the time — unfortunately featured a tennis player, and all references to tennis set Louis and Tjaart off again in their incomprehensible hysteria, considerably detracting from the suspense. I was torn between trying to concentrate on the involved plot — the tennis player's inconvenient wife is strangled by an obliging stranger, who then demands that the favor be returned — and trying not to glance back at Mr. van der Walt and Miss Rheeder. Since nobody else, not even the adults, was making any effort whatsoever not to stare, my own surreptitious glances could not have registered as any particular invasion of privacy, but by my theory of a special relationship with Mr. van der Walt, I felt convinced that he registered every furtive turn of my head.

After this it came to be accepted that Mr. van der Walt and Miss Rheeder were a "case." The Standard Fives were divided between those (mainly girls) who thought nobody was good enough for Mr. van der Walt, those (exclusively girls) who thought they made a "cute couple," and those (mainly but not exclusively boys) who commented on the relationship to each other in an undertone and with much nudging and guffawing. Only Fanie and I said nothing. I thought that under his melancholy mustache Mr. van der Walt seemed happier, and I begrudged Miss Rheeder the power to make him so. Unexpectedly, though, I found reason to channel my resentment into a much more satisfactory feeling of pity for Mr. van der Walt.

I had not thought of asking Betty the Exchange for her views on Mr. van der Walt's courtship of Miss Rheeder, mainly because I didn't enjoy the topic and had quite enough of it at school. One day, however, paging through *Die Huisgenoot*, I came across a photograph of Rock Hudson and said, "Don't you think he looks a bit like Mr. van der Walt?'

"Hmm," said Betty. "A bit. But Nico van der Walt doesn't have such a square jaw." After a pause she added, "More's the pity for him."

"Why?" I demanded. I couldn't see that anything Mr. van der Walt did not have could be worth having.

"Well, if he's chasing Dora Rheeder. ..." and Betty shrugged as if that explained everything.

"Why — does Miss Rheeder like a square jaw?"

"Yes, in a manner of speaking. Listen, between us, I happen to know that Dora Rheeder finds your Mr. van der Walt just a bit ... boring, you know?"

I was shocked and indignant. "But *why*? Everybody thinks he's the ... nicest teacher we've ever had."

She smiled. "I'm sure he's a wonderful teacher. But Dora is not in Standard Five and Mr. van der Walt is not her teacher. It's just ... you know, Dora is from the city and wants more ... excitement, I suppose. Not that you should think less of Mr. van der Walt for that."

There was no danger that I would think less of Mr. van der Walt. Miss Rheeder was another matter. "Then why does she ... play tennis with him?"

"I suppose he's interesting enough for tennis. But she'll drop him if anybody more exciting turns up. Not that there's much chance of that."

The idea that Miss Rheeder was depriving me of my tennis games with Mr. van der Walt because she had nothing better to do filled me with helpless rage. I would have pointedly ignored her if she had given any indication of being aware of my existence. I wondered if there was any point in telling Mr. van der Walt that she had killed her baby, but he would probably just feel sorry for her; besides, I knew instinctively that he would not like me the better for giving him the information. I decided that the best

150

policy was to wait for her to tell him that she was bored with him, and then to be a true friend to him in his sorrow.

For the time being, though, it seemed that Miss Rheeder couldn't find anybody more exciting, for she appeared regularly at the tennis court in the course of the afternoon. However much I prayed that she wouldn't turn up, there she was with her tennis racket and her little short dress, causing Mr. van der Walt to lose all interest in our line-call disputes.

One Tuesday afternoon, I went as usual to collect the key to the tennis room from Mr. Viljoen's office. I knocked in a perfunctory way, more out of habit than because I expected him to be there, and walked in. Mr. Viljoen was standing at his desk with his back to the door, and turned round quickly as I came in. He seemed put out to see me. "Yes?" he inquired. "What do you want?"

"The … key, please," I explained and pointed at it. "I always collect it on Tuesday afternoons before tennis."

"Of course. Well, there it is. Help yourself." I could see he was trying quite hard to be friendlier, but that he didn't want me around. I grabbed the key and left as quickly as possible. When I got to the tennis court, Miss Rheeder was standing there looking a bit lost. I was pleased to see that she was not wearing tennis clothes, although she would of course have plenty of time to go and change before her game with Mr. van der Walt.

"What time do you start your practice?" she asked.

"At 2:30."

She looked at her watch. "I haven't got time to wait. Would you please tell Mr. van der Walt that I won't be able to play tennis with him this afternoon?"

I did my best to hide my joy. "Yes — yes, certainly."

"Thank you." And she walked away toward the school building.

When Mr. van der Walt arrived, the other boys were already there, and I didn't want to give him my message in public. I didn't think there was anything particularly confidential about it, but as long as I didn't give the message I could enjoy it as a kind of secret between me and Mr. van der Walt, even though he himself didn't know it yet; and I had the tennis game with him to look forward to.

I noticed that he was looking around and at his watch rather restlessly when the time of Miss Rheeder's usual arrival approached, but I said nothing. He did his best to concentrate on our game, and under his direction our squabbles regained something of their old interest. After the game, when the other boys had left, I went up to him and said, "Miss Rheeder asked me to tell you that she couldn't play tennis with you this afternoon."

He looked at me as if he couldn't quite register what I was saying. Then he asked, mildly enough, "And when did she tell you this?"

"Before tennis, when I was waiting for you."

"And you're only telling me now?"

"I ... I didn't want to tell you in front of the other boys." It suddenly seemed a silly reason.

But he seemed to understand. He nodded. "I see. But there's nothing secret about my playing tennis with Miss Rheeder."

"Yes. I know. But ..." and I got stuck.

"Yes, I know," he said. "Do you want a game?"

"Oh yes!" I said, and gave him the balls so he could start serving. As he took them, he asked, "Did Miss Rheeder say why she couldn't play?"

"No," I said. Then I made a connection I hadn't made before. "I suppose she went to see Mr. Viljoen."

He dropped a ball, picked it up, and asked, "Why do you say that?"

"Because ... because Mr. Viljoen was in his office when I went to collect the key and Miss Rheeder went toward the school building from here."

We started playing, but when Mr. van der Walt returned a ball that was obviously way out, I realized that his attention was not on the game. He played in an absentminded sort of way, and then, just as he was preparing to serve, he stopped. "Listen," he said, "I'm not feeling very well. I hope you don't mind if we don't play any further this afternoon."

I didn't mind as much as wish I could kill Miss Rheeder for ruining even this game in her absence. I couldn't trust myself to speak, and just shrugged in what I hoped was an adult way. He came across to the net and ruffled my hair. "Shame, I expect you're disappointed. I'm sorry. But I'll make it up to you some other day. Come, I'll help you take down the net." He seemed preoccupied as we took down the net and rolled it up. As I closed and locked the door of the tennis room, he said, "You can take back the key now." He was kicking his tennis racket with his shoe.

"I always take it back in the morning," I said. "Mr. Viljoen's office will be locked now."

"Go and have a look anyway," he said.

"But ..." I said.

"What's the matter?" he said. "Don't you want to do it?"

I very much did not, but I didn't know how to explain this to him. "Mr. Viljoen seemed ... angry when I went into his office."

"Nonsense!" he said. "But if you don't want to do it I suppose I can't force you." And he turned his back on me.

"No, wait!" I cried, aghast at the idea of refusing Mr. van der Walt anything, even though I couldn't understand why he wanted it. His disappointment had more authority over me even than my fear of Mr. Viljoen. "I'll do it now."

"Good boy," he said. "Run. I'll wait for you here, then we can walk as far as the hostel together."

This seemed reward enough for even the most unintelligible errand. I ran as fast as I could to Mr. Viljoen's office. It would be locked, of course, I told myself, although it occurred to me that I hadn't seen Paulus around. I hesitated for a moment before the office door. Couldn't I just go back and say that it was locked? No, Mr. van der Walt would know I was lying to him. So I knocked quickly, not very loudly. There was no response. This was surely all that my duty by Mr. van der Walt required; but could I tell him in all honesty that the door was locked if I hadn't tried it? I turned the doorknob with only enough force to be able to claim that I had tried it. The door opened with disconcerting ease, and I found myself staring at Mr. Viljoen's black toe caps. They were standing on his desk pointing neatly toward the door. His pants were on the floor next to the desk and he himself was lying face-down on the sofa, on top of somebody who was also not wearing shoes, for two barefooted legs were wrapped around his body. The toenails were painted red. Mr. Viljoen was wearing nothing except short gray socks. I noticed that he was quite fat and that his bottom was sweating. Then I saw Miss Rheeder's red shoes on the filing cabinet, next to a neatly folded pile of clothes. Mr. Viljoen seemed to be doing push-ups on top of Miss Rheeder, and he was making grunting noises. They had evidently not heard me open the door. He changed position and I could see her face: her eyes were closed. Then she said in an out-of-breath sort of way, "This is better exercise than playing tennis with Nico van der Walt," and they both laughed in that way that I could now relate to its source. I was in the presence of The Mystery.

I turned and ran, closing the door behind me with a thump. I had a momentary vision of Mr. Viljoen pursuing me in his socks as I ran down the stoop and turned a corner and found myself holding on to Mr. van der Walt. He must have followed me from the tennis court.

"What's the matter?" he asked. "What happened?"

I was trying to hide my face against his tennis shirt but he pushed me away, put his hand under my chin, and lifted my face so that I had to look at him. "You must tell me," he said. "What did you see in there?"

"Mr. Viljoen ..." I said and then stopped.

"What about Mr. Viljoen?" he insisted. "What was he doing?" He was very pale, and I noticed that his mouth under the mustache was trembling. My mother was right, I thought, he does have a weak mouth. "You must tell me," he said. "I want to know."

Then I knew that Mr. van der Walt did know, that he had known all along and was waiting for me to tell him what he had sent me to go and find out. Something in me, a sense of fair play, perhaps, an outraged loyalty, rebelled against being forced to name this thing for which I had no name, just because this man wanted it named, wanted it named because of that woman in there, wanted it named so badly that he had sacrificed our tennis game for it.

He put both his hands on my shoulders and squeezed me quite hard. "What about Mr. Viljoen?" he repeated. "What was he doing?"

I took his hands from my shoulders. "Mr. Viljoen was having a fit," I said.

As my father had predicted, Mr. Viljoen duly got promotion to a bigger school in a more successful town. Miss Rheeder married a widowed farmer in the district and at the next church bazaar she was transferred to the meat table. But Mr. van der Walt was the first to leave, quite soon after our last tennis game — "for personal reasons," Mr. Viljoen explained. We heard that he was working in the post office in Clocolan.

December 6, 1968

The tennis match had its surprises. The Clutch Plates, it turned out, did know which end of the racket to point at us, and they did so competently enough to take about as many sets as they lost. As number one player I was expected to win all my matches, and I managed to do so, playing steadily if unspectacularly in the mounting heat. But some of my teammates were flagging badly, and were beaten not only by their opposite numbers but by lower-ranked players on the other side. In fact, Fanie was winning his games about as steadily as I was winning mine, and by the end of the day the two teams were equal, with Fanie and me having to play the deciding match.

So the tournament depended on our match, which consequently attracted more spectators than it would otherwise have done. Indeed, we attracted so many that I assumed that word must have spread that the school's tennis fortunes, indeed the cause of Civilization against Clutch Platery, depended upon my performance against Fanie, and I resolved to rise heroically to the occasion. Even Tony Miles, perhaps secretly worried about my challenge to his preeminence, had condescended to come and watch the game and, surrounded by his usual group of admiring hangers-on, was leaning against the corner post; and Gottlieb Krause, who normally affected supreme scorn for tennis, was sitting on a rock cleaning his nails.

I won the first set fairly comfortably, but not quite so much as a matter of course as I had expected. Fanie's style was unconventional, but his delivery was accurate, and he had more power than his thin frame would have led one to expect. Determined to be inspired rather than intimidated by Tony's presence, I crouched down, concentrating on returning Fanie's service. He had an odd winding action that delivered the ball at quite a brisk pace, but it was a very straightforward delivery, and if one could get one's weight behind the return, it usually went back with some force. So I hit the ball squarely with the face of the racket and returned it immediately to the far right-hand corner, well out of Fanie's reach. It was an excellent return and I glanced at Tony Miles for some acknowledgment, however grudging, from one expert to another. To my chagrin he wasn't even looking in my direction; in fact, he and his cronies seemed much more interested in Fanie than in me.

This could be taken to be natural, seeing that Fanie was once again preparing to serve; but I couldn't help noticing now that even when the ball was in play in my court, the attention remained fixed on Fanie. I might as well have been an automatic ball-returning machine for all the interest I excited.

This was disconcerting, but only made me the more determined to compel my audience's attention by an exceptional performance. I had taken three points from Fanie in his service game, and I was on the brink of breaking his service. Fanie prepared to serve, but all the balls were on my side of the court, and I trotted to the corner of the court to retrieve one of them from next to Tony Miles and his friends. I glanced at Tony, but he was talking to Leonard Williams, his particular friend.

"Hell," he said, "I've heard of Clutch Plates, but this one should be called Gear Lever," and Leonard screeched with laughter.

I pondered this comment as I passed the ball back to Fanie and, as he prepared to serve, with his elaborate winding action, my attention strayed to the general area suggested by Tony's terminology, and I saw what was so engrossing the attention of my supposed supporters. The otherwise featureless expanse of Fanie's shorts made it unignorably obvious that the OVV's charity had not stretched to the provision of underpants: Fanie having been endowed more generously by nature than by the OVV, his vigorous serving routine activated a corresponding motion of considerable proportions in the baggy shorts. I had time only to wonder at Fanie's having developed so much in certain areas and so little in

156

others, when the ball landed squarely in the court in front of me. I made a feeble attempt to return it, but it was already lying against the back fence. There were muted jeers from the Wesley sideline and uninhibited cheers from the Clutch Plates.

"Were you ready?" asked Fanie.

"Yes," I said. I couldn't very well complain that I had been put off my game by his monstrous schlong.

"Five–forty," said Fanie and walked to the baseline to serve again. I crouched down as low as possible in the receiving position, determined to ignore all distractions. But as Fanie stretched to throw the ball into the air and started his winding-up action, I had an unimpeded view of the commotion in his pants, a kind of miniaturized enactment of Fanie serving, like a puppet show under a sheet. Again the ball landed by my feet before I had time to transfer my attention to it, and again there were jeers from the onlookers, less muted this time. "Thirty-forty," said Fanie as I ignominiously went to retrieve the ball. Mr. Moore was standing next to the fence. "Keep your eye on the ball, Simon," he said, which in my by now tensed-up state brought on a convulsive fit of hysterical giggling. I didn't even try to return the next ball, just feebly jabbed my racket at it while trying to control my giggles.

The rest of the match was horrible. Fanie took his service game easily, in the face of only the feeblest resistance from me. My own service provided a slight defense against Fanie's secret weapon, in that in the receiving position his ungirded loins were less conspicuous. But if Fanie managed to return my serve and rush to the net in his heavy-footed way, his supporting team gamboled along exuberantly, obtrusively, and completely distractingly. I invariably lost the point — by now not so much because of the hypnotic effect of the uninhibitedly bouncing shorts, as through the complex discomfiture generated by the situation. I surmised that most of the onlookers knew exactly what was distracting my attention from my game, and the more I tried to prove that I was not at all put off my stroke by Fanie's puppet show, the more mistakes I made; and the more mistakes I made, the more raucous the spectators became. Under cover of applauding Fanie, they were gleefully exploiting my embarrassment, and by the end of the game their enthusiasm was near-riotous.

Fanie beat me by three sets to two, and the Clutch Plates beat Wesley by one match. From the applause of the Wesley boys you'd have thought that we'd scored a major victory; indeed, for once, in rejoicing in my defeat, Clutch Plate and Wesleyan seemed united.

We had been taught to accept defeat graciously by going to the net to shake the hand of our victorious opponent. It took all the force of instilled habit to prevent me from throwing my racket at Fanie van den Bergh and running away to hide in the bicycle shed. I walked to the net, but this was another refinement the Clutch Plates had not been taught. Fanie was already drinking water from the tap next to the court. He looked up at me as I said, "Well played, Fanie," and he smiled in a way that I could have pardoned for being triumphant, but it was worse: it was pitying. Being beaten by Fanie van den Bergh was bad enough; being pitied by him was a violation of all categories of appropriateness, a usurpation on his part of the privilege of the stronger. It was a reversal that had occurred only once before in our acquaintance.

8

Summer 1965

When old Bruno, the dog with whom I had grown up, died of old age, my parents considered getting a burglar alarm instead. Although it would cost more initially, the upkeep would be considerably cheaper and less time-consuming than feeding a big dog. Then it occurred to them that they didn't really need a burglar alarm either.

"It's not as if we're living in Johannesburg or Chicago," my father said. "Having a burglar alarm in Verkeerdespruit would just put ideas in people's heads. They'll think we have something worth stealing."

From this it was a short step to deciding that we didn't need a dog either. "It's not as if Bruno would have scared anyone away in any case," my mother said.

"Then," I said, "why did we have Bruno at all?"

"Well," said my father unwarily, "as a pet, as something to care for and for you to play with."

"Then we still need a dog, don't we?" I triumphantly concluded. "I mean as a pet and something to care for and play with."

"It's all very well for you," my mother said, "but you'll be the one who plays with the dog and I'll be the one who cares for him. You never once fed Bruno."

This was true, but only because, as I pointed out, when Bruno arrived, I was six weeks old, and by the time I was big enough to feed him, my mother had got into the habit.

"And now you've got into the habit of not feeding the dog," she replied.

"But if we get a new puppy," I said, "I'll get into the habit of feeding it and then when it's big it won't take food from anyone but me."

"I'll believe that when I see it," said my mother, which I interpreted to mean that she was prepared to risk the experiment. So when on the following Saturday I saw a Bantu man standing next to the road with a cardboard box of puppies, of which he was brandishing a specimen to passing motorists, I approached him with the assurance of a prospective buyer. I even had money, having just been given my week's pocket money. I prodded my finger at the wriggling mass of bodies, and one of the little muzzles promptly opened and seized my finger. I decided that it had selected me as its owner and lifted it out of the box.

"How old are they?" I asked the vendor, who was divided between displaying his wares to the passing traffic and attending to a possible sale.

"Six weeks," he said. "They're very good. Pedigree."

"Where's the mother?" I inquired, having been told that one should inspect the parents to see what the puppy would look like.

"She is dead," he said. "Run over," and he pointed at the passing traffic.

"And the father?"

He laughed. "The father went away," he said. "He didn't want his children."

The puppies were clearly in a terrible plight. The one I was holding was still sucking my finger and occasionally biting it with its needle-sharp little teeth.

"How much?"

"Five rand."

That was a blow. My weekly allowance was two rand, and out of that I had been intending to buy some silkworm eggs from Louis van Niekerk.

"I've only got two rand," I said, extending the crumpled blue note.

The man took the note, unfolded it, and thought for a while.

"Okay," he said. "You can have the dog for two rand." He put the note in his pocket.

"Oh, thank you!" I exclaimed, and then bethought myself of my mother and of the silkworms. "But..."

But the man was waving a puppy at a passing car and seemed not to hear my second thoughts; getting his attention was clearly going to be more difficult this time. Besides, the puppy was staring up at me in that way that nature has evolved for the survival of puppies. My natural timidity and my sentimental susceptibilities were united in urging me to take the puppy and deal with the consequences later.

These were surprisingly mild, possibly because my mother was also secretly responsive to the puppy's trick of staring at one with a mournful frown on its brow, like a very small old man. It was a very fat puppy, in spite of the demise of its mother, and had a very soft gray coat, big ears, and massive paws.

"He looks just like Dumbo!" I said. Walt Disney's *Dumbo* had been one of the more magical experiences of my filmgoing career in the Verkeerdespruit town hall.

"Mmm," she said. "I wouldn't be surprised if it had some elephant blood. Where did you get it?"

I told her, and she said, "Heaven knows what diseases it's got. You'd better take it to Mr. Vermaas."

Mr. Vermaas had a room behind his house with a sign on the door saying *Veearts/Veterinary Surgeon*, but my mother used to say that if he was a veterinary surgeon, she was a thoracic surgeon. Still, he was all that Verkeerdespruit had in the line of animal care, and he attended to all the horses and cows in the district. He was a congenitally gloomy man: farmers in the district maintained that horses went lame when they saw him; and when the milk from Koot Bothma's dairy was sour, people called it "Vermaas milk." Dogs were not normally taken to Mr. Vermaas: either he discouraged dog owners from bringing their pets to him because he found canine cheerfulness offensive, or dogs refused to be taken to him.

He certainly did not seem glad to see me or charmed by Dumbo's puppy-dog cuteness. "What's wrong with your dog?" he asked me.

"Nothing, I think," I said. "But I bought him from a man next to the road, and my mother said would you please deworm him and examine him."

"A black man?" he asked.

"Yes."

"Mmm. It's probably got all sorts of diseases." He looked at Dumbo and then at me as if this were my cue to remove the offending dog.

"That's why I'm here," I pointed out. Reluctantly Mr. Vermaas inspected Dumbo, and swore under his breath when the puppy gave him one of its mouthful-of-needles little bites. Then he gave me some deworming tablets, prodded Dumbo's fat little tummy unnecessarily hard, I thought, and said in a depressed sort of way: "He seems healthy enough. They're tough, those kaffir dogs."

I didn't much like this compliment, but accepted it as my mother had taught me to accept all manifestations of the Verkeerdespruit worldview, as the consequence of a "poor education." Besides, Dumbo certainly proved to be a tough little dog, for whatever reason. As he grew up and lost his puppy fat, he looked less like a little elephant and the name became less appropriate, but by that time it had lost all descriptive function in any case and was simply the name of my dog.

By and large I kept to my promise to feed Dumbo every evening, and I assumed responsibility for him, whether for cleaning his kennel or keeping his water bowl filled. In the drought-stricken months of the year this last was particularly important, since there were no sources of natural water available. So Dumbo's water bowl was placed under the tap in my mother's rose garden, which was the one area that remained watered, even in severe drought.

Boys and dogs are supposed to be inseparable. I can't claim this for my relationship with Dumbo, since I went to school happily enough every day without him, and as far as I know he didn't pine in my absence. Nor was he invariably waiting for me at the gate when I got home. But he was always pleased to see me, and we did spend a good deal of time together. Although I had my friends, I was not a very sociable nor I suppose a very popular child, and my favorite pastime of reading was not one that I could pursue in the midst of the throng. So I'd sit on the stoop with Dumbo by my feet, and talk to him when he seemed to require it between naps, and enjoined rational behavior upon

162

him when he exploded in a barking fit. When he was neither sleeping nor barking, he chewed my hand, which I had to leave dangling from the side of the sofa for the purpose. He liked going for walks, and when I went to the café or to Osrin's shop for my mother, he followed happily in my wake, and waited patiently if I happened to be delayed by a chance encounter. He was never a handsome dog, I suppose, but his sturdy good nature seemed to me far preferable to mere beauty. In short, I thought he was perfection, and he seemed to have something of the same high opinion of me, a mutual illusion to which dogs must owe their popularity as pets.

"He's a mongrel," said Louis van Niekerk, one day when he met me on the way to the shop.

"Of course he's a mongrel," I replied. "We're all mongrels." I had recently heard my father defend the view that we were most of us of mixed race, which caused his bridge group, reconstituted since the death of Mr. and Mrs. Brand, to depart in a huff even before tea.

"Speak for yourself," said Louis van Niekerk, which was more or less what my father's bridge group had said to him.

"Anyway, my mother says mongrels are stronger than pedigree dogs," I persisted. Since we were now in territory that could be called medical, my mother's authority counted for something, so Louis had to shift the argument onto forensic grounds.

"My father says all kaffir dogs should be shot," he said.

"Dumbo isn't a kaffir dog," I objected, selecting the most accessible and to me the most controversial part of his assertion.

"Yes, he is. You bought him from a kaffir, didn't you?"

"My father says we mustn't say 'kaffir,'" I countered with my own appeal to authority, but Louis was not to be sidetracked so easily.

"Kaffir dog, native dog, Bantu dog, same difference," he said. "My father says there are too many of them and they don't have licenses."

"Dumbo has a license, so he's not a ... native dog."

"He's a kaffir dog with a license, that's all," he taunted. "It's like ... like a kaffir with a driving license. He's still a kaffir, isn't he?"

163

This logic seemed wrong to me, even in a country that I was starting to realize had its own rules of classification. But I couldn't explain to Louis where he was wrong, and so I contented myself with patting the unconscious Dumbo and saying, "As long as he's my dog, it doesn't matter what anybody calls him."

One morning at the beginning of summer, when Dumbo was about four years old, I was sitting in my usual place, reading a Nancy Drew mystery. Dumbo got up and trotted away, as he often did when he needed a drink of water or some distraction from lying next to me. I vaguely heard him bark in the distance, but did not really register this until suddenly the barking turned to a frantic yelping. I dropped Nancy Drew and ran in the direction of the commotion. Dumbo was standing next to the tap in my mother's rose garden, trying to rid himself of a meerkat that had attached itself to his snout. Jim, our gardener, came running from the vegetable garden with a spade, and while I was still wondering what to do, he killed the meerkat with a single blow. Dumbo yelped once and ran away to the sofa on the stoop.

"That's funny," I said to Jim. "Meerkats don't usually come into the yard."

"Thirsty," he said, pointing to the tap and Dumbo's water bowl. "There's no water out there." We were having one of our perennial droughts that year.

"Poor thing," I said. "You shouldn't have killed him."

"A meerkat does not let go," he said. "I had to kill him."

"I suppose so," I said, looking at the pathetic little dead animal. "Perhaps you should bury him."

"Yes, I will bury him," Jim said. "Ask your mother where." I've often wondered what would have happened if I hadn't asked my mother where Jim should bury the meerkat. As it was, she was not happy with his explanation of how the meerkat had come to be in our yard in the first place. "A meerkat doesn't do a thing like that."

"Well, this one did," I replied, not much interested in the niceties of meerkat behavior.

"That may be because it had rabies," she said. "They go mad with thirst and attack anything in sight."

"Maybe that's why it attacked Dumbo," I said.

"It attacked Dumbo?"

"Yes," I nodded. "But he's only got a couple of small marks on his nose."

"Oh-oh," she said. "I don't like that. Tell Jim not to bury the meerkat. We must have it examined."

"But what does it matter whether it had rabies or … TB or cancer, as long as it's dead anyway?"

She looked at me and bit her lip. "I don't want to scare you unnecessarily," she said, "but if the meerkat had rabies Dumbo may get it."

This still did not strike me as a catastrophe. "Will he have to have injections?" I asked, picturing Dumbo's resistance to the process. Dumbo hated medical attention of any sort.

My mother looked grave. "I don't know about that," she said. "But let's not worry about that now. Tell Jim to put the meerkat in a bag. We have to take it to Mr. Vermaas. And perhaps we'd better take Dumbo along for a checkup."

"But I've checked Dumbo and …"

"Don't argue. Get Dumbo's collar and bring him."

Dumbo hated his collar and, it turned out, Mr. Vermaas about equally. He must have had a repressed memory of the man's treatment of him as a puppy, and snarled most uncharacteristically when Mr. Vermaas tried to examine his snout. Mr. Vermaas pulled back sharply and said, "Quite a vicious one, isn't he?"

"Oh no," I hastened to explain, "he isn't normally like that."

Mr. Vermaas looked at my mother and said, "Doesn't sound too good. Altered behavior patterns."

"It's surely too early to show?" she said. "I mean, if the meerkat really did have rabies."

"It's not a chance I'd want to take," he said, shaking his head. "But I'll send the meerkat to Onderstepoort for an autopsy. Keep the dog tied up in the meantime, and" — this to me — "don't go near him."

"Don't go near Dumbo?" I almost yelled. "What's he going to think?"

"There are more important things on earth than what your dog thinks. Like not getting rabies."

"Will I get rabies if I go near Dumbo?"

"If he's got rabies from the meerkat and he bites you, you'll also get rabies."

"But we don't even know if the meerkat had rabies," I objected.

"And we don't know that it didn't," he said, and repeated, "It's not a chance I'd want to take."

I didn't for a moment think I'd have to heed the instruction to keep Dumbo tied up: I was used to my mother's independence of mind on such matters, and I knew she did not think highly of Mr. Vermaas as a veterinary authority. So I was surprised and indignant when she said to me, "I'm afraid we're going to have to listen to the old sourpuss. If anything happens and Dumbo bites somebody, we'll be held responsible."

I objected, of course, and argued, but my mother was adamant, and when my father came home he agreed.

"You understand, don't you," he said to me, "that Dumbo may get a disease that will make him mad, and then he'll bite you?"

"He won't bite me," I said stubbornly. "Dumbo won't bite me. Dumbo likes me."

"Of course he likes you," said my father. "But when he gets this disease and goes mad he won't be Dumbo anymore, and he'll bite you, and then you'll die."

"You don't know Dumbo," I said. "He'll never bite me."

My father sighed. "And you don't know rabies."

To give Dumbo some space to run, his lead was tied to a length of wire running from his kennel. The theory was that he could exercise himself along this stretch, but in fact he just lay in his kennel moping and yelping. I took my book and went to sit next to his kennel to keep him company. My mother came out and explained that this defeated the purpose of keeping Dumbo tied up. "The idea of tying him up is to keep him away from human beings," she said.

"I don't mind if he bites me," I said.

"Don't be silly," she said. "I mind. Now come away from that kennel."

I spent the next day sitting on the stoop trying to read but concentrating only on Dumbo's mournful yelps. Sometimes he'd start barking furiously, which gave me an excuse to go and visit him.

Mr. Vermaas, of course, came to make sure that his instructions had been obeyed and that Dumbo was tied up. Unfortunately Dumbo started barking hysterically when Mr. Vermaas's van pulled up, I went to calm Dumbo, and when Mr. Vermaas opened the garden gate I was next to Dumbo, patting him while he was biting my hand in a frenzy of joy. I guessed that this would not please Mr. Vermaas — it would not have pleased him even if Dumbo had not been under suspicion of harboring rabies — and from my old listening post on the stoop I monitored the conversation.

"For how long will the dog have to be on this run?" my father was asking.

"Till the tests come back. A couple of weeks. But I wouldn't wait until then."

"You mean …?"

"I mean your son is playing with the dog and the dog can bite him at any time. I would put the dog down."

"You don't know what you're saying. The boy will never allow it."

"I don't know about you, but I don't ask my children's permission to do things, they ask mine."

"The boy loves the dog."

"And you love the boy, I suppose." He made it sound like an infinitely depressing possibility.

"Listen, just because a meerkat comes to our tap to drink water …"

"You don't know a meerkat the way I do. I wouldn't touch a meerkat that just comes out into the open like that."

"Maybe it was thirsty."

"Of course it was thirsty. Do you know how thirsty rabies makes you?"

"No, I don't, but that's not the point. I'll tell the boy not to go near the dog."

"And if he doesn't listen to you?"

167

"He'll listen if I explain to him."

"It's not a chance I'd want to take."

"I think you should leave me to calculate my own chances."

"I wouldn't want to do that. It's my duty to give you my professional opinion, however unpleasant."

"Yes, and I appreciate the fact that you do. I promise you that I'll consider your advice very carefully."

"I hope you do, otherwise I foresee a terrible tragedy in this town." Mr. Vermaas sounded quite cheerful at the prospect.

My father explained to me that I was endangering Dumbo's life by going to his kennel. I understood this, of course, but Dumbo didn't. So I slipped out sometimes when there was nobody at home and sat with Dumbo. I did not believe for a moment that he would bite me even if he went stark raving mad. And he seemed perfectly sane — upset, of course, but that was a rational reaction to being tied to a piece of wire. I saw my visits to Dumbo as a kind of conspiracy between the two of us against the rest of the world, which made the fortnight of his confinement seem almost bearable.

For two days I paid clandestine visits to Dumbo whenever an opportunity presented itself. Then, on Saturday afternoon, I decided that Dumbo needed some exercise. My father was at golf and my mother at tennis. Verkeerdespruit was drowsing in midsummer heat and Saturday afternoon torpor, and from our gate I couldn't see a soul stirring. I decided to take Dumbo for a walk; he was clearly restless and looked at me pathetically every time I went out of the gate. I took him on his lead, just in case he did suddenly go mad when he sensed freedom. He didn't like the lead, but seemed pleased all the same to be going with me.

I took him out of the village, which didn't take long, since we lived on the outskirts and it wasn't a big village. There was nobody around except Fanie van den Bergh, out on one of his inexplicable circuits of the village. I waved at him in a perfunctory way, and was slightly irritated when he crossed the street to me; I wanted to get out of the village with Dumbo.

"You're taking your dog for a walk," he said, and patted Dumbo.

"Yes," I said, and would have added something about Sherlock Holmes if I'd thought he would know what I was talking about.

"He remembers me from tennis," he said, scratching Dumbo's ears. But the dog, impatient for exercise, tugged at the lead, and I smiled a vague farewell at Fanie. As I was dragged off by Dumbo, Fanie said, "I'm sorry," but he didn't say what he was sorry about.

Once in the veld, I released Dumbo, and he joyfully started chasing whatever he could find to chase. Unfortunately around Verkeerdespruit there isn't very much for a dog or anything else to chase, so to make the most of Dumbo's outing I allowed him to chase me. This was his favorite game, but usually strictly rationed, because being chased by a dog is an exhausting and not terribly fascinating pastime for a human. Dumbo had so much pent-up energy that he ran circles around me, yapping hysterically, darting in to nip my hand gently every ten seconds or so, and then streaking off again in a circle. He in fact must have looked rather deranged to somebody not used to canine high spirits. But I was completely engrossed in the game, and I did not notice a vehicle coming along the dirt road from the location. Dumbo was the first to notice it when it stopped; he growled and I looked up to see Captain van Niekerk getting out of a police van and walking toward us, accompanied by a black constable.

"What are you doing here?" he asked, in a tone I had often heard him use, but never to me.

"I'm playing with my dog, *Oom*," I said.

"Isn't that dog supposed to be tied up?" he demanded. So he also knew. "Yes, *Oom*," I said, "but there's nobody around here for him to bite."

"And what about you?" he said. "Look at your hand; it's covered in spit." I wiped my hand on the back of my pants and Dumbo promptly licked it again.

"*Sies*," Captain van Niekerk said. "Get that dog home this minute. Can't your parents see to it that you behave like a white person?"

I glanced at the black constable, but he looked back blankly. "My parents aren't at home, *Oom*," I said, torn between shifting the blame and clearing my parents.

"Tell your father I'm coming to see him this evening," he said. "And you can tell him why, too."

I gave my father Captain van Niekerk's message. My father had never beaten me — even once when my mother urged him to punish me for eating half the teatime chocolate cake while they were having their Sunday afternoon sleep, he refused, saying, "If punishment had ever done any good I wouldn't have had a job" — but this time he took me to his study and gave me a hiding. This made me feel like a martyr and him like a tyrant, and he explained that he had been acting out of concern for me. "You realize that you're risking your life by playing with Dumbo?" he asked again.

"It's my life to risk if I want to," I replied, still much affected by my own courage and resolve.

"That's a stupid philosophy," he said. "Nobody's life is his own."

"Why not?" I asked, intrigued in spite of my sense of injury.

"Because your life affects other people."

"Oh," I said, not really understanding. "Is that good?"

"Well, that depends," he said, and ruffled my hair. "Now go to your room and don't go near that dog."

Captain van Niekerk duly called that evening, after I had gone to bed. I slipped out of bed and took up my listening post outside my father's study. I was glad that I had told my father that Captain van Niekerk would be coming, because he obviously thought I wouldn't, and was expecting to make an impression.

"I'm afraid I must tell you your son has been disobeying your instructions," he said in his gravest manner.

My father said, not very encouragingly, "Yes, the boy told me."

"Oh," said Captain van Niekerk. There was a moment's silence and then he recovered his bluster.

"And what are you going to do about it?"

"I've told the boy that he's endangering his life playing with the dog."

"And haven't you told him that before?"

"Well, yes, but this time I think he believes me."

"And didn't you think that last time?"

"Well, yes I did but … listen, what is it that you want?"

"Don't you think you should get rid of the dog before there's trouble?" For somebody who knew all the answers, Captain van Niekerk was asking a lot of questions.

"Get rid …?"

"Put it down. I'll come round later this evening when I go off duty and do it."

"Thank you but no thank you."

"I'm not making an offer. I'm telling you as commanding officer of the police station that you must put down that dog." Captain van Niekerk was even less pleasant when he stopped asking questions.

"I'm not sure that you have the authority to do that."

"If I find a dangerous stray dog in the streets I have the authority to kill it."

"The dog is neither dangerous nor a stray nor in the streets."

"The dog is a potential public danger. You're the magistrate. You have to set an example to people. If that dog bites an innocent child you'll never hear the end of it."

"And if I put down the dog unnecessarily?"

"A dog's a dog, and a human being's a human being."

"Have you tried to explain the difference to a child?"

"I don't explain things to children. They've got plenty of time to find out for themselves."

"What sort of adults will they be if we don't give them guidance?"

"Same as us, I suppose. My father never explained things to me." I could hear the chair creak as Captain van Niekerk got up. "Well, I can't stay here all night. I'm supposed to be on duty. Think about what I said, discuss it with your wife. I'll call you later in the evening before I go off duty."

"I suppose I should say thank you."

"You're welcome."

As Captain van Niekerk left, Dumbo barked at him.

My father did discuss Captain van Niekerk's visit with my mother. I listened to that, too.

"It's odd," my father said, "it's almost as if they all wanted the dog dead. He hasn't done anything to them."

"Not yet," my mother said, "but they're scared of what he may do."

"We can't kill everybody and everything because we're scared of what they may do to us."

"But a dog that may bite your own son?"

"Yes, I know. But would I be killing the dog because I really believed it was safer, or because of old Vermaas and Piet van Niekerk?"

"Do you send people to prison for pass offenses because you really believe they belong there or because of Verwoerd and Vorster?"

"That's not the same," my father said. "That's my job."

"I don't know," my mother said, and for once she sounded as if she really didn't. "I don't know what to say to you. Because if you don't kill the dog and the dog bites the boy or somebody else you'll never forgive yourself, and if you do kill the dog the boy will never forgive you."

"And you?"

"I'll forgive you whatever you do. But I can't give you advice."

I heard my mother get up. "I'll make us some coffee," she said.

"That would be nice," my father said.

I went out into the darkness of the backyard. Dumbo was lying in his kennel and came running out, his head at an angle in reluctant deference to the lead tying him to the wire in the ground. He yelped with pleasure at seeing me. I was scared my parents would hear him, and I put my hand gently around his muzzle. Then I sat down next to him and stroked his ears. "It's all right, boy," I said. "I won't let them kill you. I'll sit here with you and they'll have to kill me first."

Dumbo licked my face, then stretched himself out on the ground and went to sleep. Being a dog, he took more naturally to this position than I; without his company I became aware of the hardness of the ground under my thin pajamas. It might be a long vigil. It was a stifling evening, so at least I was not cold, but the pebbles dug into my flesh.

I had changed position several times and was wondering if I should go in and collect a pillow and blanket when my father came out of the house.

"What on earth are you doing here?" he asked. "Why aren't you in bed?"

"I'm guarding Dumbo," I said. "You're going to kill him."

"How do you know that?" he asked.

"I know it," I said. "It's true, isn't it?" And then, as he didn't answer, "Isn't it?"

"You mustn't think of it as killing Dumbo," he said gently.

"Then what is it?" I demanded.

"It's … the merciful way out," he said. "You see, if he gets sick, he'll suffer."

"He isn't suffering now," I said, gesturing at Dumbo stretched out on the ground. He opened his eyes and flicked his tail in recognition of the notice.

My father sighed. "Well, no, he isn't. But we can't wait until he starts biting people, can't you see?"

"No, I can't," I said. "If he starts biting people you can kill him." I changed position to seem more determined. "I'm going to stay with him all night," I announced. "And you'll have to kill me too."

"Don't be silly," he said. "We'll never kill you."

"You'll have to if you want to kill Dumbo."

My father looked helpless and I sensed that I was in a strong position. "You must go in now and sleep. I'm ordering you to go in and sleep."

"I won't." I had never flagrantly defied my father's authority before, and there was something oddly exhilarating about it. "I'm going to stay here all night."

"It's going to rain."

"I don't care. I'll stay with Dumbo in his kennel."

"And tomorrow?"

"I'll take Dumbo away to … to someplace where you'll never find him."

"Don't be silly," he said again, but rather absently. He came across to me and stroked my head and said, "Can't you see that it's because we love you that we're concerned?"

"You mean you want to kill Dumbo because you love me?"

"We don't want to kill Dumbo, dammit. Can't you see that?"

"Then don't kill him. Wait for the results." If the results were unfavorable I'd think of something else.

"But I've told you …" and my father shrugged. I could see the fight was out of him.

"I'll go to bed if you promise not to kill Dumbo," I said.

"Ever?" he asked.

"Not tonight. Not without my knowing."

"But …" he said, and then sighed. "Oh, all right," he said. "We won't do anything about Dumbo without telling you."

I patted Dumbo and got to my feet. I was stiff and sore from sitting on the ground. "Night, my dog," I said. "See you in the morning. Don't worry." Dumbo opened one eye and went back to sleep.

I decided not to go to sleep till my parents had gone to bed. My father had never broken a promise to me, but something warned me that he was not entirely in control of this situation. So I lay awake listening to the Saturday evening sounds: the programs on the radio, and occasionally my father and mother exchanging a few words; dogs more fortunate than Dumbo barking in the location; distant thunder building up to a storm.

"You can't expect a child to understand," I heard my father say, but I couldn't make out my mother's reply.

I must have gone to sleep then, because I didn't hear anything more until I sat up not knowing what had woken me, knowing only that I shouldn't have gone to sleep but not knowing why. Then I heard Dumbo yelping, and I knew, and as I jumped out of bed there was another pistol shot, and I realized that what had woken me was the first shot, and I ran out of the house past my mother, who was trying to stop me, and I ran to Dumbo's kennel. The kennel was empty, the collar unbuckled but still attached to the wire. I ran round the house. In the light from the front door I could see Captain van Niekerk standing in the rose garden with my father. He must have come straight off duty because he was wearing his uniform. I ran into the garden, frantic with fear and anger. Dumbo was lying next to the tap, panting and shivering. I knelt in the dust next to him. "Wait!" shouted my father. "Don't touch him! He'll bite you!"

"I don't care!" I screamed back. "I want him to bite me!"

And I put my hand in Dumbo's panting mouth. But he didn't bite me, just closed his jaws around my hand as he had always done. "I'm sorry, Dumbo," I said. I couldn't think of anything else to say. "I'm sorry, Dumbo. They promised they wouldn't kill you."

He continued shivering, then twitched violently a few times and stopped panting. Incongruously, I became aware of the heavy smell of the roses in the airless heat. I took my hand from his slack jaws. There was blood on it. I felt tears on my cheek and wiped them away, leaving, I later discovered, grotesque smears of blood and soil and tears on my face.

"A shame," said Captain van Niekerk. "The boy must have loved the dog."

There was a blinding flash, a loud crack of thunder, and the rain poured down, washing Dumbo's blood into the dust.

I was for a few days the object of commiseration and curiosity, I guessed because Captain van Niekerk had told his son, and Louis had told the other children about my performance the evening they shot Dumbo. Jesserina asked me whether I wanted a kitten, and I said no thank you I didn't like cats; Annette Loubser asked me whether I would get rabies, and I said if I did I would be sure to bite her. Fanie van den Bergh came up to me and said again, "I'm sorry," and I asked him what about and he said, "About your dog," and I said, "You've got nothing to be sorry about, it wasn't your fault." Being pitied by Fanie van den Bergh seemed to me to add ignominy to my loss.

One day after everybody else had forgotten about Dumbo, I saw Vermaas's little van driving up to our gate and reflected that it looked like a hearse for animals. But beyond that reflection I was indifferent to his visit, now that he no longer had the authority of life and death over Dumbo. Still, I was curious to know what he could have to impart, and I took up my by now customary position outside my father's study.

Mr. Vermaas sounded less assured than on his last visit. "I didn't see the dog outside," he ventured.

"No," said my father. "The dog is dead. As you said."

"I said you should keep him tied up till we had the results from Onderstepoort."

"You said …" my father started, then interrupted himself. "Oh, what does it matter what you said? The dog's dead. We had him put down because we didn't want to run the risk. The boy wouldn't leave it alone. You can't expect a child to understand."

This somewhat revived Mr. Vermaas's spirit: it gave him something to be gloomy about. "You can tell the boy it's a pity he wouldn't listen, because the tests have come back from Onderstepoort. They're negative."

"Negative?"

"Yes. The meerkat didn't have rabies. I'm sorry."

I do believe he was, too. He would have preferred the meerkat to have had rabies.

December 6, 1968

Having done my sporting duty, I turned my back on Fanie and tried to escape to some uninhabited spot to lick my wounds and nurse my grievance. I had lost my chance to distinguish myself and to secure victory for Wesley; I had lost a match that I should have won with one hand tied behind my back; and I had lost it to Fanie van den Bergh — talentless, helpless Fanie van den Bergh — with his imbecile gape and his gigantic member. I must be the first person in the history of tennis to be defeated by a bouncing dick, I thought. I cursed the OVV for giving Fanie such naively obscene shorts, and reflected with satisfaction that my mother had resigned as secretary after Mrs. Opperman had sent a Strelitzia wreath costing R79.68 "From the grieving mothers of the Verkeerdespruit OVV" to Dr. Verwoerd's funeral.

It was by now broodingly, malignantly hot, and I decided to go for a swim, partly to cool off, but mainly to avoid having to say civilized farewells to Fanie and his fellow Clutch Plates, or to listen to the condolences and even reproaches of my teammates.

I went up to my dormitory. To my relief Cavalla, my roommate, was not there: although I could normally tell him most things, I demurred at rehearsing the whole tangled set of circumstances that led to my defeat, or at explaining to him why this insignificant sharer of my past should have an effect on me so disproportionate to his gifts or his actions. We had done a Shakespeare sonnet in English class, and one phrase had stayed with me: "the sad account of fore-bemoaned moan, Which I new pay as if not paid before." Rather self-consciously, I decided that that expressed perfectly my sense of reliving the past in the present: Dumbo, Juliana, Mr. van der Walt, Steve: it seemed like a series of losses and betrayals, with nothing to show for it except this clumsy boy who had beaten me on my home ground.

I found my bathing costume and rolled it in my towel; we were not allowed to appear on the school grounds in anything less than regulation uniform. As I rolled the slightly damp costume in my towel, the dank smell and the rolling action recalled the dressing room at Bleshoenderbaai, with its half-shameful, half-exciting associations of conspiracy and innuendo. For a moment I indulged the sentimental notion that, in Shakespeare's phrase, this was the memory through which all losses are restored and sorrows end, but a sharper instinct told me that that, too, had been a loss, perhaps the greatest of all, though it was impossible to say exactly what I had lost.

9

Summer 1965–1966

Once a year we went to the Cape to stay with my grandmother, who had a beach house at Bleshoenderbaai. We had gone there for as long as I could remember, except for two years, after my mother's elder sister, in one of the periodic accesses of familial frankness that she regarded as her duty, had written to my mother explaining that she had for the previous ten years noted that we were given the best accommodation in my grandmother's house only because we came from farther away than any of the other family; those of them who "looked after" my grandmother through the year were taken for granted. I can't imagine what effect my aunt intended her jeremiad to have; but what she did achieve, whether intentionally or not, was to make my mother insist that in future we would take our holidays elsewhere. So that year we went to Umhlanga Rocks in Natal, where my father's family preferred to go. But there was a polio scare in Natal, and though my mother scornfully rejected the theory propounded by my father's sister, who was staying in the caravan park, that the Indians injected the bananas with polio germs, we nevertheless stopped eating bananas — and pineapples for good measure — and left for home after three days. The following year we went to Jeffrey's Bay in the Eastern Cape, where the wind started blowing every morning at ten o'clock. My father didn't mind, because he was used to playing golf in the wind in Verkeerdespruit, but I got tired of my toys after two days, even though my mother had given me my Christmas Meccano set early in desperation, and we left after five days, although we'd taken the house for a month. My mother decided that it would be petty to deprive my grandmother of our visits just because of my aunt's ill-tempered strictures, and when I turned thirteen we went back to Bleshoenderbaai.

Bleshoenderbaai had changed in my absence — or perhaps it was just that coming back to it after what at that age seemed like a very long time, I noticed different things. The Bleshoenderbaai coastline is famous for its cliffs, and I spent many hours wandering along the paths skirting them, exploring the shallow caves under cliff faces, the rock pools left behind by retreating spring tides, or the semiluminous labyrinthine caverns under the spreading branches of the milkweed trees hemming in the paths. There was always something intriguing about these caverns under the trees, the light filtering through the thick foliage, the pungent smell of vegetation and ozone, the soft sand on the floor, the rushing of the waves nearby. One cavern in particular held a kind of magic for me: a summer-sparse stream trickled down a rock to one side of it, and because it was quite difficult to find, it wasn't littered with beer bottles and mutton-chop bones like some of the other caves. Its sandy floor was clean and white in the mottled shade, and I used to pretend that I was the first person ever to find it.

Given the time I spent exploring, I should have found my calling as a marine biologist or a coastal ecologist; but I was completely incurious about the names of the nonhuman creatures leading their obscure existences in the pools and on the rocks, and instead of inspecting the environment with the kind of minute obsessiveness that heralds, I imagine, such a calling, I would lose myself and the details of my surroundings in imagining strange and intriguing meetings along a deserted stretch of the cliff path, meetings with strangers I couldn't quite put faces to, but with whom I had long and inconclusive conversations, and with whom I could share my special cave. The strangers, faceless as they were, were nevertheless well enough defined in my imagination to display some variation of physical type, age, and general demeanor; what they had in common was a quite unprecedented, though to me perfectly intelligible, interest in the minutest details of my existence. They asked penetrating questions and listened with flattering attention as I discussed Life or — what came to much the same thing for me — Books with them. They never volunteered much information in return, it being part of their allure that they seemed to have no antecedents and no connections: they existed only on the cliff path and only through their interest in me — and often through a shared interest in whatever book I was reading. That summer it was *Great Expectations*, which my father had suggested to me as "more grown-up" than the Trompie books that Juliana Swanepoel had taught me to despise and that all my friends were still reading. Trompie books were based upon the premise that boys were naughty but basically decent and parents were stern but loving. I had read them all before I started to despise them.

So an essential attribute of my strangers was a lively and informed interest in *Great Expectations*. Though all considerably older than I — I didn't assign them actual ages, but they seemed to range from early twenties into the unimaginable decades beyond — they treated me as an equal and invited me to call them by their first names, which always proved to be something monosyllabically laconic like Bruce, Luke, Pete (never Peter), or Dave. They were almost invariably English-speaking, possibly because in the Free State everyone was almost invariably Afrikaans-speaking, and because it was difficult to imagine a profound conversation with somebody called Sakkie or Pietie. They were in fact, I can now see, cleaned-up and suaved-up versions of Magwitch, the convict responsible for Pip's great expectations.

The beach where we went swimming was an uncomfortable walk away from my grandmother's house: by the standards of my rambles quite a short walk really, but rendered irksome by the fact that the only bathing costume in my size at Osrin's was thick and tight-fitting and took a long time to dry, especially at the end of the day, so that I would get home with a painful rash on my inner thighs. In previous years I had changed on the beach like the other children, under cover of a towel wrapped around my middle, but now the camouflage seemed precarious: what if the towel unwrapped itself at the critical moment between garments? I decided that the rash was preferable to the humiliation of a public unveiling of my incipient manhood. It didn't occur to me to mention the rash to any adult, partly because I didn't think modern medicine would bother with rashes anyway, and mainly because my inner thighs seemed too personal a part of me to be presented to view as if they were elbows or knees. But my mother was, after all, a trained nurse, and one day as I was standing in front of her drying myself after swimming, she spotted the rash.

"You've been walking in a wet bathing costume," she announced, and I was wondering how I was going to explain to her why I didn't get dressed on the beach as I used to, when she asked, "Why don't you use the dressing room?"

"Where the big men get dressed?" The sign on the door said *Men/Mans*, which I took to imply *No Boys Allowed*, just as *Whites/Blankes* really meant *No Blacks Allowed*.

"Yes. Why not?"

"I don't know. I'm shy."

"You needn't be shy. Nobody will notice you."

I was in fact less shy than intimidated. It seemed to me inconceivable that I could simply walk into an adult dressing room and not be challenged. Adults got dressed in one another's company, as they drank tea and played bridge in one another's company, because it was "not something for children." Still, my mother's matter-of-fact approach to the question at least reassured me that in a confrontation with an outraged Dressing Room Authority she would take my side, and I had enough confidence in her to believe that she would be victorious. So late that afternoon I took my little bundle of clothes and sauntered as nonchalantly as I could into the large, gloomy communal dressing room. The place smelled of wet sand and Jeyes Fluid. I looked neither right nor left, and sensed rather than saw two men in a far corner, drying themselves and talking. I felt I should try not to listen, but I couldn't help hearing that they were discussing athlete's foot, which apparently one got from using the public shower — an innocuous-looking spout in the other corner of the dressing room. "Well," said one, "I suppose we'll have to choose between athlete's foot and sandy balls," and they both laughed. I assumed that they couldn't have noticed me, otherwise they wouldn't have made such a comment in my presence, and tried to remain invisible. I tugged off my bathing trunks as fast as their wet and sandy condition permitted, got dressed without drying myself and, not even pausing to roll my bathing trunks in my towel as we had been taught to do, grabbed the soggy bundle and rushed out.

Once I got home, though, with my rash exacerbated by the walk in wet shorts, I regretted that I hadn't stolen a glance at the two men who discussed such esoteric details of their own bodies so openly in public. The following day I apprehensively sidled into the dressing room and sneaked a glance into the corner where the two men had stood; but there was now only one man, and I had no way of knowing whether he'd been there the day before. He was drying himself, and looked at me in a way that made me wonder anew whether I was committing some transgression in being in the men's dressing room. However, he didn't say anything, merely crossed the room to the shower. I wondered whether he knew about the athlete's foot, and why he dried himself before showering. This time nothing untoward occurred, and I dried, dressed, and rolled my trunks in my towel. The man was still under the shower when I left. My rash cleared up in three days.

After a week of this I was considerably more comfortable about my presence in the men's dressing room. There were never very many people in there, the dressing room having that under-utilized vacancy of most white public facilities under apartheid. Such people as there were seemed not to take exception to my presence; in fact, the man whom I had noticed on my second visit gave me a friendly sort of nod one day as he went by to the shower, and then came to dry himself next to me.

"Where are you from?" he asked.

"Verkeerdespruit," I said.

"What a sad name. Where is it?"

"In the Free State. Near Bloemfontein." I was used to explaining this to people.

"Oh, yes," he said. "Middle of nowhere."

"It doesn't feel like nowhere when you live there," I ventured, stung out of my timidity.

"I suppose not," he said. "But does anything ever happen there?"

I considered. "The postmaster committed suicide in October," I proposed. Klasie Vermaak had slit his wrists one morning with the old-fashioned razor he had inherited from his father. Betty should have been made postmaster in his place but they sent a man from Bloemfontein, and she resigned and moved to Cape Town.

"That must have been exciting. But I mean what do you do for fun?"

"I read," I said.

"And that's your idea of fun?"

"No ... yes," I said. "And I play with my friends."

"I hope you have lots of friends, then."

"No — really only one," I said. Louis van Niekerk was the only boy I could really call a friend.

"Oh well, one is all you need, not so?" and he winked at me.

I nodded. "Except for *kennetjie*."

He laughed. "Oh well, there's more to life than *kennetjie*."

"And *bok-bok*," I said.

"Yes, and *bok-bok*. But two people can play *bok-bok* quite well."

This seemed impossible, since *bok-bok* consisted of one team bending down to form a chain, and the other team jumping on their backs. I looked at him skeptically, and he said, "I'll show you someday."

On my way home I turned over the incident in my mind and measured it against my encounters with my imaginary strangers. Was this one of them, or just another grown-up? He qualified on some points: he talked to me as if he took me seriously and was interested in me; and if he seemed a bit dismissive about reading, that was no doubt because he was not used to boys who read as much as I did, and he would soon enough understand that it was more important than *kennetjie* and *bok-bok*. On the debit side, he was Afrikaans — I could tell from the way he pronounced his r's — and thus unlikely to be called Luke or Seth, but Gert or Jan might do: although hardly exotic, they had a dependable sort of straightforward quality about them. After all, Magwitch was called Abel. I decided to keep an open mind.

After this the stranger was quite often in the dressing room when I went in to change, and almost always spoke to me. As I got to know him better, I recognized reluctantly that he fell short of my ideal stranger — he never did seem to develop an interest in books, for instance, and without his clothes he didn't look like Steve. But he was certainly interested in me, and asked me many questions about myself. One day while we were getting dressed, he asked, "So what is there in this ... Verkeerdegat for you?"

"Verkeerdespruit," I corrected him. And then I felt free to say what I thought: "Not much."

"I'm not surprised," he said. "Doesn't sound like the kind of place for a growing boy."

"No," I agreed. "But I'm going to school in Bloemfontein next year."

"Thrillsville," he said, and when I looked at him inquiringly he explained: "I mean Bloemfontein isn't exactly the center of the universe."

I was taken aback. Nobody I knew had yet questioned the self-evident importance of Bloemfontein — not, of course, as the center of the universe, but, what was more important, as the commercial and educational center of the Orange Free State. "It's ..." I struggled to express my sense of the importance of Bloemfontein, and then had an inspiration. "It's a matter of definition," I announced.

To my disappointment he looked amused rather than impressed. "Oh?" he said. "I'd have thought it was a matter of population."

"No, I mean," and I tried to recall my father's lesson, "a place is ... what it is for *you*. I know that Pretoria is more important than Bloemfontein because it's" — my social studies lessons came back to me — "the administrative capital of our country, but I haven't been to Pretoria and I don't want to go there, so Bloemfontein is more important to *me*."

"Well explained," he said. "Are you going to be an advocate one day?"

"No," I said. "A policeman."

"Oh? Isn't it a pity to waste such powers of persuasion?"

I didn't know whether he was serious, but decided that it would be simplest to assume that he was. "A policeman also needs ... powers of persuasion."

He laughed. "You can say that again. But a policeman's methods are probably more direct than yours."

I tried to think of something to say. This was the kind of conversation I had imagined having with my stranger, and I didn't want it to stop. We were now fully dressed and I couldn't think of an excuse to linger, but he didn't seem to be in a hurry. He put down the damp bundle of his towel and swimming trunks, and carried on. "And why do you want to become a policeman?" he asked, in the teasing way he sometimes adopted and that made me wonder whether he took me seriously. "You like the uniform …? Or you want to be on the side of fairness and justice, is that it?"

"No," I said, "I want to be on the side of power."

He whistled through his teeth. "Tsst. And I thought you were naive. What do you know about power?"

"I know if you don't have it you lose, like … like Steve and Betty and Mr. van der Walt and Mary and … Dumbo."

"Funny names some of your friends have. Sorry, I didn't mean to be flippant. But what about turning the other cheek and all that? Jesus said the meek shall inherit the earth."

"Yes, and look what happened to him."

He whistled again. "Aren't you a bit cynical for your age?"

"I don't know," I said. "I'm thirteen."

This conversation was the last we had for a while. My stranger never spoke to me outside the dressing room, and even there not really when there was anybody else present. I thought he was embarrassed about talking to somebody as young as I, and quite enjoyed the tang of conspiracy this lent to our conversations. Then one day, toward the end of our holiday, he said, "You're always reading," gesturing at *Great Expectations*, which was taking me longer to finish than any other book I had ever read.

"Yes," I said lamely, because this was what I had been waiting for, for the stranger to manifest an interest in my ruling passion. I wished I had something intelligent to say; this was not how my imaginary conversations with my strangers had gone, but he seemed not to mind, for he smiled down at me and said: "You've almost finished it."

"How …?" I began, then noticed the end of my bookmark, an old envelope of my father's, sticking out near the back cover. "Yes," I ineptly concluded, then managed an original thought. "I must finish it before Monday. We're going home on Monday."

"Are you?" he asked. "Just when we're getting to know each other?"

"It's only Friday afternoon," I said, which suddenly sounded so forward that I could feel myself blushing. He must have noticed, because he prodded my stomach and said, "There's nothing to be shy about."

"I'm … I'm not shy," I muttered, now shyer than ever, and looked down. "Yes, you are," he said, but seemed not to mind. Then his manner retreated to a friendly distance, and he put his towel round his waist. "It's good to see that children are still reading," he said, less to me than to the man who had just entered the dressing room, and I felt relegated to the outer world of childhood, excluded from the circle in which adults had their being.

The next day, as I came in from my swim, I noticed that there were clothes hanging next to mine. I wondered why somebody should have chosen that peg out of the many available. Then I recognized the checked shirt the stranger sometimes wore. I was slightly earlier than usual, so I took off my trunks very slowly and dried myself several times before he came in. He glanced at me, smiled, and patted my bare bottom. "You're thin," he said.

"My mother says I don't eat enough," I answered.

"Nonsense. Plenty of time for that later," he said, running his hand down my side. It was the first time anybody had pronounced my mother's medical lore nonsense, and I was less incensed than impressed. "Women are always trying to feed up their men," he said, patting his own stomach, which was not as flat as mine.

He took off his wet trunks and turned to face me. He had a very big peter and it was standing up, not all the way, but so that you could see where it was going. I looked up to find him smiling at me. "Do you like it?" he asked, not leaving me much of a choice of reply. "Yes," I said; then thinking that was probably rather faint praise for something of which he was obviously proud, said, "It's very nice."

"Thanks," he smiled. "It responds well to attention." I wasn't quite sure whether this was an explanation or a hint that I should say something more along the same lines; I must have looked at him in a particularly idiotic way, for he pinched my cheek and said, "Never mind. Just joking. You've got quite a handy little pecker yourself," pointing down at my panic-stricken little peter, which was, however, showing signs of also responding to attention. I pulled on my shorts in confusion, then was sorry I had done so, but couldn't very well take them off again.

"You should see Fanie van den Bergh's," was all I could think of saying. Fanie had become the subject of ribald jokes in the changing room during physical education classes because he had suddenly and somewhat disconcertingly developed a peter that everyone agreed was as big as that of any Standard Eight boy. Even Japie Dreyer was impressed; when Mr. Viljoen decided the school should start its own museum and they found they had nothing to exhibit except a napkin ring my grandfather had carved as a prisoner of war in Ceylon during the Boer War, Japie suggested, though of course not to Mr. Viljoen, that Fanie should donate his peter, except he called it something quite common — "The napkin ring will just fit round it," he said. But I said that my grandfather hadn't spent his days in prison carving a napkin ring for Fanie van den Bergh's monstrous thing.

"And what," my stranger asked, "makes Fanie van den Bergh's so special?"

"It's …" I was going to say "bigger than yours," then thought that might be rude, and ended lamely with "the biggest in Verkeerdespruit."

"Really? Who decides that? Do they have a competition — like a dog show?"

I blushed and laughed at the same time. "No, it's just what everybody says."

"Some conversations you have in Verkeerdespruit. But where is your friend Fanie?"

"He's not really my friend. But he's in Verkeerdespruit."

The stranger made a face. "That's a bit far to go, even for a dong like that."

I was flustered. "I didn't mean ... I just meant ..."

"You just meant that you've got an interesting friend called Fanie."

"He's not so interesting," I objected, though I couldn't have said why I begrudged Fanie this misunderstanding in his favor. "He's not ... very clever."

"With a schlong like that, who needs to be clever? And is Fanie also going to school in Bloemfontein next year?"

"No," I said. "He's going to Technical School in Odendaalsrust." The OVV had decreed that Fanie should go to Technical School as "better suited to his abilities"; since this involved their paying his expenses, Mrs. van den Bergh had no choice but to accept. My mother was opposed to this. "I don't know why people assume that people who can't do anything else must be good at fixing things," she said. "That's why you can't have a fridge or a sewing machine fixed in this country." But Mrs. Opperman and her supporters prevailed, and Fanie was to leave at the beginning of the new year. He had asked me on the last day of school if he could come to visit me in Bloemfontein, and I had said I was going to be very busy because high school was much more work than primary school.

"Mm. Good place to take a big tool."

I was getting flustered. I couldn't seem to get away from the subject of Fanie van den Bergh's peter or pecker or schlong or dong or tool — I hadn't realized there could be so many words for a single part of the body. While I was thinking of something to say that wouldn't somehow involve Fanie's attributes, the man slowly put on his underpants and shorts — he took a long time to arrange his peter so that the swelling didn't show — and said, "But your hot dog is quite big enough for your age. You should just give it lots of exercise," making a gesture that Tjaart Bothma and Japie Dreyer sometimes performed in the back of the class to mutual hilarity and the indignation of the girls.

"I ... I don't know how," I said, and felt myself blushing furiously, partly because this was only half true. Apart from Tjaart and Japie's explicit enough gestures, Louis had told me that if you tugged at yourself for long enough you produced what he called "a kind of Gloy." Gloy was a sticky gray paste that we used to paste pictures on the brown paper covers of our schoolbooks.

"Heavens," exclaimed my stranger, "what on earth *do* you do in Verkeerdesloot?"

"Verkeerdespruit," I said. "I read."

"Yes, I remember. And you play *kennetjie*. But I think before you go to school in Bloemfontein we must … well, equip you for the big city, or at any rate teach you how to use such equipment as you've got. Our country needs all the trained men it can find."

We were both fully dressed now and I didn't know where to look or what to say. I knew that I was somewhere where I'd never been before, and yet it was not altogether unfamiliar either; it was like arriving for the first time in a place I had dreamed of.

"Well," he said, taking his bundle, "are you walking home today?"

"Yes," I said, breathless.

"Are you alone?" he asked. I had never been asked so many questions before, and found the attention quite flattering.

"Yes. My father's playing golf — and my mother went home early." It was Saturday afternoon and we would have a late supper.

"I'll walk with you. We can talk about *Great Expectations*."

"Yes," I said, thinking that after all my stranger was everything I had hoped for.

As we were walking, I thought it a good time to open our discussion of *Great Expectations*. "Do you …?" I started, then suddenly thought it sounded silly. But my stranger seemed unexpectedly interested in my question.

"Probably," he said and winked at me.

"Probably what?"

"I probably do whatever it is that you were going to ask me whether I do."

"Oh. I was going to ask … do you think Miss Havisham was a bad woman?" I flourished my copy of *Great Expectations*.

"Oh. That. Well …" he said, looking pensive. "That depends, doesn't it?" Then, as I looked at him inquiringly, "What do you think?"

"I think," I said happily, "I think that we're meant to think Miss Havisham did wrong because she taught Estella never to love anybody, but I don't know … I can sort of see her point."

"Oh? And what was her point?"

"Well, that the one who loves is weak and the one who doesn't love is strong."

"Mmm. You *are* cynical. What about getting married and all that?"

"Do you have to love somebody to get married?"

"I'm probably not the best person to ask, but I'm sure it helps — I mean, if you love them."

"Them?"

"Her. The person you marry."

"Why aren't you the best person to ask?"

"You don't miss much, do you?"

"No."

"Well, then I'm not going to explain." And he pinched my cheek again. In my excitement at being asked my opinion by a grown-up I had stopped, the better to explain my theory. We were standing next to one of the bushy caverns stretching into the milkweed trees. He glanced into the cavern. "Listen," he said, "have you explored these caves?"

I nodded.

"Show me," he said.

"Yes," I said, "but there's a better one farther along." At last I had somebody to show my special cave to.

"You surprise me more and more all the time. Lead the way."

"It's quite near," I said, "but if you don't know it's there you won't find it."

"And you're only showing it to me now?"

"I didn't know you'd be interested," I replied, suddenly shy.

"I would have thought I'd made my interest quite clear enough," he said.

"Here it is. The first bit you have to sort of crawl, but after that it's easy."

He patted my bottom. "You go first." So I bent down and led my stranger into the luminous gloom of my secret domain.

"Mind your head," I warned. Then I straightened up. "There," I said, pointing at the little clearing with its stream and sand, glowing in the reddish light of late afternoon.

"Mm," he said, "how very convenient."

"Convenient?" I asked, still with my back to him. It seemed a strange word for my cave.

"Yes, very convenient. Turn round." I obeyed. "You can put down your little bundle," he said, putting down his own and smiling the conspiratorial smile of the dressing room.

"Why?" I asked, for want of anything more sensible to say.

"If you didn't know you wouldn't be here," he said, still smiling. "Now put down that bundle."

I dumbly obeyed. Bending down, I dropped *Great Expectations*, and the book flopped open on the sand. I reached to close the book — we had been taught never to leave a book lying open — but he said, "Never mind that now." He had unbuttoned his shorts and there was no mistaking what he was showing me. I suddenly thought of Japie Dreyer and Fanie van den Bergh and the dog show and the napkin ring, and wondered whether it would fit round this, and giggled. My stranger frowned reproachfully and said, "What's so funny?"

I was now equally embarrassed and confused. "I'm sorry," I stuttered, "It's … it's so big."

"Thanks," he said. "But it won't stay that way if you laugh at it again. Come here before my great expectations collapse."

I stumbled the few steps to where he was now leaning against a tree. The light sifted down upon him and gave a startling prominence to his thing. He reached out and took my hand. Impulsively I closed my hand around his, but he gave it a perfunctory squeeze and then put it on his thing. I tried to pull my hand away, but he held it, smiled, and said, "This is what you wanted, isn't it?" I felt myself nodding, and then his other hand found the elastic of my shorts and slid shorts and underpants together down to my knees, revealing my body's answer to his question, sticking out from my loins in what seemed a valiant but inadequate emulation of his. But he appeared not to mind.

191

"That's very promising," he said, and put his left hand on it. I could feel his wedding ring. Then he put his other hand behind my head, and pulled my head toward his. I resisted, tried to move away from him, but my shirt was now caught in a branch somewhere, and besides, he was strong, and forced my mouth onto his. I looked at the face so close to mine; his eyes were closed. I noticed the hairs in his nostrils and saw that there were fine hairs even on the tip of his nose. I tried to pull away my head, but he held fast; and then I felt his tongue forcing open my mouth and sliding between my teeth, and I closed my eyes. I tasted the strong savor of his saliva, and felt his tongue exploring the back of my teeth while his left hand caressed and fondled and pulled at me. I had never been as close to any human being, and suddenly it was unbearable and overwhelming and my body started moving in a rhythm over which I had no control that made me think of Fanie van den Bergh and his fits; I leaned forward on my stranger and put my arms around him as my loins jerked in spasm after spasm, each more intense than the other, quicker and quicker, until I wanted to scream out the pain and the pleasure but I couldn't, and I bit his tongue as hard as I could.

"*Shit*!" he exclaimed and let go of me. Deprived of my support, and with my feet confined by the shorts around my ankles, I fell forward heavily; I could hear my shirt tearing as I fell on the sand, my body still performing its involuntary contractions, slowly subsiding into brief intermittent shudders and twitches. I closed my eyes and waited for my breath to return. When I opened them again my stranger was still standing next to me, pulling up his shorts. "Why the hell did you do that?" he asked. There was blood on his mouth.

"I ... I don't know," I blurted. "I'm sorry, *Oom*." His shirt and my body and the sand next to us were moist with the sticky fluid that my body had produced in its extremity; even *Great Expectations* was full of it. "I don't know what happened," I said.

"You've bitten off my tongue, that's what's happened," he said, rather thickly, wiping his mouth with a handkerchief.

"But this ..." and I gestured at the mess as I struggled to my feet.

192

"You've come all over the place. It happens. There, wipe yourself," and he passed me the blood-stained handkerchief.

"I can use my towel." It was some slight relief to discover that there was a name for what I had done — *coming all over the place* couldn't be completely monstrous if it had been classified as a human possibility.

"No point in adding your indiscretions to your mother's laundry. Take my handkerchief."

"I'm sorry, *Oom*," I said again as I took the handkerchief, and "*Sies*," as I saw the sticky fluid on my hand. I thought of Louis van Niekerk's description and said aloud, "It *is* like Gloy."

"There you are, then," he said. "Start a factory. You should make a fortune, once you're in full production."

Inexpertly and hastily I wiped myself, and returned the handkerchief. He was buttoning up his shorts on his now considerably diminished thing. "I'm sorry, *Oom*," I said again, clumsily pulling up my shorts. "Don't be sorry, be careful," he said, and patted his mouth with the handkerchief. He put the handkerchief back in his pocket and glanced at the front of his shorts; "Don't forget your book," he said, pointing toward *Great Expectations*. He gestured to me to stay behind while he crawled to the mouth of the cavern and looked left and right along the cliff path; then he said, "And for God's sake never give anybody a blow job."

"What's a …?" I began, but he had already slipped out of the cavern and disappeared back in the direction of the beach.

I rushed home in terror. How was I going to explain to the librarian why pages seventy-eight and seventy-nine of *Great Expectations* were stuck together? I tried to detach them, but the hideous sticky stain seemed to dissolve the paper, so that the pages threatened to tear apart as I pulled. Indeed, the very book seemed to reproach me, because all I could read of the fused pages were, at the bottom of page seventy-eight, "as if it pelted me for coming there," and, at the top of the next page, "I divined that my coming had stopped conversation": clearly coded references to my recent spectacular eruption. To add to my welter of ill-defined apprehensions, I discovered that the envelope I had used as a bookmark had disappeared: had my stranger secreted it as evidence, or as a way of getting my father's address? The letter had been redirected to my father from Verkeerdespruit, so it had our home address as well as our holiday address on it. I had wild previsions of the stranger writing to my father complaining that I had bitten off his tongue and then come all over the place. In addition to these tormenting possibilities, I was much inconvenienced by the actual physical discomfort of the sand sticking to every part of me.

Baths were not encouraged at my grandmother's house: what hot water the ancient geyser produced was needed for washing the dishes and clothes used by the considerable number of relatives spending their holiday with her, and it was usually assumed that everybody stayed clean by swimming in the sea. So I had to get rid of the sand glued to my body by wiping myself with the cloth used to clean the hand basin in the bathroom. This took a while — it was a bit like rubbing my body with wet sandpaper — and elicited complaints and queries from other family members anxious to use the place. "Why are you taking so long?" my father demanded, back from golf and the three beers he always had after the game. For a reckless moment I thought of saying, "I've come all over the place," but settled for a safer "Won't be a minute," as I'd said several times before. I emerged damp but relatively sand-free.

But more than a little water was needed to clear me of my deed. I spent a miserable night, having visions of the stranger appearing at my grandmother's house and disappearing with my father into the little sitting-room where the grown-ups went when they wanted to talk. He might even show my father the handkerchief stained with my double guilt, his blood and my fluid blended through my atrocity.

I must have slept, because I had dreams in which Magwitch and Pip and Joe and Old Orlick all did the strangest things to one another, bizarre attempts on the part of my subconscious to flesh out the concept of the *blow job* I had been counseled to abstain from; but the night seemed endless. The next day being Sunday, all it promised in the way of distraction from my fretting was the weekly church service, the dreariness of which induced depression in me even when I hadn't bitten an adult and glued my library book shut. Today it promised to be a torment.

The church at Bleshoenderbaai was always very full, because it had been built for the meager local population rather than for the augmented holiday crowds; and for those holidaymakers who felt that going to the beach came under the ambit of the Sabbath proscriptions, churchgoing was the only alternative form of socializing.

We were almost late because the car keys could not be found — my father had left them in the pocket of his golf shorts — and the only seats left were right in front, cowering under the pulpit. There would be a visiting preacher today, as often at this time of year: there were so many ministers among the holiday-makers that the local minister could have filled his pulpit ten times over with visiting preachers anxious to appear before a fresh audience. On this occasion, my mother had informed me, the preacher was a prominent minister from one of the more fashionable congregations in Pretoria, who, although relatively young, had already buried several cabinet ministers. "They say he's tipped as the favorite to bury Verwoerd one day," she had added, "which I suppose is the height of ambition in that direction, now that we don't have a queen for them to crown." My mother had no more respect for dominees than for any other figure of authority, believing as she did that they all belonged to the Broederbond, but this did not prevent her from taking us to church. "I don't suppose God can do anything about the Broederbond any more than we can," she said. My father didn't go to church: he said he saw enough of human iniquity during the week without having to countenance human hypocrisy on Sundays. "That's why I like golf," he said. "You don't go to jail if you play badly, and you don't go to heaven if you play well."

The Dutch Reformed Church is almost bereft of ceremony; one of its few procedural affectations is for the preacher to pause on the steps leading up to the pulpit for a moment of silent prayer. From where I was sitting I had a good view of the profile of the dominee from Pretoria, and noticed that he was using the opportunity to pick his nose. I was going to nudge my mother to draw her attention to this when I was struck by something familiar in the profile, which kept my eyes fixed in fascinated apprehension on the bent head. It was only when he had mounted the steep little staircase and was looming over us in his voluminous black gown over the GOD IS LOVE embroidered over the lectern that I knew definitely that the visiting dominee was my stranger. I had put my hand on the dong of a man of the Lord.

I dreaded the end of the opening prayer when I would have to lift my head toward the pulpit and meet the stern stare of the dominee, who in his black gown looked far from conspiratorial, much more like a judge preparing to pass sentence. I imagined wildly and against my own better judgment that he might use the opportunity to make a point by denouncing me from the pulpit, exposing me to the scorn and execration of the assembled children of God. He read the Ten Commandments ringingly if rather thickly, with such emphasis that I examined each one for an indictment of me and my sin; but the Lord had not seen fit to include biting His Dominee or coming all over the place in His list of prohibitions, although the reference to the jealousy of God might be taken to imply a general disapproval of people taking liberties with the person of His servant.

I was thoroughly confused. I had committed a sin so enormous that there wasn't even, as far as I could make out, a name for it in a list of sins that I had been used to regard as exhaustive. But was my sin alleviated or aggravated by the fact that I had committed it with someone who could be assumed to have a special relationship with the great Inventor of all Sin? I could see that there was something to be said on both sides, but I had been to enough church services to know that there was unlikely to be an easy way out for me.

At the best of times I found it difficult to concentrate on sermons, because they offered such a limited range of options, compared, say, with *Great Expectations*; today it would have been impossible had I not been looking in the stranger's words for a clue to my culpability. The sermon was tailored to the pre-occupations of a fair section of the congregation: a new intake of recruits to national service was about to depart, and it was the last shared church service for a number of families. The text was "And he said, Take now thy son, thine only son, Isaac, whom thou lovest," and the sermon set out to show that the

Love of God was infinite but mysterious; and in order to experience it we had to show absolute obedience to His will, having done which, we would be given proof, as Abraham found, of God's love. Against the demand for Isaac's sacrifice should be set the assurance "for now I know that thou fearest God, seeing thou hast not withheld thy son, thine only son, from me." Abraham's willingness to sacrifice his own son proved not only his love of God but also his love of his son, in that he was not deterred by a shortsighted and sentimental notion of love from dedicating his son to the will of God. The ram caught in the thicket was the living — though not for long, I thought — proof of God's love, and had to be sacrificed to seal the pact of love between God and Man. The love that Abraham felt for his son was subordinated to his fear of God; the greater love is always marked by this fear as of a higher authority; and if one yields, that authority may relent and show His true love by not requiring the sacrifice after all.

All of this helped me little with my own moral dilemma; the only role for me in the story, as far as I could see, was as the sheep. I wondered what God would have done if the sheep had bitten Abraham. I also wondered how Isaac felt about his father after being released from the altar, for that matter how Abraham felt about God after going all that way just to sacrifice a ram, and how God felt about somebody who unquestioningly set out to sacrifice his own son and as unquestioningly swapped his son for a ram. Most of all I wondered what Abraham and Isaac talked about on their way down the mountain.

But mixed with all these questions was the much more troubling speculation as to what the stranger himself could be feeling. He had not shown any sign of recognizing, even of noticing me; but that was only to be expected. Sympathetic identification was not my strongest sentiment, but somewhere in the midst of my turmoil and shame I found pity for the poor man for having to represent in his fallible person the infallible God whom he had chosen to serve — although at the time I thought of it merely as feeling sorry for a man trying to deliver a sermon while being stared at by someone whom he had pronounced the previous day to have a promising hot dog.

One of the more disconcerting aspects of my mortification was that as I recalled the appalling events of the day before, and reminded myself that it was this stranger in the black gown towering over us all whose person I had handled and who had handled my person, the glow of shame somehow spread to my belly, there to cause an insurrection so inconvenient as to make me squirm in my seat. My mother glanced at me and whispered, "Sit still." This increased my discomfort without decreasing my tumescence, and intensified my shame, which in turn further inflamed the insurrection. I tried to calm myself by listening to the sermon, but every time I looked at the dominee I imagined him reciting a litany of all the new words he'd taught me the day before. There even flashed through my mind the terrifying idea that I might get up here in church and shout these words at the dominee.

By the time the service had run its course and we had been duly blessed, with no exception made for me as far as I could tell, I was sweating with more than the January heat. I was torn between the desire to get as far away from the church as possible and a perverse wish to see my stranger for a last time. I knew, in any case, that there was little chance of getting away from the church in a hurry: as I've mentioned, church had to stand in for the beach as the center of social contact on Sundays; besides, having sat still for more than an hour, most of the faithful were counting on an opportunity to originate a sentiment of their own. This was seldom very original, the possible range of responses being limited by a sense that to criticize a sermon was to question the workings of the Lord. At most one could express mild reservations about the relevance *in this context* of any too-fervent inquiry, on the part of a mildly progressive dominee, into the identity of one's neighbor, or any too-indiscriminate application of the commandment about loving one's neighbor as oneself. In this case there were not even these misgivings: the sermon was generally agreed to have been very timely and very inspirational, though I noticed the slight tightness around my mother's mouth that meant she was trying hard not to say what she thought. She contented herself with saying, "I've always felt rather sorry for the ram," and my Aunt Dolly, my mother's brother's wife, who was known to disapprove of my mother for knitting on Sundays, said quite sharply, "Would you have felt better if God had allowed Abraham to sacrifice Isaac?"

"Well, perhaps He could just have praised Abraham for his obedience and sent him home," my mother said.

"You heard what the dominee said: God's love moves in mysterious ways," said Aunt Dolly rather more resonantly and less sharply than usual, and I realized that the dominee had emerged from the consistory to mingle with his flock.

I was rigid with the effort of not looking around, terrified to face him, but also embarrassed on his behalf that he should have to encounter me again in such different circumstances. I could feel rather than see his black presence approach; more literally so as his voluminous cloak brushed against me. The faces around me set into expressions of reverently costive panic: the dominee was pausing for a goodwill stop. There was a tight little silence, and then Aunt Dolly came to the rescue smartly if untruthfully. "We were just wondering why we haven't seen more of you," she said, and added with a coy laugh to sanction her own audacity, "You've been hiding your light under a bushel all this time." There were nervous titters: quoting scripture at the dominee was dangerously close to disrespect.

I did not turn around to face my stranger, but he was right behind me as he replied, "Ah, the Sermon on the Mount, the wisest words ever spoken. But you'll remember that in the same sermon the Lord said, 'Let not thy left hand knoweth what thy right hand doeth,'" and under cover of his black gown he put his hand on my anxiously tensed bottom and pinched it, so hard that it hurt.

When Dr. Verwoerd was assassinated later that year, I searched newspaper reports of the funeral for mention of my stranger, but he wasn't there: perhaps the untimely death had left him still underqualified. At the end of the year we went back to Bleshoenderbaai, and I saw him again. He was talking to one of the younger boys on the beach, apparently about the Trompie book the boy was reading.

December 6, 1968

Coming out of our dormitory, I was dismayed to see the floor prefect, Gottlieb Krause, come out of the bathroom at the far end of the passage. He had just had a shower, and had a towel draped round his waist. I thought I might pretend not to have seen him, but he called: "Hey Half-Ball!"

I reluctantly stopped and waited for him to saunter up to me.

"Quite a game, hey?" he asked.

"I suppose so," I said as unencouragingly as possible.

"Not that the skinny Clutch Plate was much good," he continued, scratching his bare stomach. Gott had very little sense of privacy. "Pity you lost your nerve there." I wondered if this was Gott's euphemism for my manifest demoralization by Fanie van den Bergh's private parts. But, then, Gott was as incapable of euphemism as of irony: his comment must signify that he had been the only spectator unaware of the reason for my defeat.

"Mm," I said, barely civilly, hoping to make it quite clear that I had no desire to discuss the putative reasons for my own defeat. But Gott was not to be deterred.

"I believe, you see, it is all a matter of co-ordination." He was the only person I knew who could pronounce a hyphen. He was stroking his navel with the tip of his finger. "You can play competently up to a certain level, but if you are not born with co-ordination, you just go to pieces under pressure." He stood there nodding as if, having explained it so rationally, he were enthusiastically agreeing with himself, quite apart from the satisfactory dimensions of his navel. He adjusted the towel round his loins and looked down at his left nipple with uninhibited satisfaction, as if noticing for the first time something peculiarly pleasing about its shape. He was the only boy in our class with hair on his chest. In the heat of the late afternoon the smell of soap was starting to yield to the pungent tang of freshly sprung sweat; he sniffed at his armpit and seemed pleased with the result. Cavalla once said, "Gott is the only person I know who can give himself a hard-on just by looking at himself," and indeed, Gott's self-satisfaction had something tumescent about it. My tentative adolescence was both intimidated and fascinated by his precocious, belly-scratching, armpit-sniffing sexuality. His exaggerated respect for his own

opinions seemed reinforced by the complacent way in which he explored his own well-developed body. So I said: "I'm sure you're right. You always are."

Since this was in fact what Gott believed, he could not take issue with my extravagance; but I could see that he was suspicious at my sudden conversion to his view of himself. On a sudden impulse I said, "Hicks used to think very highly of your co-ordination," and turned on my heel.

"Hey!" He shouted after me. "What do you mean, Hicks ...?" But I just shrugged and carried on walking.

"Why do you mention Hicks?" he persisted, to my retreating back. "Hicks has left; he left more than a year ago."

I stopped and turned around. "Yes," I said, "and we know why, don't we?"

1966

Bloemfontein is not one of the great cities of the world. To my restless imagination, however, it was the most accessible alternative to Verkeerdespruit; and as that it came to represent all the vaguely apprehended glamour of Life Elsewhere. Not to be Verkeerdespruit was such an enormous advantage that I was prepared to grant it almost every other charm on earth, without bothering to define with any precision the concrete details of my expectations. Few cities can live up to that kind of generalized expectation: even Paris, for the visitor expecting Light and Love and Beauty, may turn out to be, in the light of common day, mainly a place of dog droppings and rude waiters. And Bloemfontein is not Paris.

So my longed-for release from Verkeerdespruit, at the end of my primary school career, inevitably was less absolute a change of condition than I had imagined. Bloemfontein, when it ceased being the point of convergence of my various dissatisfactions, the locus of a limitless potential hitherto untested except on day visits with mixed grills in cafés and sandwiches in the zoo, turned out to be finite, a matter of a certain number of streets in relation to one another and to a limited number of points of interest, a place of regular meals and of ordinary people. This descent into the commonplace was not so much accelerated as embodied by the school I was sent to, the imperturbably respectable, *decently* second-rate Wesley College.

I had grown up believing that when I reached the proper age I would go to Free State College, a large boys' school offering instruction through both English and Afrikaans medium, thus solving the problem of deciding between an English or an

Afrikaans school. It was the oldest school in the Free State, and had produced one state president and two Springbok rugby players (three, in fact, but the third was in jail for fraud, and was thus quietly dropped out of the school prospectus). Since I had no desire to meet a prospective state president or a Springbok rugby player, it is strange that these distinctions should have spoken to me, but these were the criteria by which I heard schools judged, and I did not stop to question their substance.

Unfortunately Free State College sent my parents a brochure extolling the virtues of the institution. Apart from the luster bequeathed by the departed state president and the ex-Springboks, the school's educational offerings included, it seemed, "Citizen Training: A full course in Youth Preparedness."

"What is Youth Preparedness?" my mother demanded from my father. "Isn't Simon prepared enough?"

"Oh, you know," he shrugged. "The usual thing: the Will of God as revealed to the Educational Establishment by the Leaders of the Nation for the Good of the Country. Brainwashing."

"And doesn't it bother you that your son will be brainwashed?"

"I like to think that we've provided Simon with the means to resist brainwashing," he said, smiling at me briefly.

"It wouldn't be called brainwashing if it were that easy to resist. If you throw a sock into a washing machine it can't *resist* the process, it goes into the rinse and spin along with all the other laundry," countered my mother, who had recently acquired a washing machine. "I'm going to demand to see the curriculum for this Youth Preparedness."

The curriculum duly arrived, in the form of a booklet entitled *Education for the Future: Youth Preparedness*. My mother pored over it grimly for half an hour and then declared: "This Youth Preparedness is just another word for indoctrination. They don't want to educate the children, they just want to turn them into little Nationalists."

"I suppose that is what they understand by education," said my father from behind his *Friend*. "If you're a big Nationalist, you naturally want your children to be little Nationalists."

"And everybody else's children, apparently," said my mother. "Listen to this: 'South Africans are increasingly becoming alienated and falling prey to international opinion and a spirit of liberalism. Discipline all too often crumbles before the onslaught of the liberal idea of freedom. A deliberate patriotic preparedness action has thus become necessary. The child must once again be taught to be proud of his country and loyal to state, church, and nation. In effect, all education should be preparedness training. The child should be taught that freedom lies in the acceptance of restriction.' It's all *should be* and *must be* and *don't be*. I think Simon should go to a private school."

"What does the boy say?" asked my father, lowering his paper and looking at me over his glasses.

"I don't know," I said. I wanted to go to Free State College, but I didn't like to think of myself as a sock going into a spin cycle. "I don't want to be a little Nationalist, but I don't want to go to school with … Bantu children either." We had been told that at an English private school you might find yourself sharing a desk or a swimming pool with a Bantu. There was even a story of a little black boy inviting one of his classmates home for the weekend.

"You see," said my mother to my father. "He's a little Nationalist already."

"Then isn't it an unnecessary and belated expense sending him to a private school?" asked my father.

"No, it's not," said my mother firmly. "Attitudes like that are reversible if they're caught in time. Otherwise they become ingrained and you never get rid of them. Like your Aunt Dolly," she said, suddenly turning on me, "whose mother told her that black people were hatched from watermelons and to this day she won't eat watermelons, though she pretends she doesn't believe the story."

Her stern look seemed to implicate me obscurely in my Aunt Dolly's gullibility, and all I could think to say was, "But, I like watermelon." My mother looked unpacified by this reply, but I was saved from further remonstration by my father's intervention. "Do you know what a private school costs?" he asked.

"No, but I'll find out," my mother said. "This is not a time to count pennies."

So my mother shopped around for a private school. This did not take long. Bloemfontein had only three private schools: one Catholic, one Anglican, and one Methodist. The Catholic one was out of the running because my mother, in spite of having emancipated herself from most of her inherited prejudices, still retained from her Dutch Reformed childhood the idea of Catholicism as a sinister conspiracy. "It's the same as the Broederbond, all those men muttering behind closed doors," she said. "And they're just like the government schools really: they don't teach the children to think, they teach them *what* to think."

So I was spared the machinations of the Catholics. I didn't mind, because I didn't like the green-and-yellow striped blazer they wore. The Anglican school, St. Andrews, was more attractive, because it had nice old stone buildings and the boys wore straw boaters, but it turned out to be too expensive. My mother said a good education was all very well, but it shouldn't cost more to keep one boy at school than to keep the whole household running in his absence.

"You said this wasn't a time to count pennies," I reminded her.

"You don't have to *count* them to see how many there are," she said. "Besides, it's not only a matter of money. When school fees are as high as that, you get all the wrong sort of people sending their children there, just to prove they can afford it."

To save me from Nationalism, Catholicism, and the wrong sort of people, all that remained was Wesley College. "The Methodists aren't exactly stylish," my mother said, "but at least they're not common. They always have nice flower arrangements in church, and tea and tennis biscuits afterward. And they're unlikely to want to brainwash anybody — I mean, it's not as if they have any very strong ideas about anything, is it?"

"I don't know," replied my father, who was equally indifferent to all religions. He maintained that if God existed he was either very inefficient or very callous, so it didn't seem to matter very much from which angle you approached him. "Aren't the Methodists rather missionary?"

"Only for the Bantu," my mother said. "They're too polite to do missionary work among whites. Not like the Catholics."

So, on my mother's theory of the political and religious ineffectuality of the Methodists, I went to the slightly obscure old Wesley College, one of those relics of an English presence in the predominantly Afrikaans Free State, testimony to good intentions and reparations after the Boer War rather than of more direct colonizing ambitions. My mother phoned the headmaster, the Reverend Mr. Robinson, as he was called in the school prospectus, and he assured her that Wesley could take me.

"He sounded rather depressed about it," she said. "But it may be a good sign that they don't jump at any prospective pupil."

Wesley College, if not the Greyfriars of my dreams, looked pleasantly different from the rest of the Free State. Its red brick buildings seemed reassuringly old, and, built against one of the few koppies in Bloemfontein, it dominated the landscape with an impressive air of authority.

"It looks a bit Tom Brown for this part of the world," said my father, as we drove up to the school hostel, Milner House.

"Rather Tom Brown than Paul Kruger," replied my mother. "Look, it's got a nice rose garden. I told you the Methodists like flowers."

"That's the Garden of Remembrance," I informed them, having pored over the school brochure for the previous week. "For the boys from the school who died in the World Wars. Pro patria," I added rather grandly. I had memorized the phrase from the photograph of the memorial plaque, next to the picture of the school swimming pool.

"Pro whose patria?" asked my father.

Wesley College was run on a belief in plain cooking and plain religion and plain speaking. Although the cooking, under the grim supervision of Mrs. Cameron, was rather austere, and the religion rather dull, running mainly to moral responsibility and spiritual and personal hygiene, the plain speaking was quite comforting after the rhetoric of the Dutch Reformed Church and the flag-waving of even as undemonstrative a school as Verkeerdespruit Primary. It was admittedly a bit disorienting at first to hear Dr.

Verwoerd invoked in school prayers not in a tone of reverent adulation as meriting God's most conscientious support, but grimly, as God's inexplicable lapse, the ultimate embodiment of Them. Them, alternatively They, were the Afrikaners, who were responsible for Things Being as They Are.

"Things being as they are," intoned Mr. Robinson in chapel, "we must trust in God to deliver us from Evil and restore a culture of Christianity, civilization, and tolerance." Evil, I soon discovered, meant Them. "Things being as they are," pronounced Miss Smithers, our English teacher, "we look to great literature to deliver us from barbarism and ignorance," barbarism and ignorance once again meaning Them. "Things being as they are," said Mr. Moore, our tennis coach, "you will have little trouble beating the Ball-Bearings on Saturday," the Ball-Bearings being young male Thems, the boys of Bloemfontein Hoër, the large Afrikaans coeducational school.

I was aware, of course, of being partly one of Them. My English name spared me suspicion and rejection, but after unwisely confessing to having an Afrikaans mother, I became known as Half-Ball-Bearing, or occasionally Son-of-a-Bus, Buses being female Ball-Bearings. These appellations were no more and no less malicious than children's nicknames ever are, but I was set apart by them as, if not quite Them, then not exactly Us either. In this finely gauged exclusion I found myself thrown together with Gottlieb Krause, the son of a German cherry farmer from Bethlehem who had sent his son to Wesley College on the assumption, Gottlieb told me one day in a fit of confidence, that Methodist meant Methodical, and with David Levy, the son of a Jewish chemist from Welkom. When I asked David why he had been sent to Wesley College, he said, "Must I always explain why I am where I am?" David was suspicious of questions, maintaining that people who asked questions usually knew the answers they wanted; but after I'd convinced him that I wasn't interrogating him with a view to deportation, he said, "My father sent me to a Methodist school because he said it was where I was least likely to find Germans or Afrikaners."

The more devoutly Methodist of the boys referred to Gottlieb as the Jew-Killer and to David as the Christ-Killer, but the more secular ones favored Gott and Filter-Tip — the latter name being based on a perceived resemblance between the circumcised penis and a two-tone cigarette. Filter-Tip eventually modulated into Cavalla, in honor of a popular brand of cigarette. David said that the name was offensive because it implied that Jews, like cigarettes, were made to be burned. Gott said, "I think you're being very oversensitive," and David replied, "Heil Hitler." Gott hit him and David said, "Who's being oversensitive now?"

So the three of us, Half-Ball, Gott, and Filter-Tip, shared a dormitory and formed a kind of alliance against the forces of Christianity, Civilization, and Tolerance. The Scripture master, Mr. Chalmers, called us Shadrach, Meschach, and Abednego. When the class asked him why, he said we should look it up in our Bibles. I did so and found that Shadrach, Meschach, and Abednego were celebrated for emerging unscorched from the fiery furnace of Babylon. Gott said this meant that Mr. Chalmers thought that we were strong and incorruptible, and Cavalla said that it meant that Mr. Chalmers thought we were foreigners who should be roasted in a furnace. I thought that Mr. Chalmers was just trying to get us to read our Bibles.

We were an incongruous alliance, in that Gott was as slow and ponderous, large and blond, as David was wiry and quick, small and dark, and Gott had a deep baritone voice whereas Cavalla spoke in the as-yet-unbroken treble of boyhood. But above all it was an uneasy alliance, in that we all three suspected that the rest of the boys were right about the other two members of the alliance. It was difficult to remember to call somebody David when everybody else called him Cavalla, and I could see that at times he had to search his memory for my real name. As for Gott, he didn't bother, and just called us Cavalla and Half-Ball. I accepted this as just Gott's way, but Cavalla muttered darkly about the theft of one's identity being the first step to disenfranchisement. Cavalla was ahead of the rest of us in political thinking.

We derived such comfort as we could from calling the other boys the Stewed Prunes, after what seemed to be the school's favorite dessert, which the English boys ate with every appearance of enjoyment. About the only thing we three had in common was that we came from culinary traditions that eschewed stewed prunes. Since none of us would have dared to call one of the Prunes by that name to his face, however, we derived little power from the appellation. Secretly, in fact, we all three longed to be one with the Stewed Prunes, and there wasn't one of us who wouldn't gladly have betrayed the other two for acceptance by the Prunes. Thus when one of the Prunes, Richard Hicks, condescended to take what seemed to be a friendly interest in me — he asked me why I had such funny hair — I was flattered and pleased. I knew better than to show it too clearly, though. "I don't know," I said. "I've had it all my life. It doesn't look funny to me."

"Well it does to everyone else," he said. "It sticks up all over the place like pick-up-sticks."

"What are pick-up-sticks?" I asked, my curiosity taking over from my hurt pride.

"What *is* pick-up-sticks, not are. It's a game. If you come to my study after supper I'll show you." Hicks was in the Fourth Form, and as hostel prefect had his own little study next to the dormitories.

Pick-up-sticks was not much of a game. Its name exhausted such possibilities as it had: you threw a bundle of sticks in as tangled a pattern as possible, and your opponent had to retrieve as many sticks as he could without disturbing the rest of the pile. If any of the other sticks moved, it was your turn to pick up sticks. The winner was the one who picked up most sticks. I thought the game rather young for a Fourth Form boy, but Hicks said, "Pick-up-sticks is a much underrated game. People say it's for children, but I find it improves my concentration and co-ordination. I'm going to be a brain surgeon when I grow up, and for that you need superhuman concentration, otherwise you can make people lame and blind for life." Thus persuaded of the educational advantages of pick-up-sticks, I relaxed into my enjoyment of the game. "You see," said Hicks, pointing at the tangled heap of sticks, "that's what you hair looks like." He ruffled my hair. "You should use Brylcreem."

"My mother says Brylcreem is common," I blurted out, then realized that Hicks himself probably used Brylcreem. But he just smiled. "Your mother the Bus?" he asked.

"My mother's not a Bus," I muttered.

"She's Afrikaans, isn't she?"

"Yes," I said. 'But that doesn't make her a Bus."

"That's exactly what does make her a Bus too," he rejoined. "But I'll say that for your mother, she doesn't look like an Afrikaner. I saw her when they brought you to school."

"What do Afrikaners look like?" I asked.

"Like Buses," he said, and rolled over on his back kicking his feet in glee. Hicks was quite a funny-looking boy, very tall and thin with teeth that stuck out, and very green eyes and a lopsided smile and a raucous laugh quite at odds with his slight frame. He was an excellent cricket player, which struck me, fresh from Verkeerdespruit, as almost exotic in its strangeness. "I'm just growing into my strength," he said. "I spent my first fifteen years growing up and now I'll catch up with myself. I'm very strong really. Wiry is what they call me. If anybody tries to bully you, come and tell me. I'll sort him out."

"Thank you," I said, not entirely convinced of his protective powers, but grateful for the offer anyway. "But nobody has tried to bully me so far."

"Oh, they will," he said cheerfully. "As soon as you have something that they want."

After this I went to visit Hicks quite often in his study. For some reason Gott found this objectionable. "It is not right for you to visit an older boy," he said. "There are ranks of boys at school. You should not step out of your rank."

Cavalla rolled his eyes and started goose-stepping up and down the dormitory doing Heil Hitler salutes and shouting, "Step in rank there! *Achtung!*" Gott hit him.

Wesley College was probably as benign as a boys' school ever can be. "Floggings are few and lynching is discouraged," Hicks explained to me solemnly and not very reassuringly. The headmaster, the Reverend Mr. Robinson, was a rather remote, gloomy-looking person who sighed often, but in a fairly kindly way, as if he pitied us for being alive, Things Being as They Are. He had been a chaplain in the Royal Navy but had sent back his rank to the queen, so Miss Smithers told us, when South Africa left the Commonwealth — "as an expression of his sense of complicity in his country's crime." He seemed vague about our names and called everybody "boy." He wrote letters to *The Friend* about The Way Things Are. Cavalla said he was a Liberal. Gott asked him what this was, and I said, "My father says Liberals are people who hate the Afrikaners more than they fear the blacks."

"I don't like the Afrikaners, and I'm not scared of the blacks," said Gott. "Does that make me a Liberal?"

"Nothing could make you a Liberal," said Cavalla, and Gott hit him, though halfheartedly, as if unsure whether to feel complimented or insulted.

The most unfamiliar aspect of the new school to me was morning chapel. In Verkeerdespruit we'd had morning prayers in what served as the school hall (and also as the library and, when it rained, as the gymnasium), followed by a harangue on some aspect of our behavior that required correction or eradication, like discarding fish-paste sandwiches in the urinals or tying together two tufts of grass on the playground to trip up unwary runners. At Wesley we had Chapel four days a week, which was a less explicit affair altogether. There were scripture and prayers, of course, and a harangue, but the harangue was disguised as a sermon and tended not to identify our misdemeanors by name as much as by category: "certain irregularities in the cricket score box" meant the Sixth Form boys had been smoking, and "the disappearance of certain articles of clothing" meant that the Second Form boys had stolen socks off the line to practice French cricket after lights out in their dorm. Both practices were "distressing to your parents and offensive to God." On Mondays there was Assembly in the school hall rather than Chapel, because on Monday the weekend's sports results were announced, which could not be done in Chapel. When I asked Hicks why not, he said, "You don't think God is interested in hearing the score of the under-thirteen B hockey team, do you?" This was a novel idea to me: in Verkeerdespruit, to judge by the prayers sent up on Fridays and Mondays, God avidly followed the fortunes of the school's sole rugby team, to the extent that I had felt quite sorry for Him at the invariable defeat of His chosen team. The Methodist God, it seemed, was not interested in sport. I also learned that prowess at rugby was not by definition a Good Thing, for when we were beaten by a government school, Mr. Robinson pointed out that "Disappointing as the result was, it may have been in no small measure due to tactics on the parts of our opponents that no Wesley boy would willingly adopt merely for the sake of winning what is after all only a game." This baffling sentence was translated for me by Hicks as "He means that if you're not a Wesley boy you can only win by playing dirty."

Hicks was fond of music: he "took" it as a subject, which was another novelty to me after Verkeerdespruit, where "music lesson" meant singing, which is to say bawling everything, patriotic anthems and sentimental love songs alike, in exactly the same tone of belligerent enthusiasm, to the accompaniment of a very old piano that my mother said had probably fallen off the back of an ox wagon. Hicks had his own piano at home, he said, and he was having organ lessons after school hours. In his study he often had his little transistor radio tuned to such classical music as was available — a request program, perhaps, or a symphony concert. The other boys yowled in the background when they passed the cubicle, as implicit criticism of this affectation of Hicks's. He just smiled and said, "If you give a baboon anything he doesn't understand and can't eat, he'll piss on it to make it smell of himself." To my surprise Gott, not self-evidently a musical soul, took umbrage at what he regarded as the boys' disrespect to Culture: "What do South Africans know about music and culture?" he declaimed. I asked him if he wasn't a South African and he said no, his grandfather had come from Germany.

It transpired that Gott in fact had an impressive voice, and the organist and choirmaster, a small round man known as Meatball, coerced him into the school choir by persuading Mr. Moore, the rugby coach, to tell Gott that if he didn't sing in the choir he couldn't play in the rugby team either. I suspect Gott was only pretending to be reluctant to be in the choir; once there, he was certainly prominent enough as one of the few authentic baritones, and also for his ferocious scowl. The other boys, although hardly of seraphic mien, did manage to seem at least vaguely civil; but Gott bellowed "Nor shall my sword sleep in my hand" with truly

212

terrifying countenance. "That is splendid, Krause," Meatball, who was a mild man, once said to Gott, "but perhaps your delivery could be more joyful and less bloodthirsty." Cavalla said Gott probably didn't know the difference between joyful and bloodthirsty, and Gott hit him.

Gott, I suspect, secretly enjoyed his prominence in the choir. He condescended now and then to discuss the finer points of his technique with Hicks, but by and large affected a manly indifference to his own performances. He did achieve a major success, though, at Easter, with his solo rendering of "The Trumpet Shall Sound," with Hicks accompanying him on the organ. To listen to Gott, said Meatball, was truly to make one fear the Last Judgement.

Gott objected to going to choir practice, on the grounds of the intolerability of the whining of the other boys, the quality of the music ("Those English hymns sound like sheep bleating"), and the lack of discipline in the choir. Meatball did not in fact have very much authority. There was a story in circulation that the choir boys had discovered a pair of black fishnet stockings in one of the organ pipes, which were immediately assumed, by an illogical leap of association, to have been hidden there by Meatball, though nobody could explain, as Hicks said, "why Meatball should have bunged up his own diapason pipe with a pair of stockings he couldn't have worn in Chapel anyway." But the story persisted, to undermine such authority as Meatball ever had.

My favorite teacher was the English mistress, Miss Smithers. She taught us a new word every day because, she said, "Education is a matter of knowing the names of things. The more names you know the better you will be able to control your environment — *en-vir-on-ment*, one's surroundings, the conditions influencing the development or growth of people, animals, and plants. What is your environment, Simon?"

Before I could produce an answer to this, Tim Watkins, the class captain, chipped in with "Ball-Bearings don't have environments, miss, only people, animals, and plants." The class obligingly sniggered.

"That's not funny, Tim, notwithstanding the puerile and obsequious response of your peers."

"What's puerile, miss?"

"Immature, childish, from the Latin *puer*, boy."

Tim scored a minor victory by not asking her the meaning of *obsequious*, though he couldn't have known; but Miss Smithers had the last word when she gave it to us in a spelling test. I was the only boy in the class who got it right.

Physical education, or phys ed, was a bit of a trial. Instead of the desultory jumps in the dust that had constituted Verkeerdespruit's attempt to keep our bodies as sound as our minds, we now had various pieces of apparatus to negotiate in an assortment of unnatural positions. I could not see the educational value of a forward roll, and, one day when it rained and the school hall was being painted and Mr. Moore, who was also our phys ed teacher, said we could discuss the Theory of Physical Education, I asked him what the point of a forward roll was. He said, "The point of a forward roll is to teach you to do things without asking what their point is. The function of education is to prepare you for life. Most people spend their lives doing things they don't know the point of. Therefore the forward roll is highly educational, exceeded in this respect only by the backward somersault."

In spite of this answer, which I suspected of not being wholly serious, I liked Mr. Moore. He seemed not to mind that I didn't play rugby; indeed, he coached both tennis and rugby, and used to tell us at tennis practice that if we didn't use our heads he'd put us in the rugby team where one didn't need a head. I felt smug about this until Gott announced that Mr. Moore had told the rugby team that if they were scared of the ball he'd put them in the tennis team where the balls were too small to scare anybody, or in the athletics team where you didn't need balls.

"And you don't need brains for any of them," said Cavalla. "That's why I prefer chess."

"Only sissies play chess," retorted Gott.

"If you mean rugby players are too thick for chess, you're right," said Cavalla, and left the room quickly before Gott could hit him.

My friendship with Hicks developed gradually from pick-up-sticks to other, more varied interests. Although at times the music he liked sounded rather tuneless and pointless to me, I grew to tolerate and even like some of it. Sometimes I went to hear him practice the organ in the chapel, and he tried to explain the difference between a major key and a minor key — "It's a bit like a color, only in music" — and I pretended to be able to hear the difference, although I was terrified that he would test me by asking me to name the key of an unidentified piece of music. But Hicks was too guileless himself to suspect duplicity in others, and quite happily took my word for it when I assured him I could "feel the major key" or "see the minor key."

Gott was entirely contemptuous of my attempts to acquire a musical education. "Music," he declared, "you either have in your soul or you do not have it at all. If your ancestors didn't have it you can't *get* it by trying hard. It is not like ... like growing potatoes or ... getting high marks in mathematics." This last was aimed at Cavalla, who was best in class at mathematics, which Gott affected to despise as a useless activity. Cavalla just shrugged and said, "I can't see the point of having music in your soul if you fart like a donkey," in reference to Gott's uninhibited flatulence.

The first six months of my stay at Wesley passed pleasantly enough. I had to get used to not being best in class at all my subjects, but this loss was balanced by the relief of not being regarded as a freak for reading books of longer than twenty pages, and by the pleasure of sometimes actually meeting somebody who had read the same books as I. Hicks was one such person; although not particularly studious, he read very fast and with complete concentration, so that he could read in an afternoon a book that had taken me a week. He was happy to discuss these with me while we were playing pick-up-sticks, although he had odd perspectives on some of them. When I discovered *Lord of the Flies* he said, "Oh yes, I read that one. It's the one about the pig *braai*."

"Well, I don't think the *braai* is the point," I objected.

"Isn't it?" he asked. "I thought it was. That's where all the shit starts, isn't it? When they *braai* the pig?"

"Yes," I said, "but ..."

"But what?"

"But that doesn't mean that it's about roasting pigs."

"What's it about then?"

"It's about good and evil and ... things like that."

"Yes. It was evil to roast the pig."

I sensed, vaguely and inarticulately, that Hicks and I moved at different levels of abstraction, but our friendship proceeded happily enough in spite of this discrepancy, not to mention the two-year difference in age, no negligible thing in the hierarchy-ridden environment of a boys' school. But Hicks seemed little concerned about things that agitated or excited the other boys. "Listen," he said one day when the school was in mourning after our cricket team had lost to St. Andrews, in spite of a heroic performance by Hicks himself, "Wesley is a minor school in a minor city in a minor country on one of the smaller planets of an unambitious solar system. What does it matter whether we beat another only slightly less minor school at a completely pointless activity? It's a mouse-fart in a cathedral." And he pounded away at the Bach he was practicing. "Now *this*," he said, pulling out a stop, "this *matters*."

Although I could not in all honesty pretend to share Hicks's passion for Bach, I found his priorities congenial, and his indifference to the pieties of schoolboys and teachers refreshing. During one of Mr. Robinson's more passionate appeals to us to be worthy of the confidence our parents had placed in us by sending us to Wesley, he dropped — accidentally, he afterward maintained — a table-tennis ball in the back row of the chapel, whence it hopped perkily and noisily but quite slowly and unignorably all the way to the altar, to settle there impertinently and impenitently. It utterly ruined Mr. Robinson's plea, the more so that he chose to deal with the distraction by saying in his sorrowful manner, "I would not have expected of a Wesley boy to bring balls into chapel," which caused a near riot of ill-suppressed snorts and guffaws. The following morning somebody placed a wastepaper basket outside the chapel door with a sign saying "Please deposit all balls here before entering." The sign was smartly removed by Mr. Chalmers, and Mr. Robinson wisely pretended not to have seen it.

With my ingrained respect for authority I found Hicks's irreverence breathtaking, disturbing, and thrilling at the same time. I could not imagine what it must be like really not to care what people thought or said about one; so much of my own sense of myself seemed made up of other people's opinions. I stood in awe of Hicks's indifference, and yet found it slightly irksome, as if it made my own anxieties and concerns seem petty, without liberating me into ignoring them.

Given this discrepancy in our attitudes to public opinion, the thing our friendship was least equipped to resist was publicity. And publicity we duly got. My first inkling of something untoward was Tim Watkins's making a face at me at break and saying, "What is this we hear about our Half-Ball?" and laughing with Clive Grayling in a manner that reminded me of Japie Dreyer and Tjaart Bothma's incomprehensible jokes at the back of the class. I tried to tell myself that Tim was probably just trying to make me feel uncomfortable, and I determined not to give him the satisfaction of showing that he had succeeded. But it was clear that I was exciting comment among the other boys too; I could see some of them pointing me out to others as they had pointed out Cedric Smith the month before when his mother had been in the *Sunday Times* for doing a striptease in a church hall in Harrismith and being raided by the police. The police had confiscated a half-empty bottle of cooking oil. To be in the same league of notoriety as Cedric Smith's mother and her bottle of Covo seemed to me as unbearable as it was unmerited and inexplicable. I would rather have ignored the whole business, but it's difficult to maintain a dignified detachment if one suspects that one has, in a manner of speaking, a donkey's tail pinned to the back of one's pants. It occurred to me that Cavalla was usually well-informed on any school intrigues, without taking part in the concomitant slaughter of the innocents and the not-so-innocent.

At break I approached him where he was sitting in the sun with the miniature chessboard he always carried with him.

"Why are Watkins and Grayling laughing at me?" I asked without any preliminaries. Cavalla tended to prefer to approach things in a more roundabout way ("When people try to rush you into anything it's usually because they don't want you to think about what you're doing," he said), but I wasn't in a state to negotiate the matter as if it were a nonaggression pact.

Cavalla was not to be rushed. He checkmated himself, or at any rate made some move that seemed to satisfy him. "Well," he said, "have you had a pee this morning?"

"Yes, of course," I said. "When I got up."

"But not since coming to school?"

"No, but what does that have to do with anything?"

"Just go and have a pee and look around you," he said.

Mystified, I went into the urinal and unzipped my fly and looked around me. At first I saw nothing out of the ordinary — bubble-gum wrappers, used Band-Aids, and smoke emanating from the last cubicle where Watson Senior was known to enjoy his smoke break. Everybody knew about this, including, presumably, Mr. Robinson; but in keeping with his policy of noninterference he did nothing about it, and there was something forlorn about Watson Senior's defiance of an authority that gave no indication of feeling itself defied. Certainly that could not have been what Cavalla meant. There was fortunately nobody else around, so I could inspect the place at my leisure — and there, in large crude capitals on the wall above the urinal, somebody had announced to the world: "Half-Ball helps Hicks with his organ practice."

This seemed only cryptic to me. Why would anybody think my attendance at Hicks's organ practice a fact worth advertising? At the same time I was acutely embarrassed to have my name emblazoned in such a place, but, terrified to draw attention to it by being discovered trying to rub it out, I left as quickly as possible.

The school was equipped to deal with scrawls on walls; Jeremiah, the all-round odd-job man, had a bucket of whitewash at the ready to expunge any illicit markings, and my fame duly went the way of all the markings of my predecessors. I might have remained in my state of slightly puzzled innocence, had a boys' school been a congenial medium for slightly puzzled innocence. But the anonymous scribe, no doubt disappointed at the lack of impact of his first venture, improved upon it by writing, more concisely but in even larger capitals: "Half-Ball practices on Hicks's organ."

After a first shock of incomprehension ("Why on earth should anybody think I'd been practicing the *organ*?"), even I recognized the blatant enough wordplay; and I smarted and blushed not just for the crude accusation but also for my naive unawareness of the implications of the first declaration. The worst of it was that there was nobody to talk to about it; the first effect of the accusation was to make me realize that normally I would have discussed that kind of thing with Hicks, but now that was out of the question, since my friendship with him had abruptly lost its un-self-conscious ease, and had itself become the point at issue. All I could do was cringe and wait for Jeremiah with his bucket, and pretend not to have noticed.

To my surprise, Cavalla broached the subject. "I wouldn't worry about it," he said to me one afternoon soon after the second announcement, as we were cleaning our shoes in the dormitory for cadet practice the next day, the school's sole concession to Youth Preparedness. We practiced drilling, but rifles were taboo. We were naval cadets, presumably in deference to Mr. Robinson's naval past, in spite of the fact that, as Hicks said, "half the boys haven't seen the sea and the other half wouldn't know what to do with it if they saw it." Still, we were proud of our white uniforms, so unlike the drab khaki stuff issued to government schools.

"About what?" I asked, though I had been thinking about nothing else all day.

"You know — the writing on the wall." This was very direct for Cavalla.

"Oh that. No, I'm not worried about that."

"Yes, you are. You've been shining the same shoe for the last twenty minutes."

"I don't want to get into trouble tomorrow for not having clean shoes."

"Then you should polish the other one as well. The person who wrote on the wall … is, you know, not a very nice person."

"How do you know?"

"How do I know? Do you think a very nice person would write things like that on walls?"

"No. But I thought you meant you knew who it was."

"No, I don't," he said.

"Yes, you do."

"If I did I wouldn't tell you. But I don't know."

"You can guess."

"If I guessed it wouldn't be fair to tell you. I could be wrong. Besides, why do you want to know? What would you do if you knew?"

"I'd go to him and ask him what it was to him what I did or didn't do with Hicks's organ." I tried to sound casual about it but it came out, I thought, very awkwardly.

But Cavalla just nodded as he spat on the tip of his shoe. "He couldn't tell you. He probably doesn't know himself."

"How do you know?" I challenged him, irritated at his calm assumption of knowledge.

"I don't *know*. I said *probably*. But my father has told me about people who want to make other people suffer."

"What does your father know?"

"He knows about people who make other people suffer. He says we must believe that most people don't know what they're doing, otherwise we must believe that they are monsters."

"So what?" I said. "Perhaps they are monsters. I bet the person who wrote that on the wall about me is a monster."

"Well, then," Cavalla said, "you should know who it is. Just think of somebody you know who is a monster."

I considered this for a moment, but although there were people I didn't like, like Tim Watkins, there was nobody who seemed actually *monstrous*. I shook my head.

"See?" he said. "You don't know any monsters. So the person who wrote that isn't a monster, just a human being like you or me."

"Speak for yourself," I said.

Helpless to do anything about an accusation that seemed to come from nowhere and have no reason for existence, I decided to confine its power as much as possible by avoiding Hicks. Or rather, I did not decide this in so many words; I just tried to avoid him without explaining to myself why I was doing so. But he was not a person who was easy to avoid: he was much too direct for that.

"Well, young Half-Ball," he said, "I see somebody's been saying things about us."

"Yes," I muttered, not sure how to respond.

"Does it bother you?" he asked; and then as I hesitated, "I suppose it does. It bothers me too, because it's a damn nuisance, but in the end, if you think about it, it's just somebody who's jealous of us, and that's a sort of compliment, isn't it?"

"I don't know," I said, not really convinced.

"Well, I know," he said. "So don't let it bother you. After all, so what if somebody has a problem with your chatting to me while I practice? It's just baboon-piss again."

But here too I couldn't adopt Hicks's pragmatic interpretation. I was particularly sensitive to the accusation, after my encounter with the stranger in Bleshoenderbaai. I was haunted by the fear that somehow somebody would find out what I had done; and the announcement on the urinal wall suggested that somebody had at least a suspicion. So I stopped drifting into the chapel when Hicks was practicing, and even stopped going to his study for pick-up-sticks. Direct as he was, he was also too tactful or too proud to say anything. He remained cheerful, and stopped to talk to me when he saw me, but he never said, "Come for pick-up-sticks" as he used to, or "See you in Chapel." So I effectively stopped seeing him, though I walked past his study quite often. There were no more notices on walls after this.

In September of that year Dr. Verwoerd was stabbed to death in the House of Assembly. Wesley College took note of the fact, as it could hardly avoid doing, though the note was hardly an unambiguously elegiac one. Mr. Robinson's address in Chapel on the morning after the assassination seemed to regret mainly the fact that the whole cabinet hadn't been assassinated. "We must deplore," he said, "the violent means chosen by the assassin to express his dissatisfaction, nay, his hatred of a man who to many has come to stand for everything that is evil in this country, who has by many been held largely responsible for the way things are.

But we must remember that he was only one man, and that one man has a limited potential for both good and evil. Dr. Verwoerd is dead, but the principles that he professed are very much alive. While deploring, as I have said, the means chosen by the assassin, we must in our own way continue to resist those principles."

As Hicks said, pausing outside Chapel to strike up a conversation, "He means that we mustn't think we can relax just because Verwoerd is dead." I nodded, still slightly awkward at being seen talking to him, and went to my dormitory to change into "after school" dress. The day had been declared a holiday — or rather, a national day of mourning, but to us that simply translated into no school. After the chapel service we were left free to pursue what Mr. Robinson called "constructive leisure of a quiet kind, so as not to offend our neighbors. You may wear Number Threes." Number Threes were the least formal of our uniforms, and consisted of a short-sleeved shirt and shorts with running shoes. It was the uniform we wore for sport, but "leisure of a quiet kind" ruled out sport; indeed it ruled out almost everything except reading and pick-up-sticks. The latter of these was no longer an option for me — besides, I noticed that Hicks wasn't in his study — and even reading seemed a bit flat on this windy September morning. I thought that Hicks would probably be practicing organ; the short conversation with him that morning had left me feeling that perhaps I had been a bit rude to him, and I might just go and sit with him for a few minutes while he practiced, to show that I wasn't angry with him.

The decision cheered me up surprisingly, and after changing into my Number Threes I skipped across the lawn to the chapel, which was kept open at all times to encourage us, as Mr. Robinson said, to give ourselves a space to think in and to be alone with God. Cavalla said it was typical of Christians to try and be pally with God, and that Jews wouldn't presume to take such liberties with Him: the Jewish God wasn't interested in people feeling sorry for themselves. In practice few boys availed themselves of this privilege, so I did not expect to find anybody in the chapel, except Hicks practicing.

But as I pushed open the swing door there was no sound of the organ briskly pumping away under Hicks's energetic hands and feet. I felt strangely disappointed, and stood still for a moment, wondering whether I should go somewhere else to look for him. While I was considering, I heard a sound from the vestry. It was a very slight sound, but I thought it might be Hicks on one of his tours of exploration — he was insatiably curious — and I walked closer. The vestry also had a swing door, but the two halves didn't meet exactly, and there was a slit through which it was possible to peer.

I'm not quite sure what made me do so, but instead of opening the door I leaned forward and peeped through the slit in the door. I recognized Hicks almost immediately, though he was standing with his back to me. His shorts were round his ankles, his long thin legs and his white buttocks exposed under the short tail of his shirt. He was facing somebody, with whom, it was clear from his posture and actions, he was doing the thing that I had done with my stranger in Bleshoenderbaai. I watched, appalled. Hicks seemed to have his left hand around the back of the other boy's neck and his right hand was moving faster and faster, while his buttocks were contracting and relaxing, contracting and relaxing in a rhythm whose outcome I now knew. The other boy's hand reached round Hicks's back and under his shirt. They were both breathing very fast. Hicks's buttocks twitched sharply and started jerking spasmodically; the breathing was now so loud that I felt no danger in changing my position to get a better view.

"Jeeez!" Hicks cried, and he leaned forward over the other boy, who was quite a bit shorter than he. He stood like that, panting; the other boy removed his hand from Hicks's back. Hicks's body relaxed. The two bodies moved apart, but they stood still facing each other. For a while there was just the sound of their racing breaths, and then the other boy said, "I have gone all over the place," and I recognized Gott's unmistakable baritone.

"Wipe yourself with a choirboy's gown," said Hicks, giggling, still out of breath. "They probably do it all the time themselves."

"No, thank you. I have been taught always to use a clean handkerchief," said Gott.

"Jeez, you mean you've had lessons in wiping up gizm?"

"No, I mean I have been taught personal hygiene." He sounded offended, probably by Hicks's aspersion on the habits of choirboys.

I didn't stay to hear what method of purification was agreed upon; I turned around and ran out of the chapel with no attempt not to be heard, ran without really knowing where I was going until I found myself in the bicycle shed behind the school hall. Here I paused and waited to recover my breath. I was trembling, but I couldn't tell why. I felt a mixture of things: a kind of shame at what I had seen, but also a strange excitement; and anger, and resentment of Hicks, and hatred of Gott, the shame and anger and excitement and resentment and hatred all mixed up with one another in a conviction that I never wanted to see Hicks again and yet had to see him immediately in order to tell him so.

In my experience, any irregular situation was eventually sorted out by an adult. I had not always enjoyed the means found by adult authority to restore order, but in this instance the consequences would be visited upon Hicks and Gott; I would surely be on the side of right in reporting them. Also, doing that sort of thing in a chapel clearly had religious implications, which could best be handled by a religious expert like Mr. Robinson. Besides, I wanted Hicks to be punished.

Mr. Robinson's house stood on the school grounds; the Garden of Remembrance doubled as his own garden and was tended by his wife, a flustered-looking, pink-cheeked woman known to the boys as Dotty Robinson. Mr. Robinson's study had a door into the main corridor of Milner House, and we were encouraged to regard it as "always open to anybody in need of support or advice," although I had never actually seen it open.

I paused for a moment outside the heavy wooden door. My first excitement had abated somewhat, and I wasn't quite sure what I was going to say to Mr. Robinson. But I assumed that he would take charge of the situation once I had conveyed to him the nature of the atrocity committed in his chapel.

I knocked at the door, but the wood was solidly unresonant, and I had no way of knowing whether my timid knock had penetrated it. So I waited for a while and then, using four fingers instead of just the knuckle of my index finger, rapped on the door in what I hoped was a firm and assertive manner. The door opened almost immediately; Mr. Robinson must have heard my first knock after all.

He removed his glasses and looked down at me. He had little round brown eyes that gave him an air of surprise; or perhaps he really was surprised that somebody should actually have knocked at his study door.

"Yes, boy?" he said. "Can I help you?"

"Yes, sir," I said. "Please, sir, there's something I have to tell you."

"Come in, then," he said, and opened the door for me to enter. I had never been into Mr. Robinson's study before, and I was astounded at its size. It had a huge brick fireplace with two easy chairs in front of it. Mr. Robinson walked to his desk, a massive mahogany structure in one corner, and gestured me toward a chair facing his swivel chair. Behind him on the wall hung a picture of the queen. Below it on a bookshelf was a tasteful etching of Christ, obviously distressed, but with no gashes or thorns or Catholic agonies, just well-bred reproachful Methodist self-sacrifice.

"Sit down," Mr. Robinson said, and I did so. The radio was on, broadcasting yet another speech extolling the virtues of our dead prime minister. Mr. Robinson seemed to be listening to the speech and to have forgotten about me; but after a while he looked up at me, sighed, and said, "With Verwoerd gone, all we have to look forward to is Vorster, God help us." I must have looked at him in some puzzlement because he drew himself together, smiled vaguely, and said, "Never mind about that, boy. Why did you want to see me?"

"I ... I ... saw something today that I think I must tell you about," I said.

"Yes, my boy?" he said. "Is it something that upset you?"

"Oh, no," I lied, "it's just that I don't think it's right."

He seemed lost in thought again, and I wondered whether he'd heard what I'd said. "I ... I thought I should tell you what I saw," I said, in an effort to repeat what I'd said without appearing to do so, in case he had after all been listening. He startled me by breaking out of his trance, leaning forward and fixing me with his small but sharp brown eyes. "You've come to inform on one of your friends?" he almost snapped. This was not very encouraging, but I had to carry on now.

"No," I said. "Or yes. Or no, it's not one of my friends. It's Richard Hicks."

"Hicks in Fourth Form?"

"Yes, sir," I said.

"Fine young cricket player," he said, in a tone that disconcertingly seemed to conclude the conversation.

"Yes, sir," I said again. "I ... I saw him in chapel this afternoon."

He looked puzzled. "Playing cricket?"

"No, sir. You see, sir ... he wasn't alone, sir."

He looked at me and sighed. "Are you trying to tell me that Hicks was committing an indecency?"

"Yes, I think so." There was something disconcerting about the way Mr. Robinson seemed to be able to anticipate my information.

"You think so? Aren't you sure?"

"Please sir, what's an indecency?"

He sighed again. "I'm not sure I can define it for you, it means such different things to different people. But let's say it probably means, in this context, any form of sexual behavior." He seemed to drift off into his own thoughts again. On the radio somebody was saying, "And oh Lord, may this country arise from its grief with renewed determination to combat the forces of evil." Mr. Robinson spoke softly, as if talking to himself: "I have often wondered whether it is a lack of respect or an excess of awe that makes the chapel so ... exciting to our boys." Then suddenly he leaned forward again and said in a much sharper tone: "With whom?" As I stared at him blankly, he said, "You said that Hicks was indulging in sexual behavior with somebody else?"

"Oh. Yes, sir. With Gott, sir."

He leaned back in his chair, looked at me over his glasses, pressed the tips of his fingers together and sighed heavily. "You saw Hicks committing an indecency in the chapel with ... *God*?" he asked.

I was shocked. "Oh no," I said. "With *Gott*. Gottlieb Krause. He's in my dormitory."

"Young Krause? Fine young rugby player." He seemed about to start pondering Gott's qualities as a rugby player, but as abruptly as before he leaned forward again and asked me, "But what exactly were Hicks and Krause doing?"

"Well, as you said, sir, er … indulging in …"

He relapsed into his ruminative mode. "Yes, but you see, or possibly you don't, there are various kinds of sexual behavior, and perhaps somewhat illogically we discriminate degrees of seriousness. Perhaps you can just give me some … er … indication of the general nature of the activity."

One of the educational advantages of living in a boys' hostel was that I was no longer at a loss for names for things that six months earlier didn't have names for me. Certain practices were much referred to, though of course only as the kind of thing that others, hilariously, indulged in. Thus I had at my disposal a rich vocabulary of suppressed prurience; the only difficulty was selecting a term proper to the occasion. Bullying the Bishop obviously wouldn't do, and Polishing the Pulpit might be misleading in this context. "Yes, sir," I said. "They were Punishing Percy."

He looked grave. "Really? That is serious." He paused for a moment. "Percy who?"

"No, not like that," I stammered. "They were … you know, sir, milking their lizards." As he still looked at me blankly I added: "Pulling pudding, sir. You know, beating …"

"Yes, yes, yes," he said, holding up his hand. "No need to go on. I assume you are referring to mutual masturbation. Is that right, boy?"

"Yes, sir. I think so, sir."

"You think so? Don't you know?"

"I know what they were doing, sir, but I don't know what you mean by … mutual … maturation, sir."

"Right. I'm assuming that the boys involved were touching each other's persons?"

"Yes, sir."

"Were they facing each other?"

"Yes, sir."

"And were all four of their feet on the floor?"

"Yes, sir."

"Were their heads at the same level relative to the floor?"

I considered. "No, sir."

"No?"

"No, sir. Hicks is much taller than Gott, sir."

"Of course. I mean allowing for the natural difference in height, were their heads in the same position relative to their bodies?"

"Yes, sir." I was now thoroughly bewildered but guessed that an affirmative would let me off further questions.

"And they touched each other's persons in that position until the process reached its ... natural terminus?"

This was obscure, but I was learning fast. "Yes, sir. They ... came all over the place, sir." I considered telling him about the choirboy's cassock, but realized that I couldn't say with absolute certainty that it had been used for the purpose Hicks had suggested.

He nodded, apparently satisfied. "Yes. Mutual masturbation. It is of course a serious misdemeanor but not, I am thankful to say, of the first degree of iniquity. In the Royal Navy it used to be called Plain Sewing."

"Plain Sewing, sir?" I said, not knowing what else to say.

"Yes," he said, "in reference, I imagine, to its relatively un-complicated nature."

I felt like somebody who had reported an earthquake, only to be told that it was a relatively uncomplicated effect of the earth's motion. I felt cheated by Hicks and Gott's lack of initiative — their Plain Sewing was paling into insignificance compared with unimaginably exotic enormities of the first degree of iniquity, orgies of intricate embroidery, performed with the participants' feet in midair and their heads levitating in acrobatic relation to the rest of their bodies. So I dumbly waited for Mr. Robinson to go on. But he just sat staring in front of him, apparently lost in thought again, unaware of me. Then once more he leaned forward suddenly and fixed me with his little round brown eyes. "Now tell me, boy," he demanded, "what is it that you expect me to do with this information that you've brought me?"

"Do with it?" I asked, taken aback. In my experience adults *knew* what to do with information, without asking advice from children. "I don't know, sir."

"You don't know?" he said. "You come and deliver this information to me and then tell me you *don't know* what you want me to do with it?"

I was now completely confused. "Yes. I mean no. I mean ..."

"You mean you just wanted to get your friends into trouble?"

I shook my head dumbly.

"Well, let me tell you the kind of trouble you've got them into," he said. "Hicks, because he is the older, will be assumed to have led young Gottfried ..."

"Gottlieb," I muttered.

"Young Krause into sexual misconduct."

"Oh but. ..." I broke in. He held up his hand. "Don't interrupt. You will be given an opportunity to put your point of view. It will be assumed that young Krause was the innocent party, and he will be talked to very seriously and warned about such matters and sent back to the dormitory he shares with you. Hicks, on the other hand, will be expelled."

"Ex ...?"

"Expelled. Kicked out. Sent home in disgrace."

I looked at him dumbly.

"Have you told anybody else about this incident?" he asked.

"No, sir."

"Nobody at all?"

"No, sir."

"No?"

"I mean yes, sir. I told nobody at all."

He looked at me pensively. Then he said, "I'm going to give you a choice." He stopped, as if that were all that he wanted to say, and I wondered whether he was waiting for me to thank him. But he carried on. "If you promise that you'll tell nobody what you saw today, I'll speak to Hicks and Krause, and tell them to refrain from further indecencies inside the chapel and out of it."

Again he looked at me expectantly. I wanted to shout *but that's not why I came to you, for you to let Hicks and Gott go, I came to you to punish them.* But Mr. Robinson was continuing, talking very slowly and clearly: "On the other hand, if you cannot give me such an undertaking and you tell anybody, anybody at all …" — he took off his glasses and tapped them lightly on the massive desk — "… even somebody who swears to you that he'll tell nobody else, then word will spread very quickly, and the parents of the other boys will demand that Hicks be expelled. The choice will then be out of your and my hands. But for the time being it is your choice." He put his glasses on and looked at me sternly.

I thought of Hicks practicing to become a brain surgeon. Then I thought of Wesley College without Hicks.

"Couldn't you expel Gott and keep Hicks?" I asked.

"I'm afraid justice is not a means of getting rid of people we don't like, boy, notwithstanding the example of our government," he said.

I sat in indecision. I had wanted to punish Hicks and now I had been given the power to punish him beyond my wildest imagination. I wished that it were possible to punish him just a little, and then to show mercy and be thanked for it. And then I thought that perhaps Hicks deserved to be expelled, not so much for what he had done with Gott as for what he had done to me. He had exposed me to the gossip of the school, and then he had gone and done with somebody else what I was accused of doing with him, and what I would be proved to have been innocent of if it became known that Hicks and Gott had done mutual masturbation together. Obscurely, too, it seemed to me that my own sexual misdemeanor, as I now knew it to be, would in some measure be expiated by my delivering these other miscreants over to justice.

"I don't know, sir," I said.

"What is it you don't know, boy?"

"I don't know if I … I can give you my word."

"Oh," he said. "Why not?"

"Isn't it dishonest, sir? To hide something you know?"

"It is not the whole truth, certainly. But a certain humane

230

suppression may be less offensive to God than the relentless pursuit of truth."

This argument was beyond me. My mystification must have been written on my face, for he shrugged and said, "Let it pass. What you are telling me is that you think it your duty not to suppress your knowledge of Hicks and Krause's misdemeanor."

This sounded like a respectable sort of opinion to have, and I nodded.

"You are sure?"

I nodded again.

He sighed, and started talking in his private way to himself again. "There is a famous experiment," he said, "in which a group of people were told that they could control the intensity of an electric shock administered to people whom they could see behind glass. The object of the experiment, they were told, was to see how much pain human beings could stand. They were told to increase the current steadily, in spite of the obvious suffering of the people on the other side of the glass. In fact, of course, there was no current, and what was being tested was their willingness to obey commands, even when to do so visibly caused distress to others. The experiment was intended to explain how deference to authority could have caused people to do the unthinkable, like execute the commands to kill millions of victims in the Nazi death camps. Do you understand that, boy?"

"Yes, sir, I think so, sir." In fact I had absolutely no notion what he was getting at, but I didn't want him to explain in any more detail.

"Well," he said, "my own theory is that what the experiment proves is rather that, given the power to hurt or harm other people, people will use that power only because they have it."

Then once again his manner changed from the detached, abstracted air of somebody thinking to himself, and with a kind of eagerness that oddly reminded me of Mr. de Wet at the moment of striking, he leaned forward again and said, "Your response to the choice I gave you supports my theory. I put no pressure on you to harm your friends; it was enough to give you the power. If a boy of — how old are you, boy?"

"Thirteen, sir."

"If a boy of thirteen is prepared to betray his friends just because he has the power to do so, is it any wonder that things are the way they are out there?" and he gesticulated to the radio, which was still broadcasting the grief of the nation at the loss of its leader. I sat transfixed, staring into his eyes. "Is it, boy?" he asked again.

"I ... I ... no, sir," I said, though I had no idea what I was saying. I had a startled sense that the blame for Things Being as They Are had abruptly shifted from Dr. Verwoerd and the Nazis to me.

"I gave you the choice," he continued, "because I believe that it is better to appeal to a boy's own sense of responsibility than to force or threaten him. But your choice leaves me no choice. This country has enough spies and informers without our schools breeding them too. I shall not tolerate telltales at my school. If you're unhappy with that, you can go to one of the many schools where you will be rewarded for informing on your friends and comrades. But if you stay here, and if I hear anything again about this incident, anything whatsoever, from whatever source, I'll know that you are responsible, and I'll punish you. I'll punish you in ways that only you and I will be aware of, but I promise you that you *will* be aware of them; and if anybody should ask about this, your parents for instance, I shall deny your story. I will be believed and you will not. Do you have anything to say, boy?"

"No, sir." I felt as if I had been run over by a bus that I had in good faith been trying to board. I must have looked very miserable, for his manner became less stern.

"I don't think you are an evil boy," he said almost gently. "But you have grown up in an evil society and you must be taught that it is evil."

"Yes, sir," I said.

"And the best way to recognize evil is to acknowledge its presence in oneself," he continued.

"Yes, sir."

"No, sir," he snapped suddenly, "you do not understand what I'm telling you. But one day you may, and I pray that it will help you. The reason for Things Being as They Are is seldom deliberate evil — it is lovelessness." He paused, while I stared at him blankly. "And there are as many forms of lovelessness as of love," he continued, more pensively again. "And I sometimes think that lovelessness is just the desire for love gone wrong. Aren't you ... the boy who came to us from ... Verneukpan?"

"Verkeerdespruit, sir."

"Yes, yes," and he waved aside the difference between Verneukpan and Verkeerdespruit. "The point is that your ... background has taught you to regard evil as normal. I want you to recognize it for what it is."

"Yes, sir."

"Do you have any questions, boy?"

"No, sir."

"Well, then. I trust that you have learned something from this unfortunate incident." He looked at me expectantly.

"Yes, sir," I said, since that was clearly what I was expected to say. I hoped that he would be content with this rather bare affirmation, but he was not.

"What?" he asked

"What ... what, sir?"

"What have you learned from this incident?"

I sat in dumb mystification, trying to think of something to say that would satisfy Mr. Robinson. He was looking at me as if he were preparing to pounce again. It did not occur to me that his question might actually have an answer; it seemed to me merely a trap: either he wanted me to say what he wanted to hear or he wanted to punish me for not saying what he wanted to hear. I felt that all I had learned was never again to go to Mr. Robinson for any reason whatsoever.

"Well, boy?" he asked, and something in the near eagerness with which he leaned forward reminded me again of Mr. de Wet interrogating a class of terrified children, reminded me of Mr. van der Walt trying to force me to say what he dreaded to hear, and of my stranger asking me all those questions that I thought meant that he was interested in me; and I thought of Cavalla saying people who ask you questions usually know the answer they want.

So when Mr. Robinson said again, "Well, boy? I'm waiting," I said, "Yes, sir, please, sir. I learned what Plain Sewing is."

December 6, 1968

In the stifling air of late afternoon I floated in the tepid water of the pool, deserted in spite of the heat: most of the boys were preparing in various ways for the evening's sociabilities. Since we had to wear our Number Ones, that is, our white shirts and gray flannels, there were shirts to iron for those too fussy to accept the standards of the school laundry (Mann and Scott, known as Mangle and Scorch), and perhaps even pants to press, though that was regarded as an affectation bordering on the suspect. Even those boys who scorned such refinements as newly ironed shirts were shining their shoes well beyond the level deemed adequate for daily inspection. As for me, I had no preparations to make, since I would be attending the film unaccompanied.

I drifted in the pool for a long time, long enough, as I judged, to give the Clutch Plates time to return to their proper medium, taking Fanie van den Bergh with them forever. I took my time dressing, reluctant to return to the stifling dormitory, and yet vaguely restless in the chlorinated seclusion of the pool. Crossing the lawn at last to my dormitory, I was dismayed to see the Combi still parked in front of Milner House. The Clutch Plates, freshly showered and dressed in their school uniforms, were sprawled on the lawn, looking bored. Fanie saw me and jumped to his feet.

"I was looking for you," he said.

"I was swimming," I replied.

"Yes, it's hot," he said, and relapsed into a Fanie silence.

"I must go and get dressed," I said. "I suppose you'll be on the point of leaving."

"No." He shook his head. "Mr. Sanders says we're staying for the evening. He and your teacher have gone to have a beer somewhere."

I felt an irrational irritation. Mr. Moore knew how we felt about the Clutch Plates; he had no business to impose them upon us for the evening. But for the time being my first concern was extricating myself from the inarticulate solicitation of Fanie van den Bergh.

"You must excuse me," I said. "I have to go and get dressed."

"Yes," he nodded happily. "I'll see you later. We're going to see a film."

"I know," I said gloomily and left. I could have decided not to go to the film. But somehow I still stopped short of a certain level of rudeness to Fanie: whereas his vulnerability infuriated me, it also inhibited me — and then infuriated me even more for inhibiting me. So I refrained from hurting him and resented him for making me refrain.

I made my getaway to the dormitory that I shared with Cavalla. Cavalla was polishing his shoes.

"Listen," I said to him, "you must go the film with me tonight."

"Why?" he asked. "Are you scared of the Nazis or of Julie Andrews?"

"Neither," I replied, "but there's this chap, one of the Clutch Plates, who was at school with me in Verkeerdespruit, and he seems to want to attach himself to me for the evening."

"And why is that such a terrible prospect? You're not otherwise accompanied, are you?"

"He's … you know, rather simple."

"Is that a problem?"

"Well, yes. He's not, you know, exactly good company."

"And he finds you good company?"

"He seems to, though heaven knows why. It's not as if I've ever given him much to like me for."

"You must have given him something, otherwise he wouldn't like you."

"I told you he was simple."

"And I'm supposed to protect you against the simplicity of your Verkeerdespruit past?"

"Well, you can just keep me company so that he can't slobber all over me like a … like a Labrador puppy."

"I'm not sure that I'd have done that even if I could. I think it's time you confronted your origins." He spat on his shoe and polished it carefully. Cavalla could be maddening at times. "But it turns out I can't. I'm partnering Helen Murdoch."

"What!" I exclaimed. Helen Murdoch was supposed to be the prettiest girl in Victoria Girls: she had blue eyes, freckles, and real breasts. "You're taking Helen Murdoch?"

"You needn't be so unflatteringly astonished. She may prefer brain cells to mere muscle."

"From what I've heard of Helen Murdoch she wouldn't recognize a brain cell if she found one floating in her porridge. But what I mean is I thought you wouldn't be seen dead in The Sound of Music."

"I would still prefer not to be seen dead in The Sound of Music," he replied, "but I'm running the risk as a favor for a friend." He paused for my question, but I wasn't going to give him that satisfaction, so he continued: "Peter Emery, if you must know."

"Why can't he go himself?" I asked, wondering to myself how Helen Murdoch was going to react to being claimed by a small, bespectacled, ironical, intelligent partner instead of the tall, broad, blunt, stupid Peter Emery; in short, Peter was what was regarded as a catch at the girls' school, whereas Cavalla was absolutely not.

"Can't you guess?" he asked, and spat on the other shoe. I should have known better than to expect a straightforward answer from Cavalla.

"No, I can't," I said. My humiliating defeat at the hands, as it were, of Fanie van den Bergh had driven most other circumstances from my mind. "Why don't you stop spitting on your shoe and tell me?"

"It's quite simple really," Cavalla said. "You know how hard the hall chairs are?"

"Of course I do."

"And you can't have forgotten why Peter Emery couldn't play tennis today."

"Of course not."

"Well, if he couldn't play tennis, how the hell do you expect him to sit through four hours of The Sound of Music? I mean, music hath charms to soothe the savage breast and all that, but there are limits to what it can do. So I have to sit through it for him. Greater love hath no man."

"You're not supposed to quote that," I said. "It's from the New Testament."

With Cavalla otherwise occupied, I had no option but to submit to Fanie's companionship, which he lost no time in imposing upon me

236

when I appeared at the school hall. After the public spectacle of my defeat I was not eager to appear in public with the victor. However sporting this might seem to a charitable observer, to me it appeared not unlike Macbeth having his head publicly displayed by Macduff, except that Macbeth was mercifully dead at the time. Fortunately the school hall had only two light settings, either blinding or pitch-dark, so once the film started I would be relatively anonymous.

The heat had steadily increased during the day, and was now at the point where the very air was crackling with static electricity. It was a dry, thundery night, building up to one of those storms that periodically relieve the heat and restore sanity to the Free State. But as yet it was oppressively hot and close, and the room was stifling. The unofficial but stringent rules of the occasion demanded that those boys without partners had to take the front seats in the hall, so as not to inhibit the partnered ones by their prurient and vociferous presence behind them. From my celibate's seat in the front rows I pitied the tightly packed rows of nominally courting couples, a miasma of aftershave lotion, teenage perfume, and pheromones, almost visibly steaming in the torrid atmosphere of lust, embarrassment, and honest sweat.

After a few false starts with the 35mm projector that had been specially hired for the occasion, the film got going, and a large and restive audience settled down to the idyllic atmosphere of Austria under the Anschluss. Mr. Chalmers discreetly padded up and down the aisle in his crepe-soled Hush Puppies, pretending to be checking whether the windows were open, but he needn't have bothered: any active display of passion in that atmosphere would have ended in heat exhaustion or asphyxiation. Besides, for all their posturing, most of the boys were secretly as much under the spell of the preposterously melodious Von Trapps as the most susceptible of the girls.

Fanie was enthralled, or so I assumed from his half-open mouth, which I remembered from Verkeerdespruit as his most vivid expression of emotion. A childhood in the smaller villages of the Free State had not equipped him with very much English, and he could not have followed even such elementary subtleties of dialogue as The Sound of Music *aspires to, but he was rapt. I was thankful that he seemed too engrossed to talk — or was until the* nuns came on. Then I could see from his slight frown that there was something puzzling him, and he turned to me and asked in a loud whisper, "Is hulle Roomse?" Are they Catholics?

"Yes, of course, Fanie," I said in a tone that tried to dissociate itself as much as possible from the question.

Now Fanie looked really unhappy, and I thought I knew why: I shared enough of his background to know that, in the popular mythology of paranoia that was called a primary education, Catholics were only slightly less sinister than Communists, and considerably more sinister than Nazis. He was clearly having problems processing a Catholic Julie Andrews. Then he turned to me, and there was relief written all over his face; he had solved the dilemma: "Is she running away from the nuns?" he asked.

I nodded, not wanting to commit myself too publicly to this interpretation, but not wanting needlessly to deprive him of this pacifying illusion either. The nod sufficed for Fanie, though, and he settled back happily; he could handle the nuns if they were the villains. He had some problems with Climb Every Mountain, which even he could recognize as Uplifting, but he solved that by deciding, as he told me in a loud and happy whisper, "The chief nun has been converted."

By this stage I had become uncomfortably aware of giggles behind me. Since most of the older boys had partners and were thus in the favored back rows, we were surrounded mainly by younger boys, who didn't even have the rudimentary politeness that in an English school does duty for consideration; they obviously found Fanie hilarious.

I was embarrassed, and furious with Fanie for exposing me to the callow giggles of the Second Formers, for implicating me in his Clutch Plate imbecility. But part of my anger, too, was directed at the mindless mockery of the boys, their scorning of a simplicity that they could not understand. It put me in mind again of Hicks's baboon-piss. But then again, this anger redirected itself at Fanie, for allowing himself to be the butt of the smart little boys behind him, for laying himself, and me too, open to the smug snobbery of privilege and the assumed superiority of a cultural tradition that had produced, as its crowning achievement, The Sound of Music.

And then again, part of me sided with the boys, wanted to be classed with them rather than paired with Fanie as a Ball-Bearing.

When it became unambiguously obvious, even to Fanie, that the Nazis were bad news for the Von Trapps, he seemed puzzled again, and I had just conceived the hope that his mystification might keep him silently occupied with his own thoughts, when he turned to me with an air of happy discovery and asked: "Did the nuns send the soldiers to fetch her back to the convent?" Although this version of the plot was no more intrinsically ridiculous than the real thing, our neighbors found Fanie's question sidesplittingly funny, all the more so, I suspected, because several of them were having problems with the plot themselves. Their hilarity was so loud and so sustained that even Fanie became aware of it. "Why are they laughing?" he asked.

The strain of the day, the disappointment of my defeat, the tension of hoping that Fanie wasn't going to disgrace me even further, the heat, the stuffiness, the embarrassment — all these suddenly overcame my restraint, and I knew only that I had to get out. Fortunately I was sitting on the aisle.

"They're laughing at you, you fool!" I said, and made my way out of the hall, past a worried Mr. Chalmers, past the rows of sweaty and intent couples. I didn't really know where I was going, but the relatively fresh air outside was a relief, and without really thinking about it, I sought out Mrs. Robinson's rose garden. The inane good cheer of The Sound of Music was still clearly audible from here, but it was more bearable when you didn't have to watch it as well. I took a deep breath. There wasn't much fresh air around, but it was like an alpine meadow compared with the atmosphere in the hall. The thunder muttered darkly in the distance. The smell of the roses was vaguely troubling, reminding me of something pushed back, out of reach of my daytime self, and yet demanding to be recognized.

There was a dim light over Mr. Robinson's front door, in which I must have been more visible than I knew, because I hadn't been there for five minutes when a shadowy figure came trundling toward me with what I recognized only too well as the deliberate gait of Fanie van den Bergh.

239

I was tempted to turn my back on him and leave, but some in-hibition prevented this. I simply stood, and Fanie came up and also simply stood, kicking the dust with the toe of his shoe. The smell of his sweat, innocent of the various volatile aromas the Wesley boys had hoped would subjugate the natural odors of their armpits, mingled with the scent of the roses. I thought he would ask me what I had meant, saying that the boys were laughing at him, but he did not. He said nothing for a good two minutes, and then, with more steadiness of voice than I was expecting, he said: "This after-noon, when all those other boys laughed at me …" He paused.

So he had noticed. "Yes."

"I didn't mind because …" He didn't mind?

"Because …?" Fanie had never been good with reasons.

"Because it doesn't matter if people laugh at me. But you …"

"But I …?" I felt like a teacher dragging answers out of a slow pupil.

"I'm sorry that you … you played badly so that I could win."

I took a moment to digest this novel interpretation of my defeat. At least it was more flattering than Gott's. "You think I deliberately played badly so that you could win?"

"Yes."

"Why would I do that?"

"I don't know." He shook his head, but he looked more self-assured than I had ever known him. "But I know you play better than that." He paused again. "I think perhaps you felt sorry for me."

"Why would I feel sorry for you?" I became aware of the scent of the roses, cloying in the heat.

"Because I'm … you know, not clever."

I didn't feel called upon to contradict this proposition. "And why would I feel sorry for you because you're not clever?"

"I don't know. I can't answer questions. But I wanted to say that you mustn't feel sorry for me, because it's not necessary. Steve told me …"

He stopped. The thunder rumbled again; a hot wind had come up, and the night was now unbearably close. From the open windows of the hall a sound of yodeling came oozing like treacle. The smell of the roses was almost overwhelming.

240

"Steve told you …?" I resented Fanie's bringing up the name of Steve again, as if he had some copyright on the sayings of Steve.

"… when they came to fetch him …"

"You were there?" It had never occurred to me that Steve would have been arrested in Fanie's presence.

He nodded. "Yes. I was staying with him. They took me back to Verkeerdespruit, but they brought him here … to Bloemfontein. And I was angry because the policeman said that you had told them where we were, and I said I … I hated you, but Steve said I shouldn't because you … you were jealous …"

"Jealous? Of you?"

"No, of Steve. That's what he said."

"Why would I be jealous of Steve?"

"Because you liked me, he said. He said I must remember that you like me and will look after me when he is gone."

"And you believed him?"

"Yes." Fanie's affirmation was as flat and incontrovertible as always, as confident in its blunt presumption as the most subtly argued oration. I had a sudden, stark vision of the wastes of love-lessness that could have made my perfunctory attentions figure as care or affection or anything remotely consoling to the various deprivations of Fanie van den Bergh. But the vision yielded to my annoyance with having to catechize Fanie on his quaint theories of my conduct. I had never given him reason to suppose that I regarded him as anything but a faintly irritating presence; and here, where I had thought I was safe from Verkeerdespruit and all its demeaning associations, he had followed me to confront me with his absurd claim.

Fanie was facing me in the dim light. He licked his lips and I could see him swallowing. His clumsy figure, with its uncoordinated assortment of arms, legs, and genitalia, embodied all the ineptitude of his youth and mine, its ignorance in the grip of processes and experiences it had not learned to understand or control. And yet he had a strange self-possession, too, that I found even more irksome than his abject deference.

"I don't feel sorry for you, Fanie," I said deliberately. "I've never felt sorry for you. Don't you know that I never even liked you? That from the day you first came to Verkeerdespruit you

241

were nothing but a nuisance to me? Don't you know that? Didn't I show you that in almost everything I did?"

In the dim light Fanie shook his head. "No," he said. "It's not true."

"It's not true? How do you know it's not true?"

"I don't know. I mean I don't know how I know. But I know you like me. Steve told me."

Steve had told him: his sole legacy to the boy who had worshipped him. "Steve is dead," I said. "You must believe me now."

"No."

"Then what must I do to convince you?"

He shook his head again. "Nothing," he said. "There's nothing you can do. Steve said you didn't know you liked me."

With the strange abruptness that I had seen only twice before, he smiled. And then, quite deliberately, he took my left hand in his right. It was surprisingly cool and firm; I had always imagined Fanie's hands as limp and damp. For a moment Fanie's hand in mine, trusting, imploring, reassuring — it was impossible to tell from its gentle pressure — made the whole terrible day fall into place, make sense, simplified into a kind of truce between my anxious present and that hungry past with which Fanie had confronted me so insistently all day, between the manifold betrayals of adulthood and the dumb gullibility of childhood. The offered hand asked, demanded, claimed nothing but to be accepted on its own terms, a pledge too inarticulate to betray or be betrayed.

Then I came to my senses and registered the enormity of Fanie's gesture, the peril of being found in the rose garden holding hands with a Clutch Plate. "You ... you ..." In my agitation I couldn't find the words for what I wanted to say. But my education came to my aid with a formula. "You Clutch Plate pervert," I said, pushing him out of the way.

In the dim light his pale blue eyes and his slightly open mouth seemed idiotic, completely vulnerable and very beautiful. I felt a vicious surge of pleasure in my groin and, closing my hand lightly, struck him under the chin as hard as I could. His eyes closed in pain as he bit his tongue.

242

"I … I … you … you …" he said, and licked his dry lips; there was blood on his tongue. Then he turned and ran into the night, across the school courtyard, in no direction at all.

A blaze of light froze the night into a brilliance devoid of shadow or nuance: objects seemed to emit light rather than absorb it, and motion was frozen as if by a giant photographic flash. An infinitesimal fraction of a second later the light exploded in a crack of sound that obliterated all other sensation, so that I did not know whether I was hearing light or seeing sound.

In the eruption of light and sound nothing seemed to move except the figure of Fanie running across the courtyard. He was eerily bathed in light, his blond hair shining light against light, his movements lighter and quicker than I had ever seen them. He ran and ran, and as a second bolt struck the earth, he stumbled and fell and crumpled to the ground. Then all the lights in the school buildings went out at once with a startled yelp from the Von Trapps, and for a moment there was absolute blackness and a terrible hush, and then voices and shouts and screams from the school hall, and I started running in the direction where I had seen Fanie fall. Another flash of lightning showed me Fanie's shape on the ground and I ran through the darkness and I thought of Dumbo and I knelt by Fanie and said, I'm sorry Fanie, Fanie please, I didn't mean for you to be struck by lightning, but the wind and thunder swallowed my words and I was dumb to tell Fanie how sorry I was. The lightning flickered across the walls, showing Fanie lying on his back, his eyes open, seeming to watch me. Then he closed his eyes and his body started contracting and relaxing, contracting and relaxing, contracting … Fanie was having a fit.

I knelt by him. I remembered that I must turn him on his side, but I was entranced by the rhythmic convulsion so impartially suggestive of an extremity of pleasure and a torment of pain, the blind face in its transport of oblivion; the frail body punishing itself in its fierce assault upon the earth, the image of all love under the spell of the passion it cannot tame or deny or even articulate. And as I knelt over Fanie van den Bergh the rain came. In the wind and the rain and the wide glare of the sky, I was enclosed, alone with Fanie. I put my hand over his mouth, wet with spittle and *blood and rain, and I searched for the separation of his clenched lips, forced open the contracting mouth, felt for a moment the mutely writhing tongue, and waited for the agony of the jaws closing possessively around my fingers in dumb absolution.*

About the Author

Michiel Heyns grew up in South Africa and studied at the universities of Stellenbosch and Cambridge. After the publication of his first novel, *The Children's Day*, he began writing full time, publishing *The Reluctant Passenger* in 2003 and *The Typewriter's Tale* in 2005. In 2006 he translated two works by Marlene van Niekerk, *Memorandum* and *Agaat*, and in 2008 he won the English Academy's Sol Plaatje Award for Translating. He has also translated *Equatoria* by Tom Dreyer, published by Aflame Books (UK, 2008). His latest novel, *Bodies Politic*, was recently published by Jonathan Ball.